THE SOMERS TREATMENT

The Somers Treatment

Gillian Bradshaw

Severn House Large Print
London & New York

This first large print edition published in Great Britain 2006 by
SEVERN HOUSE LARGE PRINT BOOKS LTD of
9-15 High Street, Sutton, Surrey, SM1 1DF.
First world regular print edition published 2003 by
Severn House Publishers, London and New York.
This first large print edition published in the USA 2006 by
SEVERN HOUSE PUBLISHERS INC., of
595 Madison Avenue, New York, NY 10022.

British Library Cataloguing in Publication Data

Bradshaw, Gillian, 1956 -
    The Somers treatment. - Large print ed.
    1.   Language disorders - Treatment - Fiction
    2.   Suspense fiction
    3.   Large type books
    I.   Title
    813.5'4 [F]

ISBN-10:   0-7278-7486-1

Printed and bound in Great Britain by
MPG Books Ltd, Bodmin, Cornwall.

I think we would try to open the box of species that encloses us even if we knew that it was an inside-out Pandora's Box, and that once we had broken free of it, all the terrors of the universe would rain down upon our heads.

Derek Bickerton, *The Roots of Language*

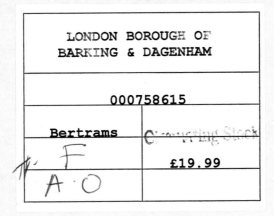

One

'What are you waiting for?' asked David Somers impatiently. He set a hand on the consent form and looked up irritably. 'A guarantee that it's a hundred per cent safe and absolutely certain to work? You can't get one – even a *general practitioner* knows that.'

He pronounced the title as though it were the equivalent of 'tea lady'. Janet Morley, GP, bit her lip, irritated, then reminded herself that to a neuroscientist of David's stature doctors with medical degrees but no specialist training were probably an annoyance: they knew enough to think that they understood things they didn't. She became embarrassed that her last-minute misgivings were so obvious. 'I know,' she said hastily. David lifted his hand off the form again, and she smoothed the paper uneasily. 'I know it's the best chance he'll get, and I'm grateful to you for providing it. It's just that...'

She glanced over to where Madhab sat attentive and alert on the edge of the examination table. Small for his fifteen years but

7

strong and compact, he was wearing the Science Museum T-shirt she'd bought him as a souvenir and his new blue trainers. He might have been any ordinary boy – Britain contained enough immigrants, after all, for a Nepalese face to be nothing to remark on. He looked normal.

'It *is* his best chance,' David agreed condescendingly. He leaned back in the desk chair, relaxing again. His round, high-coloured face was full of satisfaction; his china-blue eyes glowed with self-regard. 'He's been very lucky.' He smiled smugly, not quite meeting her eyes. 'First that you found him, and then that you knew me.'

Smug, slimy bastard, thought Janet, and then almost reflexively tried to amend the thought: David was just trying to reassure her; he was offering Madhab the chance of a normal life; he was a brilliant and a very busy man, and she was lucky that he was bothering with Madhab at all.

The fact that she'd thought him a slimy bastard ever since they were at med school together was neither here nor there.

She looked at Madhab again. He caught her glance this time and smiled eagerly, raising his eyebrows in a silent question. She smiled back, but shook her head: not yet. She wondered if Madhab's *real* mother would have signed him up for this.

Probably not. Madhab's real mother, by all

8

accounts, had considered his affliction to be the result of bad karma – atonement for the sins of another life, to be endured, like all the world's evils. When she'd realized that her son was deaf, she had never taken him to a clinic to check the cause, never enquired about schools for the deaf, never tried to teach him sign language or learn it herself – and none of that was her fault, really, because such things had been unheard of in rural Nepal until very recently, and were still vanishingly rare. An uneducated and impoverished widow in a tiny Himalayan village was simply expected to care for a deaf child at home as well as she could. She was dead, though, and Madhab was living in a different world now.

She signed the consent form: *Janet Morley, Legal Guardian.*

David smiled and handed her two more forms. One was the waiver, acknowledging that she understood that this was an experimental treatment, undertaken because of clinical need but not guaranteed to work; she signed with a nervous gulp. The other was another version of the secrecy agreement she'd signed before: a promise not to reveal any details of the treatment to anyone without David's written permission. That one she signed without a tremor. David had been guarding his discoveries jealously all along, and she knew why: he planned to patent his 'Somers Treatment', and reap the profits, along with the fat research contracts and the academic glory a successful trial would bring. He was welcome to all of them, if the treatment worked.

David smiled again. 'That's all set, then,' he said, with satisfaction. Then he looked uncomfortably at Madhab. He never liked trying to communicate with the boy.

Janet stood up; at once Madhab was on his feet as well, tense and eager. 'Ye-es?' he asked her, in his slurred, uncertain voice. 'Give word?'

She made herself smile. 'Yes, Madhab. They will try to give you words now.'

Madhab grinned hugely and bounced a little on his toes, and she felt her doubts dissolve. Whatever Madhab's mother would have done, there was no doubt that Madhab himself wanted this – and he did understand what was involved. He was very bright; she'd known that from the moment she'd watched him fix the pump.

The pump had been at a medical clinic in a Gurkha village in the Kosi Hills above Dharan in Nepal, where she'd gone to do a year's voluntary work for a medical charity. The clinic had had a little diesel generator for electricity and a hand pump for water, but four months into her stay the pump had stopped working. She'd appealed for help to the *pradhan panch*, the village mayor. He had brought his deaf-mute servant over, demonstrated that the pump wasn't working, and gone off again. Madhab – then a skinny boy of twelve – had carefully stripped the pump and examined it. One of the seals was broken, and he had improvised a new one by stapling plastic packaging material around a circle of wood. As she'd watched his quick, deft hands shaping that spare part, she had suddenly been struck by the fact that he could never have *heard* anyone explain how a pump worked. He must have figured it out for himself.

She'd been vaguely aware of Madhab before then – she'd seen him about, working in the fields or carrying firewood or fodder for his master – but she'd assumed that he was simple-minded. As she had got to know him better, in the wake of the pump incident, she had become aware of his bright, fierce intelligence, trapped in a world without words. She had begun to long to free him.

He was, she discovered, some sort of cousin of the *pradhan panch*: his parents were dead, and the mayor had taken him in out of charity. Yes, of course he was the mayor's servant as well: everyone had to work! No, no one had ever checked what was wrong with the boy. Everyone *knew* what was wrong with him: he was deaf; he'd been born that way. Oh yes, he was clever with his hands:

he'd fixed other pumps; once he'd fixed a sewing machine. He liked machines; he would watch them for hours, the lazy thing.

She hadn't had the right equipment to do a proper hearing assessment at her clinic, so she'd persuaded the *pradhan panch* to allow her to take Madhab with her to Kathmandu when she next went to the capital to collect some supplies. It was the first time the boy had left the hills, and he had clung to her desperately, staring at the big city with a mixture of terror and exhilaration. Sitting in the hospital in Kathmandu while the doctors examined his ears, he had gripped her hand and glanced continually at her face, watching her expression, trusting that what was happening was all right because he trusted her and she wasn't alarmed. Nobody had ever trusted her like that before, and she had been amazed by the protective pride that she'd found rising in her in response.

The ear specialist in Kathmandu had reported that Madhab did, in fact, have some hearing: his inner ears and nerves worked perfectly, and he was able to hear some sound through the bones of his skull. The problem lay in his middle ear. The three tiny fragments of bone which should have conducted vibrations from his eardrums to the fluid-filled chambers of his inner ear were fused. It was perfectly possible, however, to perform an operation to separate them. In an affluent Western country that would probably have been done while Madhab was still a tiny child, and he would have grown up hearing normally.

'Could you operate on him now?' Janet had asked the ear specialist eagerly.

The doctor – an Indian-educated Kathmandu Brahman – had been taken aback by such haste, and had fluttered his hands uneasily. 'It would be better to have it done in London,' he had told her. 'It needs microsurgery, you understand – very delicate, very specialized. In London they have much better equipment for that than we have here. You are from London, yes?'

'Actually, I'm from Leicester,' she told him, 'but probably I could get him into a specialist unit at an English hospital, which is what you mean, isn't it?'

'Yes,' agreed the specialist, and smiled.

So when Janet left Nepal, Madhab went with her. It had required a lot of paperwork, even though the *pradhan panch* had supported her: Nepalese officials had wanted bribes, and British ones sweeping declarations that she would see to Madhab's financial support in the event of anything short of the end of the world. She had done everything officialdom demanded. She had known that the villagers thought she was taking so much trouble because she had no children of her own and nobody else claimed this one.

13

Perhaps they had been right – though she liked to think that Madhab would have impressed her whatever her own status.

What she hadn't understood, when they left Nepal, was that the operation alone would no longer be enough to free Madhab from his prison of silence. He had been thirteen by the time it was done; he had grown to the edge of adolescence without learning to speak. During the agonizing year after the operation, the psychologists and the speech therapists had all informed her that there was a critical period for language acquisition, and it ended at puberty. Hearing wasn't the issue: sign language would've been just as useful to Madhab as Nepali or English; but he hadn't learned it. Now he was unlikely ever to speak more fluently than a two-year-old: he was doomed to a life of impairment.

That was why she'd consulted David Somers. That was why she'd just given her consent to another operation for Madhab, one even more delicate than the micro-surgery that had successfully given him his hearing.

'Don't promise too much,' David said now, sharply. It was obvious that he disapproved of her grand promise: 'They will try to give you words now.' Probably he thought that Madhab would expect to be speaking fluent English tomorrow. 'All we're going to do

14

today is put in the microshunt. Can you keep him calm for that?'

Do you think he's an idiot? wondered Janet irritably – and again tried to amend the thought: David didn't know Madhab, and the question was legitimate enough. 'I don't think anybody could keep him *calm*,' she said carefully, 'but he knows what to expect, and he'll keep still.'

David gave her a sceptical look, then snorted, 'Good. We're going to use a general anaesthetic for the first part of the operation, but he'll have to be conscious while the shunt is positioned, and we can't have him panicking. Is he capable of understanding that?'

She sighed, raising her eyebrows. She thought of saying, 'David, he's more than *capable*! He's learned maths up to secondary-school level in just the past two years!' – but did not. Instead she went to Madhab.

'We – will go upstairs – now,' she told him, speaking slowly and gesturing to make her meaning clear: Madhab had grown up interpreting body language in place of speech. 'They – will give you a medicine – to make you sleep...'

'Fix ear,' said Madhab, nodding and using the wobble of the hand that meant 'sort-of' or 'like that'.

'Like when they fixed your ears,' agreed Janet.

15

'Cut hair!' said Madhab, grinning. 'Open head!' She grinned back: he was running through what he'd been told would happen – for David's benefit, she was sure; he'd noticed that sceptical look, too.

'Wake up, Madhab,' the boy went on, holding a palm against the left side of his head. 'Lie still. Talk, talk. Put tube, little tube, talk-talk place. Give med' cine, brain-med' cine. Madhab talk-talk place...' He held up pinched fingers to show how small it was. 'Spill word.' He sloshed an invisible tiny cup. 'Brain-medicine...' He measured out a huge expanse with his hands. 'Yes?'

'Yes!' Janet agreed. She glanced at David, and was satisfied. He wasn't exactly embarrassed – he had too high an opinion of himself for that – but he was certainly disconcerted.

Madhab stopped smiling, and his eyes met hers. 'Janet stay?' he asked, and she saw that, for all his eagerness, he was at least as apprehensive as she was. She wanted to give him a hug to comfort him; but he was fifteen and Nepalese. Fifteen-year-old boys do not want to be hugged by foster mothers, except in truly exceptional circumstances and in private, and Nepalese men are expected to be dignified and undemonstrative.

She contented herself with a nod, solemnly holding his eyes. 'I'll stay with you the whole time.'

He smiled again. 'Le's go!'

David had wanted to do the operation at his lab to the south of Oxford, but hadn't been able to get insurance cover for it, and had had to settle instead for a private arrangement at Oxford's main hospital, the John Radcliffe. Janet had been glad of it: she'd done some of her own medical training on the Radcliffe's overcrowded wards, and when she'd arrived with Madhab from Leicester that afternoon, the familiarity of the place had been comforting.

The Neurology Department, however, was new to her. When she had been a student it had still been based at the old Radcliffe Infirmary in town; it had moved out to the big modern hospital in Headington only a couple of years before. It was still clean and shiny-looking, the walls a fresh unscuffed cream and the carpet tiles barely beginning to grey in the most trodden patches – not much like the Radcliffe she remembered. On this sultry July evening it was quiet, too – eerily so, as though the noisy mobs who peopled the hospital in her memories had been snatched away by some catastrophe, leaving this strange, clean, empty hush. She knew, however, that it was quiet only because she was in an outpatient area and it was now after hours; the hospital trust scheduled all private operations in the evenings. During the working day Neurology was undoubtedly full of bored and anxious NHS patients waiting their turn to see a specialist; but just now it was hard to imagine them.

To meet David they had made their way through the silence to the office of a consultant friend of his. Now, with the paperwork finished, the three of them made their way back through the empty waiting rooms and up a flight of stairs to the operating theatre.

David had arranged two theatre assistants and an anaesthetist – members of the hospital staff willing to do private work after hours, like the facilities they employed. Janet had nerved herself and offered to pay the bill, but to her relief David had said that his research grants would cover it. She had disliked the reminder that to him Madhab was research – the first human trial of a new treatment devised by the great David Somers! – but she was glad that she wouldn't have to remortgage the house.

The anaesthetist and the two nurses were already assembled in the prep room, dressed in their green surgical gowns, though not yet masked and gloved. They looked at Madhab with open curiosity; he smiled at them shyly. Janet shook hands and thanked them for helping.

David checked that the team understood

the operation; the anaesthetist confirmed that Madhab hadn't eaten during the previous six hours and that he was in good health and had no known allergies. There was the routine business of assigning hospital numbers, checking the labels on all the paperwork, fitting Madhab with his surgical overall and plastic bar-coded bracelet. Then it was time.

Madhab lay down on the trolley without fuss and rolled up his sleeve for the needle. Then he glanced over at Janet – that same trusting glance that had bound her to him in Kathmandu. She came over and took his free hand. 'I'll stay right here,' she promised him.

He did not smile this time, merely watched her – seriously, with complete trust – as he lost consciousness. His hand relaxed in hers, and his eyelids fluttered once, then shut. She pressed his limp fingers, her throat tight.

'Is he adopted?' asked one of the nurses sympathetically. The woman already knew he wasn't Janet's own.

Janet shook her head, then cleared her throat so that her voice wouldn't catch. 'I want to adopt him, but I haven't been able to, so far.' She gave the nurse an appeasing smile. 'They're very strict about adoptions from overseas. I'm his legal guardian, though.'

'Come on!' said David impatiently. 'Let's

get started.'

Janet stepped back to let the theatre team work.

They allowed her to put on a gown and mask and join them in the theatre. The operation went very much according to plan. Madhab had the left side of his head shaved and swabbed. A flap of scalp was sliced open and retracted, and a powerful surgical saw cut out a panel of the bone beneath. His head was positioned and immobilized in a special headset; a screen was set up to give a magnified view of the exposed section of brain. The three layers of the meninges – the tough membranes encasing the brain itself – were carefully sliced open and peeled aside, shining with blood and cerebrospinal fluid.

Janet stood quietly by the wall, trying to stay out of the way. The closest she usually got to brain surgery was to refer a patient to a consultant: she'd never been ambitious for anything beyond the ordinary dramas of general practice. She felt ... no, not queasy – she'd lost all her queasiness long ago, much of it in this very hospital – but she felt ... was there a word for it? Like a voyeur, watching unseen as some beautiful stranger disrobes: that mixture of tenderness with an awareness of violation. Madhab's living brain was a delicate pink, not the famous grey of dead tissue; it was, she knew, tender, soft to the touch. The standard comparison was 'like scrambled egg', but she wished someone would find a better simile: it seemed wrong for an object of such profound complexity and mystery to be described by a phrase so graphically mundane. The surgical team revolved about it like Parsee priests, robed and masked, tending a sacred flame. In the magnified view she could see the pulse of blood in the innumerable tiny vessels; the pulse of information along the synapses was enormously finer and more complex.

David superimposed the magnified view on the screen with a 3-D computer graphic obtained from scans he had made over the weeks before. He marked points on it with a cursor, then marked the brain, very delicately, with droplets of a harmless short-term dye. One of the assistants moved the small electrical probe closer to his hand, and he nodded. 'Let him surface,' he told the anaesthetist, and the man nodded back and made some adjustment to the drip feeding into Madhab's arm.

Janet came forward and took Madhab's hand again – his right hand, on the other side of the table from the surgical team. 'Wake up, Madhab,' she whispered.

His eyes fluttered open and found her, then drooped almost shut again. Janet was relieved to see that, despite the gaping hole in his skull, he did not appear to be in any pain. He'd been given a local anaesthetic, of course, on the site of the wound; no anaesthetic was needed for the brain itself, which is insensible.

'It's the middle of the operation, Madhab,' she told him. 'We need you to talk now.'

'Tal-talk,' slurred Madhab, still half asleep. 'Give word.'

'Try and talk, Madhab,' Janet urged. 'Tell me about an engine. Just in words, remember. You mustn't try to move.'

''C' linduh,' said Madhab indistinctly. 'Piston. Up'n' dowwn...'

Madhab tried to describe the working of a car engine in clumsy, half-asleep toddler's English. David moved the electrical probe carefully across his exposed cortex, applying a weak electrical current. Every now and again Madhab's voice stopped abruptly: the electrical current was interfering with a part of the brain he needed to produce speech. Whenever that happened, one of the assistants would apply another dab of dye to the site. In that way they confirmed their map of the portions of his brain most crucial to the production and understanding of language – the parts of his brain that were deformed, stunted by his long exclusion from language.

'OK,' David said at last, 'put him back under.'

The anaesthetist adjusted the drip again,

and the boy lapsed once more into deep unconsciousness.

Janet stayed where she was, holding Madhab's hand, watching as David arranged the microshunt. This device was of David's own devising, a radical improvement on everything that had gone before it – or so David claimed; she couldn't judge. It looked a bit like a dead insect: a small steel-and-plastic valve sprouting five thread-like tubelets. David positioned the valve at the edge of the incision in Madhab's skull, secured it with a dab of a special protein glue, then gently attached the tubelets to the sites he had marked out. A notch to fit the shunt was cut in the edge of the piece of bone that had been cut out, and then membranes and bone were replaced, the membranes stitched and the bone fixed in place with a set of hypoallergenic plates. The scalp was drawn back over the bone and stitched around the plug of the shunt.

David breathed a sigh of satisfaction and stepped back, pulling off his surgical mask. The anaesthetist began to remove the needle from Madhab's arm.

'That's that, then,' said David, stripping off his gloves. 'I'll see him on Tuesday, at my lab, and we can start the treatment.'

Janet nodded. 'Who do I contact if there are any complications?'

David was airily dismissive. 'Oh ... the hospital will look after you.'

'Who's his doctor here? Your friend Dr Bhattacharya?' That was the consultant whose office he'd borrowed.

David nodded. 'Not that you'll need him.'

'I've never met Dr Bhattacharya,' Janet pointed out. 'Does he know what's going on?'

David was affronted. 'Of course! But I very much doubt you'll ever need to meet him. There shouldn't be any problems, but if any should arise, he's got a GP on call, hasn't he?' He grinned: he knew that Janet herself was Madhab's GP. 'Now I'm going to go home and have a drink. I deserve one!' He paused, then gave her a speculative look and asked, 'Join me?'

She tried to be gratified rather than irritated that he'd invited her. She failed: his complacent assumption that she could leave Madhab, with his limited language skills, to wake up alone in a hospital in a foreign country, spoke of a callousness that disgusted her. 'I ought to stay with Madhab,' she said mildly. 'He'll want me with him when he wakes up.'

'Suit yourself,' said David, shrugging. 'See you on Tuesday, then.' He went off.

The two nurses helped Janet take Madhab to the recovery room, which was in another part of the hospital entirely. There he slowly woke up, and was transferred to a general

24

surgical ward before midnight. There were, as David Somers had anticipated, no complications, and after another night the hospital was happy to discharge him. It was a Friday.

Madhab was quiet on the way back from Oxford, curled up in the passenger seat of the old Datsun with his bandaged head wedged between the headrest and the window and pillowed in a raincoat. Janet suspected that the wound was giving him a lot of pain. He hadn't said so – but then, he never did complain: he was, after all, a Gurkha, born and bred to courage in adversity. *Kaphar hunnu bhanda mornu ramro chaa*, went the Gurkha motto: 'It is better to die than live as a coward.' Madhab had never heard the saying, but he had certainly grown up with the ethos.

She twiddled the radio and found some piano sonatas on Radio 3 which were quiet and relaxing, and was rewarded by a brief smile.

She wondered again whether she was doing the best thing for him – whether, in fact, his real mother's attitude might not actually have been wiser and kinder. True, he'd had a pretty miserable life in Nepal, dependent on his cousin the *pradhan panch*, working, unpaid, at whatever dirty or menial jobs his master assigned him, dressing in hand-me-downs and cast-offs; but nobody had actually been unkind to him there. Everybody in the village had known who he was, he'd had enough to eat and he had, after a fashion, supported himself. True, he'd had to work hard, but so had everybody else in the village. He hadn't had the education he craved, but without language, he couldn't get the kind of education he wanted in England, either. She had taken him away from his community and everyone he'd ever known, shown him a thousand new things to want that she couldn't give him, and made him suffer quite a lot of physical pain – twice now. She'd destroyed his old life, and what had she given him in its place? A stammering half-life as a disabled teenager in a world that despised him. He attended a special school, where he had suffered the humilia-tion of being put in a class with children much younger than himself. He had no friends his own age, and she knew – though he never complained – that he was teased and occasionally bullied.

She had twice nerved herself to ask whether he wanted to go back to Nepal, but he had been adamant that he did not. She could see that his old life would now seem stifling: he was a bright boy, eager to learn and to understand, frustrated only by the barrier of language. David's experimental treatment still seemed his best chance. If it worked, oh God, if it worked!

They reached Leicester about midday. The house was a modern semi on the west side of town, part of a middle-class housing estate developed in the 1970s. Returning to it after an interval away, Janet gloomily noticed all the things that needed doing to it which were unlikely to get done in the near future. The paint on the window frames was flaking, the pebbledash was crumbling, the guttering needed replacement and the roof, though not yet leaking, really should have been attended to a year or so before. Since returning from Nepal she'd been working as a locum for a primary care trust; it did not pay as well as full-time work with a practice, but Madhab's appointments with specialists and teachers had taken up a lot of her time as well as all of her savings, and she'd needed the flexibility. The result was that she didn't have either time or money to spend on maintaining the house.

The small front garden was tidy, though, the lawn neatly clipped and the small flower bed free of weeds. Madhab looked after it.

She helped Madhab out of the car, then unlocked the front door.

She didn't at first realize that anything was wrong. She stood aside to let Madhab go in, then went back out to the car to collect the luggage. When she came back with the two overnight bags she found him still standing

27

in the front hall. He was frowning.

'What's the matter?' she asked anxiously.

He waved a hand helplessly at the book-case that stood in the hall, and she noticed, for the first time and with a shock, that some of the books were scattered about the floor while the rest stood in untidy stacks on the shelves. Moved by a sudden sick suspicion, she went to the door that led to the kitchen.

The window in the back door had been smashed. There was glass all over the floor, and the door itself was unbolted.

'Oh shit!' she exclaimed in disbelief and disgust.

'Bad?' asked Madhab, coming through the kitchen door behind her.

She grimaced. 'Yes. We've been burgled. Oh God.' She glanced back, noticed the way he was clinging to the door frame, and how pale his face was. She went over to him hurriedly. 'You better lie down, my love,' she said concernedly. 'You're not well.'

He started to shake his head, then stopped with a wince. 'Help,' he insisted. 'Fix.' He pointed at the broken window.

'Later!' she ordered. 'Once you've had a lie-down. We'll want to show that to the police anyway.'

She made Madhab lie down in his room upstairs, phoned the police, then went through the house to see what was missing.

Both the computers had gone – the old one she used to keep track of her locum work and the newer one she'd bought for Madhab. So had the answering machine, which was new. The burglars hadn't bothered with the television, which was ten years old, or the CD player, similarly worthless. They'd taken her jewellery box, however, and that hurt – that really did hurt. The computers were probably more of a loss – she depended on e-mail to arrange her work, and she kept some notes on patients on file – but her wedding and engagement rings had been in the jewellery box, together with earrings her husband had given her on various occasions while their marriage was still happy, and the opal necklace handed down from her great-grandmother. Looking at the empty spot on the dresser where the box had been accustomed to sit, she found herself gulping tears. She sat down heavily on the bed. Her reflection watched her from the dresser mirror: a thin, nervous thirty-six-year-old whose untidy brown hair was beginning to grey, whose face was red and swollen with grief.

Madhab must have heard her, because he came in; in the mirror she could see him standing in the doorway, his face anxious and concerned. She turned away from the mirror and the missing box, and he came over, sat down beside her and hugged her – not like a child, wanting comfort, but like an adult, supplying it. 'Poor Janet,' he said.

'Sorry,' she said vaguely, sniffing and looking about for a tissue. 'It's the jewellery box.' She waved at the spot where it used to stand. 'The bastard took it. Stupid git probably won't get more than a couple of quid for a used wedding ring, so why couldn't he just have left it?'

She knew that the sentence was too complicated for Madhab's limited grasp, but he patted her on the back and repeated, 'Poor Janet.'

The police were slow to arrive: a crime that had been committed hours or days before obviously wasn't urgent. Janet wasn't sure whether or not she should clean up before they came. She doubted very much that anybody would ever be caught, but still, it seemed irresponsible to destroy evidence. On the other hand, the burglar or burglars had made a dreadful mess. She suspected that they'd realized that she was a doctor – the shelves of medical texts were probably a giveaway – and that they'd ransacked the house looking for drugs. They'd emptied all the drawers, thrown books off shelves, and dumped the contents of the filing cabinet in the kitchen unceremoniously on to the floor. She realized that they must have got the credit card number, and phoned the company to cancel it. She thought about phoning the bank as well, but decided that her account should be safe enough – the smartcard had been with her, not in the house, and the passcodes weren't written down anywhere. It would be massively inconvenient to change the account: she was going to need money herself over the next few days.

She decided not to clean up until after the police had had a look. She made herself a stiff drink – the burglars didn't seem to have hit the liquor cabinet, fortunately – brewed some tea for Madhab, gave him a painkiller, then went round to ask the neighbours if they'd noticed anything.

By the time the police arrived, at about supper time, she was reasonably calm again. The two officers examined the mess and dusted for fingerprints in a desultory fashion; they found nothing useful. She gave them a statement about what had happened, and told them that she'd spoken to the neighbours, none of whom had noticed anything. They replied gloomily that people often didn't, that there'd been a lot of break-ins in the area, and that they couldn't promise anything. They suggested a couple of second-hand shops where her goods might turn up, and told her what to do if she spotted them. Then they advised her to have the window fixed and the locks changed at once: burglars often returned to a house a couple of weeks after first breaking into it, knowing that by then the owners would have replaced stolen electrical goods with brand new ones. They gave her an incident number to report to her insurance company and departed.

Madhab fixed cardboard over the window, as a temporary measure, while Janet cooked supper and did some of the tidying-up. They ate together at the dining-room table, and Janet suddenly found herself very glad that Madhab was there – glad of his companionship, his silent, uncomplaining support. If it had been her husband George sitting there, she would have had to comfort him and try to calm him down. He would have been outraged, have complained loudly to the police, demanded to know what they were going to do, fumed over the missing items and shouted at the insurance company over the phone. Probably he would have shouted at her, too, angry because she was 'so fucking calm – how can you sit there like that, don't you *care*?'

Suddenly, and almost for the first time, she was glad that he was gone. She smiled at Madhab gratefully, and he smiled back.

The next few days were spent dealing with the aftermath of the burglary and arguing with the insurance company. Janet arranged for a local handyman to fit new locks and replace the window with a wooden door panel, over Madhab's protests that he could do it himself if she just bought the necessary equipment. 'We need it done right now,' she said firmly, 'and you're recovering from *brain surgery*, Madhab; there's no way you should be fixing the door!' She also bought a new computer, on credit, and worried about whether she would have to approach the bank for a loan before the insurance came through.

On Monday afternoon she found Madhab doubled up on the sofa. Her first stricken thought was that the operation had caused some serious damage to his brain, and that he was suffering a cerebral haemorrhage. She ran over, struggling to suppress her own panic and guilt, and to her relief found him alive and conscious. She asked him what was wrong.

He couldn't tell her. No, he said, when she asked if his head hurt; but what the matter was he couldn't manage to explain. He gestured at the ceiling and touched his side: 'Up!' he said, and 'Ouch!' She asked if he felt dizzy, if his stomach hurt. He seemed to agree.

Nausea and giddiness, she thought: *possible infection of the brain*. She ran to the phone in the hall – only to have him get up and follow. He grimaced unhappily and pointed at the phone. 'No, no!' he declared emphatically. Scowling in misery and frustration, he tried to mime an explanation.

She eventually understood that he'd simply bumped his side. He'd been tidying up the box from the new computer, which he'd filled with miscellaneous bits of electrical cable; he'd decided to put it in the loft, which was reached through a trapdoor from the landing at the top of the stairs, and he'd stumbled coming down the ladder again. He'd been a bit shaken and had had the breath knocked out of him, but he wasn't badly hurt.

'You shouldn't have been climbing ladders!' Janet scolded. 'Not so soon after brain surgery.'

He shrugged, still scowling. In his eyes she could see the deep pain of his isolation: he had a mind full of ideas, and he couldn't communicate even that he'd slipped on a ladder.

'Never mind,' she told him, then bit her lip, knowing that of course he minded: anybody would mind. To be unable to speak was to be less than human.

He shrugged again, then suddenly looked at her and smiled. His hand came up and hovered for a moment over the wound in his skull, and his eyes were suddenly full of hope.

On Tuesday morning they put the new computer into the boot of the car, to keep it safe, locked all the new locks, and headed off again for Oxford.

David's lab was, in fact, south of Oxford, one of the many medical research establishments between the university city and Didcot. It was officially named 'Somers Synaptic', and operated as a private research company, getting its funds from medical research boards and pharmaceutical companies interested in cutting-edge neurobiological research. It occupied a converted farmhouse and barn on a country lane: a pair of solid nineteenth-century brick buildings facing each other across a gravel yard, with nothing to tell the casual passer-by that the site produced anything more exciting than dairy products or eggs. The first time she had taken Madhab there, Janet had driven right past it, and had to cruise back along the road, checking the numbers on the infrequent gateposts.

'We can't put up a sign because of the animal rights people,' David had explained to her when they'd finally arrived. 'We used to use monkeys.' He'd snorted in disgust, and added bitterly, 'The little beasts were well treated: there's more animal cruelty on a *real* farm than ever went on here; but we got death threats, and we had to spend a fortune on security.'

The monkeys had been in the barn, but they were gone now. 'Sold 'em to another place up the road,' David had informed her.

'They only take you so far. Apes would've been better, but you can't use apes any more, not in Britain.' The security, however, was still there. There was a chainlink fence around house and barn, with warning signs about guard dogs; but those could be matched by fences and signs on many genuine farms. Less obtrusive, and less routine, were the security cameras and the electronic locks on all the reinforced doors and windows.

Arriving on that Tuesday, Janet gave her name to the receptionist from the intercom at the gate, and the receptionist pushed a button that opened the tall gate and allowed her through to the yard. Parking was easier than usual; normally there were six or seven cars in the small enclosed space, but today there were only three: David's Mercedes and two others.

Madhab climbed out of the Datsun by himself and stood leaning against the door while Janet locked up. He was recovering well from the surgery, though he still went pale and needed to sit down after any exertion or excitement. That morning Janet had found him examining his scar in the mirror. His dark hair was still only a faint down across the shaved patch of scalp, and the wound stood out, a dark red horseshoe of scab and stitches. The plug of the microshunt gleamed in his left temple, unnatural and clean. They had been wiping it twice a day with antiseptic on some cotton wool.

Madhab had noticed her watching him, and had grinned at her, then mimed putting petrol in the microshunt. 'Vroom, vroom!' he'd exclaimed cheerfully. She'd laughed, and helped him put on a fresh bandage.

'Le's go!' he said now, when she'd finished locking the car, and together they went to the house door.

Somers Synaptic was a small establishment. David employed one other full-time researcher, a balding, tongue tied molecular biologist by the name of Jeremy Firsby. There were also three laboratory assistants and a receptionist cum-secretary. (Presumably there had once been another employee who'd looked after the monkeys, but, if so, he'd departed with them.) The receptionist was a slight, fierce, dark-haired woman called Elena Simonson. She opened the door to them by pressing a button on her desk and, when they entered her office, nodded without speaking. She looked angry and offended about something – but then, she often did.

After a moment David appeared, holding a coffee mug in one hand. With him was another man whom Janet had never met – a short, thin, dark-haired man in a suit. He had a long, quizzical face, slightly too dark to be English stock: he might have been of Middle Eastern descent, or perhaps just from the Mediterranean south. He wore thick spectacles with a heavy black frame, and looked to be about forty. He gazed at Janet and Madhab with an air of surprise.

'Ah!' exclaimed David triumphantly, 'here they are.' He gestured at them – Exhibit A – and did not introduce his companion. 'As I was saying, Janet and I know each other from when we were studying Medicine at Oxford, which is how she knew to contact me about Madhab. I saw at once that he'd be the perfect test of the Somers Treatment.'

'Hello,' murmured the stranger, holding out a hand. 'Michael Shahid. Um. I'm glad to meet you, Dr Morley.' Despite the vaguely Arab name, his voice was Estuary English.

They shook hands. Shahid turned to Madhab and offered the hand again. 'And you're Madhab Limbu? I've heard a lot about you. I'm delighted to meet you.'

Madhab smiled shyly and shook the hand. Janet, who had been prepared to dislike Shahid as a friend of David's and an intruder, revised her assessment. 'Are you a neurologist, Dr Shahid?' she asked.

'*Mr* Shahid,' he replied at once. 'Uh, no, I'm afraid not. I'm responsible for overseeing our funding of Dr Somers' work, and, uh, obviously we're very interested in this trial. I asked Dr Somers if I could meet you.'

She knew that David got money from a

number of different companies and organizations and was about to ask Shahid which one he represented when David interrupted with a brisk 'Let's get started, then!' and held open the door leading to the main part of the lab. Shahid gave Janet an apologetic look and went through.

Two

Somers Synaptic's labs were on the ground floor of the converted farmhouse; the upper floor was used for offices and storage. The rooms retained their original narrow windows and high ceilings, but not much else. Flat white walls met flat black linoleum-tile floors, and the lighting was provided by fluorescent strips. The main room contained an examining table, computers and two brain scanners, as well as some cages for the departed monkeys. There was a chemistry lab in what had probably been the kitchen, and the remaining two rooms, which might have been the cloakroom and dining room, were now given over to tissue samples and microscopes. The bleak functionalism of the decor was not broken by so much as a pot plant or poster. Janet had disliked the place from the first time she saw it, and familiarity had not improved it.

'You can take the bandage off him,' David told Janet, going to the X-ray machine in the corner of the main room. The technicians who were usually in attendance did not

40

appear to be around; presumably that was why the car park was so empty. 'The first thing is to check that the shunt's still in place.'

Madhab went over to the examining table, sat down on the edge of it, and began unwrapping his bandage. Janet came over and collected it from him as he finished, rolling it neatly and securing it with the safety pin that had held it.

'Gruesome,' remarked Shahid, also coming over, his hands in his pockets. He eyed the scab with respect. 'Does it hurt much?'

Madhab looked at him warily. 'No hurt. Sleep.'

Shahid cast an uncertain glance at Janet.

'He has trouble recognizing tense,' she explained. 'He thought you were asking about when it was done.' She turned to Madhab. 'He means, does it hurt *now*?'

Madhab shrugged, embarrassed. 'Little hurt.'

Shahid smiled. 'Does that mean that it doesn't hurt much, or that you're being brave about it?'

'He won't understand that, either,' interrupted David, wheeling the X-ray machine over. 'The grammar's too complicated for him. He has the language skills of a two year-old.'

Madhab flushed slightly: he obviously understood the gist of the interruption

41

perfectly.

'He's being brave about it,' Janet answered quietly, ignoring David. 'He is very brave.'

David dismissed Madhab's courage with an impatient snap of the fingers. 'Tell him to lie down and turn his head to the right, so I can get a look at where the shunt is,' he commanded.

Shahid gave Janet and Madhab another look of apology. His courtesy was soothing, next to David's abrasive arrogance.

Madhab lay down and let David take his X-ray. The picture was instantly scanned into the computer. David beckoned the party round, and they all came over to look at the screen. David pressed some keys on the computer and brought up an image recorded during the operation: Madhab's brain marked out with spots of dye.

Madhab made a small *mmh* noise expressive of interest and surprise. 'Me?' he asked Janet.

She nodded. 'During the operation.'

The computer mapped the two images on top of one another, and at once it was clear that the microshunt's tubelets were all still in place.

'You can see there that we have five delivery sites,' David told Shahid, pointing to the filmy tendrils of the shunt, just visible on the X-ray: 'two in Broca's area, one in Wernicke's area, one along the arcuate fasciculus, which connects the two, and one on this site on the lower edge of the Sylvian fissure, which was found to be significant in this case. Because of Madhab's early language deprivation, all of these areas are smaller than they would be in a normal person. An adult brain – and Madhab's brain is effectively adult – cannot grow new cortical cells. So – obviously – if we want to improve Madhab's condition, we have to repair the damage to his brain.'

He was giving this spiel to impress a source of funding, of course. Janet, who had heard it all before, surreptitiously rolled her eyes at Madhab. He smiled.

'Other researchers,' David went on, visibly expanding, 'have been trying to repair damaged brains by injecting stem cells, either into the blood or directly into the cortex. While they have sometimes had good results, the procedure is haphazard and wasteful. It's like painting with an aerosol can on a teflon wall: things will stick here and there, but only in the gaps, and as for fine detail – forget it! What *I* am going to do, in contrast, will be like painting in oils: fine detail on a specially prepared surface.'

He touched one of the dye-spots on the screen lovingly. 'The first step will be to treat the language centres of the brain so that they become receptive to the implantation of new cells and to cell growth. An adult brain, as I

43

said, is not receptive. The remedy is to apply the neural growth factors and hormones that are ordinarily present during embryonic development, when the brain is first taking shape.'

Shahid stirred. 'This was one of the questions we had,' he said politely. 'Where are you getting these neural growth factors, if they're only present in embryos?'

'My associate Dr Firsby has been able to synthesize some of the factors,' replied David calmly. 'He extracted the rest of what I'm going to use today from animals. Fetal pigs, to be precise.'

Shahid looked uneasy. 'Is that safe?'

'Hormones are essentially the same in all mammals,' said David airily. 'You're thinking about the fuss over xenotransplantation, aren't you? Frankenstein's genetically modified pigs spreading all sorts of pig diseases to humans! Scaremongering rubbish, but this isn't the same thing at all. This doesn't involve transplanting anything, genetically modified or otherwise. It's just a chemical extraction from pig tissue, processed and prepared for medical use. It's as safe as eating pork.' He glanced sideways at Shahid, and his lip curled. 'If you eat pork. If you don't – well, some of us do.'

Shahid looked at him thoughtfully a moment. 'I eat pork,' he said shortly. He was still frowning. 'The other question we had was about the stem cells. We understand that you intend to use fetal stem cells.'

David nodded. 'In due course. They're the most potent kind.'

'I thought it was possible to use stem cells extracted from bone marrow,' said Shahid diffidently, 'or from the umbilical cords of newborn babies. I'm not trying to be diffi- cult, Dr Somers, but you must know, we'd prefer it if this didn't involve anything con- troversial.'

David rolled his eyes in disgust. 'You know what a stem cell is, don't you? It's a cell that hasn't differentiated – that hasn't yet de- cided whether it's going to be a muscle cell or a nerve cell or whatever. Embryos obviously have a whole lot more of them than adults do! Adult bone marrow still has a few, it's true, but they aren't as flexible – for example, they might be willing to turn into blood or muscle, but won't turn into nerves for you, and mostly they just fuse with existing cells in a way that's actually dangerous. Stem cells harvested from the umbilical cord are safer and more flexible, but they aren't as active as fetal stem cells. When you're working with the brain, you really need a cell that's going to get in there and grow.' He shrugged. 'This technology is in its infancy. In future we'll probably be able to use stem cells cloned from the patient. At present, though, we have to make do with the best we can get.' He put on a sanctimonious look. 'It would be unethical to subject a patient to this sort of invasive treatment without doing everything possible to ensure its success.'

Janet set her teeth. She was sure that was rank hypocrisy – even though she agreed with the sentiment itself. She tried again to amend her dislike, telling herself that she had no right to be so suspicious of David. He might well believe what he'd just said. He had an abrasive manner, it was true, but that didn't mean he was dead to morality.

'So where are you obtaining these fetal stem cells?' asked Shahid patiently.

David named an Oxford fertility clinic. 'They have a licence to harvest the cells,' he added. 'And I have a licence to use them in research. Everything's perfectly legal. You don't need to worry.'

'We would, um, *prefer* it if you could assure us that the stem cells you'll be using were not obtained from aborted fetuses,' Shahid said apologetically. 'That could cause trouble for us in some quarters.'

David rolled his eyes again. 'Oh, it would be *controversial* even for *you*, would it? You know how *stupid* that is? Nobody's talking about performing abortions just to supply the stuff: there are thousands of abortions in Britain every month, and if the material from them isn't used it's incinerated. Why should it be wasted like that, when it could be used to improve people's quality of life? But, in fact, the cells I'm going to use come from embryos prepared for fertility treatments, and frozen at the fourteen-cell stage; if they aren't used, they'll be destroyed.'

'Thank you,' said Shahid. 'I'm relieved to hear that.'

'To proceed,' David resumed, expanding again. 'As you can see, I've inserted a micro-shunt – my own revolutionary new design! – into the patient's brain. It allows me to deliver the treatment precisely to the sites where it's needed, and to no other sites. Today I'm going to give Madhab a cocktail of growth factor, immune suppressants, and selected neural hormones – again, a mixture of my own devising. In three days' time, when the hormones have had time to work, I'll deliver more growth factor, a different set of hormones, and a solution containing human stem cells. If all goes well, some of those stem cells will implant in the prepared regions of cortex, differentiate into neurons, and begin to grow. Madhab's hearing is now normal, of course; if all goes well, he should soon begin to grasp the principles of language as easily he would have done if he'd been exposed to it as a child.' David smiled in self-congratulation. 'You're aware, I hope, that between the ages of two and five a child learns an average of ten thousand words –

one for every waking hour – and grasps hundreds of grammatical principles so complex that highly trained linguists find them hard to enunciate. Ordinarily we're never that skilled at language again.'

'I'm aware of that, yes,' agreed Shahid, so mildly that Janet at once suspected it was the reason his company was funding the research. Well, if the treatment worked, it had great potential as a therapy for those who suffered language impairments, from victims of stroke and brain trauma to autistic children. It was not surprising that a medical research board or pharmaceutical company was interested in it. She wondered again what organization Shahid represented; medical research charity was her guess. A pharmaceutical company wouldn't have been so squeamish about the source of the stem cells.

'If you're satisfied, then...' began David.

'Actually, I'm not,' said Shahid. His diffident, apologetic um- ing and ah- ing were suddenly gone, replaced by an air of severe determination. 'We have one other, very serious question: about the patient. One of our managers is uneasy with the fact that this experimental treatment is being carried out on a minor – one whose comprehension is limited, and who cannot be presumed to have an informed grasp of the risks involved. What is more, your patient is a foreign national with no right of residence in the United Kingdom, whose parents are dead and whose guardian is a friend of the man doing the research. Our manager is concerned that a vulnerable patient might have been strong-armed into cooperating with this research, and that he might have been chosen to minimize the risk of litigation if something goes wrong.'

Janet felt the blood rush to her face. 'What are you suggesting?' she demanded angrily: 'that I'm allowing David to use Madhab as some kind of *experimental animal?*'

Shahid looked at her levelly. His eyes, behind the spectacles, were serious and very dark. 'Are you?'

'No!' she exclaimed furiously. 'Madhab is ... is *extraordinary*. Do you have any idea what it must be like, to be so brilliant, and to be trapped – unable to understand, unable to communicate?'

'Janet?' asked Madhab, understanding that an accusation had been made, that it concerned him and that it angered her, but unsure what it involved.

'What sort of future does he have if this treatment doesn't work?' Janet demanded. 'All he can look forward to is dirty and menial jobs or the dole – or being sent back to Nepal, if they won't let me adopt him, to live on his cousin's charity as an unpaid servant. All his life he'll be treated as though he's mentally defective, when actually he's exceptionally intelligent! He has the potential—'

'Janet!' repeated Madhab, and she stopped. He reached across and touched her hand, looking intently at her face. 'What?' he asked softly.

'He asked if...' she began – then schooled herself, and broke the idea down into the units he could comprehend, gesturing to make her meaning clear. 'He thinks – you don't understand – you don't know what this is.' She indicated the microshunt, and Madhab's hand flew up and hovered over it in response, his eyes wide. 'He thinks – *that* – may hurt you. He thinks – David and I – want to know, "Does *that* work?" He thinks – we do *that*, to you, because we want to learn "Does *that* work?" He thinks – *I* agree to hurt you.'

Madhab glared at Shahid. 'No,' he said firmly. 'Janet good. Me good mother.' He touched the microshunt gently. 'This. Give word. Me want. *Me* want. Me say Janet, me want, please, me want.' He slapped his chest with a fist and continued fiercely. 'No stupid. Want word. No word, all over, Madhab. Want word, here!' He touched the side of his head over the scar. 'Brain-med' cine, give word. Me unnerstan'. Me want.'

'I believe you,' replied Shahid, after a silence. He looked from Madhab to Janet. 'I

50

apologize.'

Her anger vanished as suddenly as it had come. 'No,' she declared unsteadily. 'It's better you should ask. It's good you should be concerned about it.' Her eyes were stinging. Madhab's words sang within her memory: *My good mother.* She looked at the boy, who was still glaring suspiciously at Michael Shahid, and thought, *My beautiful son!*

Only he wasn't, of course, any more than she was his good mother. She had no children, his real mother was dead, and perhaps Shahid's suspicion was right, and she *was* allowing David to use him as an experimental animal. David probably regarded him as one.

She didn't know that. She had no real basis for believing the worst of David; and even if it were true, David was their best chance.

'Now that's settled,' David said smoothly, 'shall we proceed with the treatment?'

The treatment was, in fact, entirely lacking in drama. David attached a ten-millilitre ampoule of his growth hormone cocktail to the microshunt, and allowed it to diffuse through – very slowly, over half an hour. It did not appear to cause Madhab any pain or, indeed, to have any effect on him at all. Madhab was required to speak as the drugs diffused, to ascertain that they were not doing him any harm; he described a visit to the Science Museum with no more clumsiness and hesitation than usual.

'That's it, then,' David said, when the injection was complete. 'Call me if you notice anything. Otherwise, come back on Friday, and we'll start the next stage.'

Madhab and Janet went back through the office and out to the car. Feeling a bit flat, Janet unlocked it. 'You OK?' she asked Madhab.

'OK,' agreed Madhab. He smiled suddenly and held up both hands with the fingers crossed.

Janet crossed her own fingers back at him.

'Dr Morley!' a voice called. She glanced round and saw Michael Shahid hurrying from the building.

He stopped a few feet away. 'I, uh, wanted to apologize again,' he told her. 'I, um, got the wrong end of the stick. I can see now that you're ... that is, that you'd never allow what I was worried about. I'm sorry if I offended you.'

'I thought it was a "manager" who was "uneasy",' Janet responded drily.

'Well. Um,' replied Shahid, and looked away.

'It was just you, huh?' She found that she was not surprised. 'You got worried and you came here, off your own bat, and asked to meet us before David actually started the treatment. You were all ready to stop us if you thought we were exploiting Madhab.'

He looked back ruefully. 'Yes. I confess, I find Dr Somers ... that is, he doesn't strike me as the most responsible person I've ever met. Probably I'm being unfair to him, but it worried me.'

She leaned against the side of the car, smiling. 'Sometimes I get suspicious of David, too.'

'Oh?' He looked at her quizzically. 'I thought he was a friend of yours.'

'Sonovha bitch,' Madhab reminded her mischievously.

Janet laughed. 'Yeah, that's what I called him. Look, David's helping Madhab when nobody else could, and I'm grateful for that. I think he's probably nicer than he seems: it's just that he has an abrasive manner, and never notices when he says something offensive. I don't think *he'd* call himself my "friend", though. I mean, he's aiming for a Nobel prize and I'm just a lowly GP. We happen to have gone to med school together, that's all. I was looking for someone who could help Madhab, and I heard that David was working in a relevant field, so I contacted him.'

'I see,' said Shahid. He put his hands in his pockets, then took them out again. 'Um. I obviously don't have a very good idea what's going on. To tell the truth, I just switched jobs a few weeks ago, and until then I didn't even know we were involved in something like this. I'd, uh, like it if we could talk a bit more. Could I buy you two some lunch?'

Janet checked her watch, and found that it was just after twelve. Lunch would have to be bought soon, anyway, so why not? She looked at Madhab. 'Lunch with him OK?'

Madhab gave Shahid a look of cool assessment, then shrugged: 'OK.'

They ate at a country pub a few miles down the road. It turned out to be quite a grand place, with an oak-beamed restaurant and an award-winning chef. Janet would never have ventured into it if she'd been paying; since coming back from Nepal she had rarely eaten anywhere that used real linen on the table. She found herself enjoying the whole ritual: taking a seat at a table decorated with flowers, inspecting the menu, debating the merits of grilled brook trout versus pasta primavera, giving the order to an attentive waiter. Madhab, however, was tense and wary, still suspicious of a man who had upset Janet, and did not seem to enjoy the treat.

'First off,' said Shahid, when they'd placed their orders, 'can you give me some idea how much Madhab can understand? Madhab, did you understand what I just said?'

The boy looked at him a moment in silence, then shook his head and held up both hands, squeezing the palms together. 'Little bit.'

'He *can* understand most things,' Janet supplied, 'but you have to take time to explain – in little bits, like he said. Mostly people just talk to me, and I explain things to him later. It's quicker that way. He can normally grasp words in groups of three or four at a time, and usually he has to express himself in two-word phrases. The big problem isn't the vocabulary – he memorizes words all the time! – it's the grammar.' She smiled ruefully. 'I used to think grammar meant saying "and I" instead of "me and", and not splitting infinitives, but I've learned better. I mean, consider what you just said: "Can *you* give *me* some idea what *he* can understand?" That's really a very complicated sentence, and to understand it you have to be able to grasp how all the pieces fit together. If you were going to write it out the way the linguists do, you'd have a whole tree – "He understands *x*" and then "He can understand *x*" – which puts an auxiliary verb in, to confuse things – and then, "What can he understand?", which reverses the subject and the object, and then you have to embed all that in a whole mess of indirect objects and direct objects and auxiliaries in the wrong order – and on top of that, you have to remember that the pronouns reverse, that, from Madhab's point of view, "he" really means "I"! Language is a lot harder than it looks. We don't realize how hard it is, because it comes to us naturally, but when you start to analyse it, you start to wonder how *anybody* can make sense of it.'

'You're saying that sentences are like jig-saws,' said Shahid, frowning. 'That we have a thing inside our heads that automatically assembles the pieces, but for Madhab, they all come out at random, and he can't make sense of them.'

'Yes,' agreed Janet, with a glance at Mad-hab. 'At least, I think that's how it is for him. He *is* very bright, and he works very hard at it, but it's a constant struggle, and he often gets things wrong. If you take time, and give him the pieces one after the other in the right order, he can understand most things – and he understands more than he can express.'

'How much of this is just because he's still learning English? I mean, after all, he's only been in Britain – what, two years?'

'Two years and a few months. Mr Shahid, English is his *only* language. He never heard Nepali or Limbu – that's the language they spoke in his village – and he doesn't speak either of them at all.'

'Isn't Limbu his surname?' Shahid asked bemusedly.

'Yes. Yes, it is. It's also a language, a Gurkha tribe and – because it's the name of a tribe – a very common Gurkha surname. Look at a list of Gurkhas some time – Victoria Cross winners, for a good example. Most of them are called Magar, Rai, Gurung or Limbu. Those are the names of the Gurkha tribes.'

Shahid was amused. 'So Gurkhas are like Scottish highlanders in more ways than military distinction? They're clansmen?'

'Not *exactly*. Tribes are bigger and more distinct than clans. They all have their own languages, for example – though they're all related Tibeto-Burman languages. *Very* difficult for a poor Indo-European speaker to learn. That's one reason I haven't tried to teach Madhab to speak Limbu. I know, probably I should have – but I never could speak more than a few words of it, and we've been in England since he had his ears fixed. It seemed ... I don't know – just more complication than anyone should have to handle, to face *two* languages when you've never had experience with *any*.'

Shahid let out his breath with a little hiss, blinking slowly. 'I find it difficult to imagine how someone could *think* without language.'

'It is hard to imagine,' she agreed. 'But ... well, imagine you're trying to do something mechanical – fix a door, maybe, or work out how to fit a bulky object into a small space. You don't use language to do that; you sort of visualize things, how they fit together, one step after another. That's one kind of thinking we do without language. Or there's mathematics – that's pure reasoning, and it doesn't use words, either. Madhab's very good at both of those things. I think probably he relies on those methods of thinking more than we do. There's nothing wrong with his mind, but he's trapped in it, unable to communicate.'

Shahid shook his head wonderingly. 'Still, very hard to imagine. I never thought about it before.' He was silent a moment, then began to smile a little. 'I suppose, though, that even when we use words, the *meaning* must be separate from the words themselves. I was brought up bilingual – my father's Egyptian and my family spoke Arabic at home – and sometimes I'm aware of the meaning I want to express as something that isn't English or Arabic, because you'd have to express it differently in the different languages.'

'One of the linguists I've read argued that we all think in something called "mentalese", and translate it,' Janet said warmly. 'I think that's right. Sometimes even in English we have translation difficulties. The other day I got into a discussion about whether angling was a sport.'

Shahid nodded enthusiastically. 'Yes! Whether or not you think it is would depend on your mental concept of a sport. It's really the opposite situation to what happens to me with English and Arabic. There I have two ways of expressing one meaning, but you had two people with different meanings for one word!'

They smiled at each other. Then Janet glanced at Madhab and saw the sad resignation on his face. He was excluded, as ever, from the rapid exchange of ideas, from the flow and rush of information between two minds, from all the richness and delight of conversation. She reached over and caught his hand, in a vain attempt to draw him in; then squeezed the hand and let go again. 'Like I said, Madhab has a natural ability to think mechanically,' she told Shahid. 'He can see at a glance how a simple machine is supposed to work – something that I often have trouble understanding even when somebody explains it to me! He's turning out to be very talented at maths as well; but so much hinges on *verbal* reasoning, and he can't do it.' She paused a moment, then added, 'His English probably will improve some, even if David's treatment doesn't work, but all the people I've consulted say he'll never be able to speak and understand normally. It's like songbirds: apparently they have to hear the song of their own species during a critical period during their development. If they don't, they'll still try to sing, but they'll never get it right.'

'And you're trying to help him sing.'

'Yes,' she agreed, blushing and looking down. 'I know, you're probably wondering

59

"What business is it of hers?" It looks pretty suspicious, this middle-aged Englishwoman snatching a Nepalese orphan away from his home and his relatives and pushing him into a lot of high-powered experimental medicine. I can understand why you're worried. All I can say is that Madhab's the most extraordinary person I've ever met. Once I realized what he was like, I didn't really have any choice. You can't just ... just turn your back on somebody like that.'

'Plenty of people do,' said Shahid quietly.

She was saved from having to think of a reply to that by the waiter arriving with the food. When the bustle of plates had settled, Shahid ate a forkful of trout and then asked, 'What were you doing in Nepal, anyway?'

'Voluntary work,' she explained. 'With a charity that sends British doctors and nurses out there for a year. The rural areas are short of trained doctors – it's a poor country, the government can't afford expensive staff for clinics outside the towns, and it's hard for rural people to get into the towns. The roads are mostly non-existent: sometimes the only way to get to hospital is to walk for a week. People die of things nobody ever dies of in the West. Madhab's mother, for example: she cut her foot and died of septicaemia – *died*, because she was a poor widow and couldn't even get antibiotics! That was before our clinic was set up; if it had happened a couple of years later, we could have saved her. I ... well, the truth of the matter is that I'd just been through a miserable divorce, and I wanted to get right away from everything and do something really *worthwhile*. I met Madhab when he mended my pump.' She smiled at Madhab, who had been listening watchfully, barely touching his curry. 'You remember, Madhab? How you fixed my pump?'

At that he smiled back. 'Good rememba.'

They talked about Nepal for a bit, and Madhab finally began to relax. He was even able to join in the conversation a little, supplying details of life in the Himalayas: the perpetual chore of fetching firewood, the endless labour on the terraced fields. From this they passed to life in Leicester: Madhab's place at a special school; Janet's struggles with bureaucracy to get him there; hi startling progress in everything which did not involve language; his struggle with everything that did; Janet's frustration in her bid to adopt. Shahid – Michael, as he asked her to call him – was intelligent, perceptive and sympathetic, and Janet found herself enjoying the meal more and more. She was sorry when it ended.

Michael paid the bill, and they went back to their cars.

'Well,' said Michael, putting his hands in his pockets. 'Um. Thank you. I enjoyed that.'

Janet abruptly realized that she had done nearly all the talking, and that she had not discussed David's research, which had, after all, been the point of the exercise. She had eaten lunch under false pretences! Her face burned. 'I ... I'm sorry I wasn't more informative!' she stammered. 'I was supposed to tell you about what David's doing.'

Michael smiled, eyes creasing behind the specs. 'I wouldn't have enjoyed that nearly as much. I don't get to hear about *good* people as often as I'd like.' Then he shifted uncomfortably. 'Anyway, mostly I just, uh, wanted to be sure you weren't still offended.'

'No, no!' she protested. 'I overreacted anyway. I should've been *pleased* that you were thinking of things like that. I was just tense because ... well, because of the whole business – not knowing how it will turn out, worrying in case something goes wrong. We had a burglary, too, which didn't help.'

Michael took his hands out of his pockets, straightening to sudden concerned attention. 'A burglary? When was this?'

She waved it away. 'Oh ... while we were in Oxford for the surgery. We came back to the house and found we'd been burgled. I was pretty upset.'

'Horrible thing to come home to,' agreed Michael. He was frowning. 'Did you lose much?'

She shrugged. 'Our computers. My jewel-

lery box, with some sentimental stuff in it –
that's the worst of it. Not much else, though.
I think they knew I'm a doctor and were
looking for drugs – not that I keep any in the
house. They turned everything upside-
down.'

'Well,' said Michael, looking helpless and
concerned. 'Well. I'm very sorry.'

She smiled. 'It's not your fault, is it? But,
anyway – thank you very much for the lunch.
I hope we meet again some time.'

He offered his hand, as he had when they
had met. 'I hope we do.'

She wondered, as she drove home, whether
he really hoped that. She doubted it. The
more she thought about the way she'd talked
over lunch, the more she cringed with
embarrassment. Why had she gone on about
Madhab's school like that, or about the
stupidity of the council social worker who'd
interviewed her about the adoption? What
possible interest were those things to
Michael Shahid? He'd only been there because he had doubts about funding David's
research! She hadn't asked him anything
about himself, either – she still didn't even
know what organisation he worked for. All
she knew was that his father was Egyptian,
and that was only because he'd volunteered
it. He must, she concluded gloomily, consider her a very boring woman. A pity,
because she really *liked* him.

She realized, with a wave of hot shame, that she knew that he wasn't wearing a wedding ring. She could not remember noticing it, but her mind had retained it as a salient fact. How stupid! It didn't even mean that he wasn't married, let alone that he might be interested in a boring middle-aged Leicester GP.

She swore silently that she would not, *not*, turn into some caricature of a Desperate Divorcee, frantic to hunt down a new husband before it was too late. She would work hard at the things she had – at looking after Madhab, at her friendships and her family and her job – not fling herself into a struggle to grab the things she lacked. A perpetual chase for things beyond your reach was not the way to be happy. Love and marriage might well be beyond her. Her last attempt at them certainly hadn't worked out very well.

They arrived back in Leicester in the middle of the afternoon. There were no nasty surprises awaiting them: either the new locks had worked, or else the burglars hadn't yet got round to trying the house again. Janet spent the rest of the day trying to get her new computer hooked up to her old e-mail, while Madhab watched television and played at maths puzzles.

The next two days passed quietly. Janet had

decided not to take any work while Madhab's treatment was at such a delicate stage, so that she would be free to rush him back to hospital if there were any signs of danger; but in fact David's cocktail still seemed to have had no effect at all. Madhab continued to recover well from the brain surgery; his natural energetic cheerfulness started to come back, and his scar began to itch. On Friday morning they once again headed south toward Oxford.

The car park at Somers Synaptic was, once again, nearly empty: two cars, one David's, the other presumably belonging to Elena, the secretary, since she was the only other person in the lab. When they'd been admitted, Janet asked David what had happened to his staff.

'Oh – the others took the day off,' said David dismissively.

'It's not a holiday – is it?' Janet asked dubiously.

David gave her a sharp look, then said, 'I think there's some local thing on in Didcot. Once a couple of them say they want the day off, they might as well all go.'

'Oh.' She looked at his face a moment, wishing that the china-blue eyes were less opaque. 'What about on Tuesday?'

'What *about* on Tuesday?' demanded David impatiently. He leaned against the examining table, looking put-upon.

'There was nobody but you and Elena here on Tuesday as well,' Janet pointed out.

'And that man Shahid,' said David, suddenly fierce. 'If you want the truth, I suspected he was nosing about trying to find some excuse to shut down my funding, and I didn't want my people gossiping to him. Huh!' The fierceness faded, and he added, more brightly, 'You shut him up very nicely.'

'He had a perfectly valid worry,' said Janet mildly. 'He was just mistaken.'

'Mm,' agreed David. 'Anyway, I gave my people Tuesday morning off, and today they're off at the Didcot Festival, or whatever it is, and I'm here alone for the sole purpose of treating Madhab. Tell him to lie down and let me have another look at the shunt.'

The delivery of the stem cells should have been momentous. In a film it would have been done in slow motion, with soaring violins and a menacing beat on the timpani. In reality, of course, it was boring. Madhab lay on the table, talking – this time about his maths class – while the solution oozed slowly through the microshunt into his brain. After half an hour the ampoule was empty, and David disconnected it and tossed it into the bin.

'Good,' he said, with satisfaction. 'Now, you take this...' He ducked into the biological section of the lab and came back with a

66

rack of three more ampoules, chilled from the refrigerator. Janet had been expecting this, and eyed the drugs with respect. These were more neural growth stimulants – a different and simpler mixture from the 'priming' dose. The idea was to give one ampoule to Madhab every other day. He would receive regular doses over the next few weeks, their frequency depending on how well he was responding, and perhaps another batch of stem cells after a month or two.

'I presume you know how to insert these into the shunt?' asked David, and she nodded.

'Store them at between 5 and 15 degrees C?' she asked, checking it, and received an impatient nod. She put the rack of ampoules into a refrigerated case to take home.

'Right,' concluded David. 'Now all he needs is lots of exposure to language. Come back in a week. I don't expect there to be any change before then, but if there is, tell me. Next time I'll have the linguist in to do some tests, and then we'll decide on the maintenance dose of the growth factors. OK?'

'Right,' said Janet. She felt unsettled, almost cheated: after so much anxiety, there should have been something eventful to report.

Three

They drove back to Leicester, pausing to buy some lunch in a Little Chef off the M40. When they arrived home, Janet was surprised to see a vaguely familiar car parked in the street outside the house.

She pulled into the drive and parked. At once the doors of the other car opened. Michael Shahid emerged from the driver's seat and came over to her, while a fat young man in a frayed jumper exited from the passenger side and hesitated in the open car door.

'Hello!' said Michael. He seemed anxious and unhappy. 'I, uh, need to talk to you.'

'Hello,' replied Janet, caught between pleasure and alarm. She eyed his companion uncertainly.

'This is my colleague, Simon Gorce,' Michael informed her, and waved the other man forward.

Simon Gorce closed the passenger door, then went to the boot and took out a battered overnight bag.

'I've asked Simon to check your house,'

Michael explained. 'I, uh ... well, please would you allow him to do that?'

'Check my house?' Janet repeated in bewilderment. 'Check my house for what?'

'Bugs,' Michael answered unhappily.

'What?' Janet demanded indignantly. 'Look, my house may be a bit *run down*, but it isn't *infested* – and even if it was, I don't see what business that would be of yours! Maybe I gave you the wrong idea when I told you about my fights with Social Services. I *am* a doctor, I *do* know how to look after—'

'Not that sort of bug,' Michael interrupted.

There was a silence while she tried to take this in. Simon Gorce came over, carrying his case. He was in his early twenties, stout rather than obese, with a pale, acne-scarred face and greasy fair hair.

'Hi,' he said cheerfully. 'Where do you want me to start?'

'What?' asked Madhab, also out of the car and gazing at the visitors with open hostility.

'I don't know "what",' Janet told him. She looked hard at Michael Shahid. 'Maybe you'd better explain.'

He put his hands into his pockets. 'I, uh, have reason to suspect that your house may have been bugged – that the burglary you mentioned wasn't what it seemed. I'd, uh, just like to check it. Please.'

'That isn't any sort of explanation!' Janet

objected angrily.

'Um,' said Michael uncomfortably, 'let me show you something.'

He went over to his car and opened the boot. Janet stayed where she was, rigid with surprise and indignation.

Michael came back, carrying something – carrying a wooden box ... a carved wooden box about twenty centimetres square ... a box she had purchased in India on the way back from Nepal. 'Is this yours?' he asked, offering it.

'My jewellery box!' she exclaimed in a strangled voice, and took it.

Her great-grandmother's necklace was missing, likewise some of the good earrings George had given her for birthdays and Christmases in years past; but the wedding ring was there, a simple gold circle lying amid a jumble of cheap costume pieces. She fished it out and held it tightly, remembering the way George had looked at her when he had slid it on to her finger.

'I, uh, found that,' Michael said awkwardly, 'in some rented accommodation here in Leicester – well, uh, to tell the truth, in the skip behind it – anyway, I found it behind a building that was used by some people whom we ... that is, by the people I suspected of being behind the burglary. It is yours, then? Oh, dear.' He sighed deeply. 'Were you aware that Dr Somers' research is currently being funded by the Ministry of Defence?'

Janet stared at him in consternation.

'No,' supplied Michael, with an air of satisfaction. 'Somers said he hadn't told you, but I wasn't sure – he'll say anything if he thinks it will improve his funding.'

'What on earth has language impairment got to do with the MoD?' Janet demanded – then swallowed, because her voice had come out shrill.

'I think he sold his research proposal as a means of improving intelligence effectiveness,' Michael replied apologetically. 'That's why our department was called in to oversee it, anyway. If the treatment works, it would mean we could train our own people to speak any language we liked with the fluency of a native speaker and with whatever accent we chose. That's obviously, um, a very desirable thing for an intelligence service.'

'I...' began Janet – and found she had no idea what to say. Michael Shahid watched her with a kind of resigned anxiety.

'Who's "we", anyway?' she demanded. 'I thought...'

He dug his wallet out of his pocket, riffled through it, extracted a card and handed it to her. It bore a digitized photo of him, had a magnetic strip down the back and carried his name printed across an image of a winged sea horse surmounted by the royal portcullis and crown. Below the crest were the words: 'MI5. The Security Service.'

'Good God,' she said numbly, looking up at his bespectacled face. 'You're a card-carrying *spy*?'

'Well...' he said in embarrassment.

'I didn't even know spies carried cards!'

'Only bureaucrats like me,' he said. 'Not the field operatives, obviously.' He sighed again. 'I'm sorry; this is, obviously, something of a shock to you. Look – please can you let Simon have a look at the house? I'll take you and Madhab off somewhere where we can talk.'

'We could talk in the house...' she began, but he was already shaking his head gloomily. 'Oh. You think it's bugged.'

'I'm afraid so.'

'Janet?' asked Madhab anxiously. 'What, "bugged"?'

'Oh, God!' she exclaimed. She swallowed several times, fighting a sense that this couldn't really be happening: it was too far removed from the ordinary pattern of her life even to make sense. She remembered having felt the same way when George had told her he wanted a divorce.

'Madhab, I'll try to explain later,' she said at last. She looked up at Michael Shahid, and found him still patiently waiting for her to compose herself. A card-carrying spy! 'Yes, all right,' she said numbly. 'I'll let

Simon have a look at the house, and then yes, please, explain what's going on!'

She unlocked the house, admitted Simon Gorce, put away the jewellery box, and unpacked the rack of drugs into the fridge. Then – moved by some absurd impulse of conventional courtesy – she put on the kettle and made tea for Gorce. He thanked her, opened up his case and took out equipment, setting the mug to one side, for all the world like a plumber come to fix the drains. She left him to it and went back outside the house, trailed by Michael and Madhab.

'Madhab, how are you feeling?' she asked, when they were back in the front garden. 'Does your head hurt? You can go lie down, if you want. I'll explain later.'

He shook his head. 'OK. With Janet.' He gave Michael a look of deep distrust.

'You OK to walk, then? Or shall we sit in the car?'

'Walk OK.'

She glanced around the quiet suburban street. A woman was walking a dog on the other side of the road, but no one else was about. Where was the nearest place to sit and talk? She gestured vaguely towards the right. 'If we go this way we come down to the river,' she explained to Michael Shahid. 'There are places to sit there.' He nodded.

For a few minutes they walked in silence. It was a cold day for July, overcast and breezy.

The leaves of the birches and rowans in the suburban gardens along the road flashed white in the wind, and the rose bushes spilled petals on to the trimmed lawns. Michael walked with his hands in his pockets and his head bowed; Madhab watched him suspiciously. Janet struggled to put her thoughts into some kind of order.

The road ended in a T-junction, and beyond it was the strip of green land and the footpath that followed the course of the River Soar for miles. There were benches placed beside the footpath at intervals, looking out over the river toward the city centre. They made their way to one and sat down under a willow tree.

'So,' said Janet at last. 'Why is the Ministry of Defence funding Madhab's treatment? I mean, I guess I can see why ... *your* people ... might be interested, but I can't understand why David would've agreed to it. I mean, I can't believe you're going to let him publish, and I *know* he wants to be rich and famous. He made *me* sign a secrecy agreement, but I thought that was just to protect his patent rights until he published it himself with a lot of noise. Did you just find out about it, think it might be useful and – what is the term? – D-notice it, or something?'

Michael cleared his throat uncomfortably. 'Umm ... the project is D-noticed now, but I believe Dr Somers approached the department, not the other way around. He'd lost his licence to perform animal experiments, and he thought the MoD could get it back for him.'

'He lost his licence?' Janet repeated. She remembered David's angry and self-righteous comments about the monkeys; the empty barn; the empty cages. 'Oh, God!' She should have suspected, but she had not. 'What did he do?' she asked, with dread. Cruelty to animals sickened her. It was too close to cruelty to humans: most serial killers began with it. David had done God-knew-what to those poor monkeys, and she'd trusted him to put his gloved fingers and his probes into Madhab's *brain!*

'I don't really know the details,' Michael told her. 'I think it was more in the line of carelessness and callousness than active cruelty. Filthy cages, unsuitable food, inadequate pain relief – I know there was a whole catalogue of breaches of the guidelines. All I really know, though, is that last autumn he lost his licence to work on animals. Since all of his work involved animal experiments, this meant that he lost his funding from more conventional sources. So he went to the MoD.' There was a silence, and then Michael went on, 'Actually, he was wrong to think they could get him his licence back. They operate under the same constraints as anybody else. He was delighted when you provided him with an acceptable case for a clinical trial.' He noticed Janet's horrified expression and added quickly, 'He'd done a lot of testing *before* he lost the licence. He applied for approval of a clinical trial through the normal procedures, and he got it. He didn't lie to you about that.'

Janet said nothing. She was appalled and ashamed. She told herself that she should never have sought out this treatment from a man she'd always felt was untrustworthy. She had failed to care for Madhab properly, failed to protect him. God, she should never have tried to play mother! She wasn't up to the job.

Madhab caught her shoulder. 'Janet,' he said concernedly.

She threw her arms around him and hugged him fiercely. 'I'm sorry,' she choked. 'I'm sorry, Madhab.'

He disentangled himself with hasty teenage dignity. 'What?' he demanded, distressed and frustrated. He turned angrily to Michael. 'What?' he asked again. 'David Somers, what? Bad man? This, bad?' He touched his microshunt.

'Ah,' said Michael. 'No. That is not bad. As far as I know, that is good. David Somers ... is not so good.' He hesitated, as though trying to think how to put it in 'little bits', then went on, with gestures, 'David Somers did not tell – your foster-mother – important

76

things.'

Madhab frowned. 'Sonova bitch,' he commented bitterly. 'Bad man.' He was silent a moment, then asked, 'Hurt Janet?'

'She fears he might hurt *you*.'

Madhab shook his head. 'OK, me. Fine.' He again touched Janet on the shoulder gently. 'OK, me. Bad David Somers, good give word. OK.'

Janet sniffed and wiped at her eyes. 'I should have asked more questions.'

'You were desperate to give your foster-son a full and free life,' Michael said gently. 'And Madhab is right: the treatment is as good as it ever was.'

'Oh, yeah!' she said bitterly. 'If it's so good, why weren't your spies queueing up for it? Why did you wait until David had Madhab to practise on?'

'Actually, we considered recruiting a healthy volunteer,' Michael replied unexpectedly. 'But, as I said, when it comes to our dealings with other bureaucracies we're operating under the same constraints as anybody else. The medical establishment won't approve an experimental treatment for trial unless there's a demonstrable clinical need, and we really couldn't claim a clinical need for someone to speak Arabic with a Saudi accent. And if we'd done it without medical approval – well, if anything had gone wrong, our agent could've sued. We worry about things like that these days much more than they used to in the past.'

She wiped her eyes again and swallowed. 'Why are you telling me this? Because of the burglary?'

He nodded. 'It represents a breach of security. Ordinarily, I wouldn't even have told you who I work for. The official line is that we're only supposed to tell our immediate families – though most agents take that about as seriously as they take the speed limit, I'm afraid. I'm not a field operative, though, so I have a bit more latitude. I need to ask you about what was stolen and how much the people who stole it will have learned, so that means I need to identify myself. Um ... I don't want you to get the wrong impression. The Somers Treatment *is* technically an official secret, but it's not highly sensitive, strategic, defence-of-the-realm stuff. As classified material goes, its classification is pretty minimal. It's very likely that Dr Somers will eventually be allowed to publish his results, if not quite as soon as he'd like. Still, the fact that somebody burgled your house is a breach of security, which means that we have to investigate.' He tentatively offered a smile. 'Standard procedure. We *are* a bureaucracy.'

'You said the burglars were people you suspected.'

Michael nodded and leaned back against

the bench. 'When you said that you'd been burgled and that the burglars had made a mess of the house as though they were searching for drugs – well, obviously, that set off all sorts of alarm bells. I went back and did a check on known suspects.' He paused, giving her his apologetic look. 'We, um, have a lot of people on the computer. That's one of our ways of justifying our existence these days: we have a big database on our computers, so we can help the police keep track of terrorists and drug-dealers ... or we could, if we could find some way to cooperate with the police. Anyway, I started asking the computer questions, and eventually I found a pair of suspects – or rather, a German couple thought to be a possible match for a pair of suspects – in Leicester. So I came up here to check them out – only, of course, they were gone by the time I arrived. I found your jewellery box, though, and a couple of other items in the rubbish from their room – enough to make me think the German couple had been correctly identified. So I asked Simon to come along and check your house for bugs.'

'Germans?' Janet echoed in bewilderment.

'Mm. Ex-Stasi freelancers.'

'What ... that is, who ... I mean, the whole East German state hasn't existed for *years*; anybody who used to work for them must be...'

Michael smiled. 'Yes, they're getting older; but the Stasi employed a lot of people, and obviously the post reunification German intelligence service wants nothing to do with them. Nor does anyone else. A lot of them went into freelance work, and many are still there: private investigating, corporate surveillance, industrial espionage – and regular espionage, if for some reason the, uh, interested party doesn't want to do an operation itself.' He paused, then added, 'In this case I'm afraid I've got very little idea of who the interested party could be. I'm pretty confident that the Americans and the Israelis wouldn't have hired ex-Stasis, but apart from that, the field is wide open. It could even be industrial rather than political – though, given that it's happened *after* we got involved, that's unlikely.'

Janet imagined the sinister, black-clad agents of some unknown foreign power poring over the files on her computer. Or the *German spies*, for God's sake, like something out of the Second World War! What would they make of her list of what Madhab needed for school, her letters to the phone company about a mistake in the billing for her mobile, her rant at the Immigration Service over their suspicions of Madhab? She wasn't sure whether to burst out laughing or fly into a rage. 'Why would whoever-it-is be interested?' she asked. 'For the same reason you are?'

'Possibly,' replied Michael. 'To tell the truth, though, I suspect that whoever it is knew only that *we* were interested in this, and commissioned the burglary to find out what was going on. Will the material you lost be enough to tell them?'

She considered that a minute. 'I think so,' she concluded. 'All my letters were on the computer – all the ones I printed, anyway. There was a lot about Madhab. I'm sure I told the authorities that he was having a treatment for his language impairment. The Immigration people admitted him to Britain "for medical treatment", see, and they keep trying to tell me that the treatment's complete and he should go back to his relatives in Nepal. I had to explain that he was still receiving treatment, and what it was for. Obviously I didn't give them the technical details, but I must've told them pretty much everything else.'

Michael nodded resignedly. 'What I expected. And I take it you hadn't encrypted the files on your computer, or passworded them? No, of course not. What else did they get?'

'My answering machine – but there probably wasn't much on that, just talk about locum work. Um ... they threw all the letters and bills from my filing cabinet on the floor. That means they must have seen all the letters people had sent to me about Mad-hab.'

'They'll have checked those, maybe photographed a couple of them. Anything else?'

'My great-grandmother's necklace,' said Janet bitterly, 'and nearly everything of real value that was in my jewellery box. If they were really spies, why did they bother with those?'

'If their employers ask them that, they'll probably say "To make it look like a burglary"; but I'm perfectly certain they pick up stray cash and valuables whenever they get a chance. These are not honest people, Dr Morley. As far as they're concerned, your jewellery was a bonus. I'm sorry. Well, on the bright side, whoever hired them probably isn't *interested* in a treatment for language impairment.' He snorted unhappily. 'On the other hand, they probably won't believe that *we're* interested in one, either, and they'll suspect that this is cover for something else. I'm sorry. I'm very sorry.'

For a moment she didn't take that in. The possibility of being affected by the manoeuvrings of foreign spies seemed so melodramatic as to be ludicrous. Then she realized that Michael did not find it melodramatic – that, to Michael, it was a matter-of-fact reality. Such things did happen; in his circle they happened all the time. Now they were happening to her.

'What are they likely to do?' she asked with dread.

He frowned. 'Well ... as I said, I suspect that they left a few bugs in your house. Somebody's likely to be monitoring you, trying to work out what's really going on. Possibly it will be the Germans; possibly it will be whoever it is that hired them.' He looked at her for a moment, intently and unhappily. 'If you could bear it, it would probably be best if you just let them listen. From what you say, they wouldn't learn anything more than they've learned already, so all it could do would be to confirm that what they've learned is true. As I said, I very much doubt they'll be interested in a treatment for language impairment, and once they're convinced that that's all this is about, they'll lose interest.'

She bit her lip. 'Am I in danger? Is Madhab?'

He seemed shocked. 'Oh no! Nothing like that. I don't ... that is, it's highly unlikely that we're dealing with terrorists here. It's not their style at all, not their sphere of operations. No, I'm sure this is the work of an established intelligence service – unless, as I said, the whole thing is industrial after all. Established intelligence services these days aren't likely to engage in violence – particularly not in a suburb in the middle of England! I won't try and tell you that this is nothing to worry about – I know you've had your property stolen and your privacy violated, and of course you're worried and upset – but I don't think you need to be *afraid*.' He hesitated, then added, diffidently, 'Though you're very welcome to phone me any time if you want help or advice.'

'Thank you,' she said, and tried to think of something else to ask. She was sure that as soon as he was gone she would think of a thousand questions, but just now her mind was numb. 'Can I also phone you with questions?' she asked at last.

'Yes,' he said, smiling eagerly. 'Yes, please do.'

He gave her his office, home and mobile phone numbers, and his e-mail address; she carefully wrote them down in her address book. There was a moment of awkward silence, and then he said earnestly, 'I really am sorry this has happened.'

She thought of saying, 'I'm not sorry if it means I see a bit more of you' – but no, she couldn't possibly say that: it was far too forward, and anyway, she didn't know that it was true. She, too, was sorry this had happened, and she wasn't at all sure she did want to see any more of him. He wasn't what she'd thought he was, and probably that meant that what she'd seen in him was false, an act he'd put on to baffle her. A cover story – or, in other words, a pack of lies.

'Yes. Well,' she replied instead. 'It's not your fault.' It was the conventional thing to say, but even as she said it, she decided it was true. Michael Shahid was just doing his job. David was the one who'd got *spies* involved in this. Not knowing what else to do, she got up and began walking back toward the house.

'Janet?' asked Madhab, hurrying up beside her. 'What?'

'Oh, God!' she exclaimed, her heart sinking. 'It isn't easy to explain.'

She tried to explain it anyway, and after a while Michael tried to help her. They were still working on it when they arrived back at the house.

Simon Gorce met them in the entrance hall. He put a finger on his lips and beckoned them into the kitchen.

'Two,' he told Michael, 'both on the phone; one a wire tap, and the other a pretty standard trip that will feed down the wire. The rest of the house is clean. My guess is they aren't willing to collect.'

'Good. Good,' Michael said, with evident relief. He caught Janet's look of puzzled suspicion and explained, 'Your house phone's tapped, and there's a listening device attached to it that will record sound in the hall and relay it down the telephone line. Simon couldn't find anything else, and he's very good. The fact that they haven't planted any listening devices in the rest of the house is a good sign. It means they aren't willing to set up a local base or move in a van to collect the signal. Probably they don't have the resources for it. This isn't a high priority for them, either. Probably they'll soon conclude that it's exactly what it appears to be, and go away.'

'And you think I should leave the tap on the phone,' she said.

'If you can bear it,' he replied. 'If you take it off, they'll know that we're aware of them, and the whole business is likely to last much longer. We'll come and take it off for you as soon as they've given up.'

'How will you know when that is?'

He was mildly surprised. 'Obviously we're going to follow this up. We have to find out who they are.'

She sighed unhappily. She thought of foreign spies listening in to her conversations with the health authority. She imagined James Bond abseiling in to the local hospital. She pictured a pair of TV Gestapo threatening Madhab: 'Ve haff vays of making you talk!'

Madhab would be delighted if they had a way to make him talk. How *stupid!*

'OK, leave it on!' she snapped; then, suddenly struck by it, 'How am I supposed to phone *you*, if you don't want them aware that you know about them?'

86

'Ah. Well, don't use the house phone, obviously. I think a pay phone would be best for routine questions; use your mobile in an emergency ... or, no, no, they probably know the details of your mobile from the burglary. I'll get you a new mobile. Our expense. I'll post it to you tomorrow.'

'Thank you,' she said, unhappily.

Michael Shahid left shortly afterwards, taking Simon Gorce with him. Janet watched them leave from the doorway, then turned back into the entrance hall. The phone sat on its table against the wall, listening. She glared at it in disgust and went into the kitchen to make herself a drink.

She spent an uncomfortable weekend avoiding the phone. Madhab, irritatingly, seemed to have shrugged off the whole business, and was in good spirits, even though the treatment still didn't seem to be having any effect. He watched more television than usual – undoubtedly in an effort to increase his exposure to language – and enlisted Janet's help to struggle through some of the reading primers he'd been given at school. (They rewarded themselves after each simple booklet with four pages of his favourite book, a humorous, lavishly illustrated tome called *The Way Things Work*.) On Sunday morning she gave him another ten millilitres of the growth factors, and once again the drugs diffused into his brain without, apparently, doing anything at all.

The new mobile arrived on Monday morning, by first class post. It was a good one, very small and neat, with a twenty-pound prepaid card. With it was a note: *Don't use this except in an emergency. Pay phones are more secure. Call me when you get it, and I'll try and answer any questions you have. Again, I apologize for the disruption. Michael Shahid.*

She telephoned his office number from the pay phone at the local shops when she went to buy groceries. A woman's voice answered: 'Research and Training.'

'Uhh...' gasped Janet, taken aback. Somehow she had never expected that you could just dial up MI5 and be answered by a *departmental secretary*: it seemed far too mundane for the world of spies. 'Can I speak to Michael Shahid, please?'

'Who's calling, please?'

'Dr Janet Morley.'

'Oh, yes!' The voice was suddenly warm and amused. 'He's been waiting for you to call. I'll put you through.'

There was a pause, and then Michael's voice said eagerly, 'Janet?'

Part of her registered that it was the first time he hadn't called her 'Dr Morley', and she was not sure whether to be pleased or irritated. 'Research and Training?' she asked.

'Well. Yes. That's my department – though, like I told you, I only moved here a few weeks ago. What can I do for you?'

'I got the phone,' she told him, and hesitated.

'Oh, good!'

'Though I'm calling from a pay phone now. Is there anything else I should be doing, or anything I shouldn't be doing?'

There wasn't, not much. If she thought she was being followed, she should stick to public places and phone as soon as possible; she should report anything suspicious; she should try not to worry unduly, 'though I know that that may be hard to carry out'. When he had finished giving the advice, such as it was, Michael asked hesitantly, 'When are you next seeing Dr Somers?'

'Friday.'

'Ah. I was thinking of coming along again. Would you object?'

'No, though he might. You know that last time you came he sent all his staff off so that they couldn't gossip to you?'

'*Did* he?' asked Michael, in surprise. 'He told me that they'd gone to a festival in Didcot.'

'That's what he told me last Friday! There was nobody but him and Elena there then, too.'

There was a silence on the other end of the line. Janet heard in it the echo of her own suspicions. She hadn't really believed David's explanation even at the time. He'd always been a liar in med school – 'Oh, I missed the deadline for that project because I had flu,' when she knew very well it was because he'd drunk himself silly at the Dog and Trumpet; and 'I'm not involved with anybody else,' when there were at least two girls who thought differently.

'Probably,' said Michael at last, 'he's dismissed most of his staff. He probably gave them their notice as soon as he had the clinical trial set up, and he isn't admitting it because he wants to carry on collecting their salaries. After all, they are people he recruited when he was able to work on animals, and they've probably been underemployed ever since he lost his licence. I expect that's all it is.'

'What else are you afraid of?' she asked – because it was there in his voice, that he was afraid it might be something worse.

There was another silence. 'I don't know,' Michael said heavily. 'Some kind of deal involving the people who commissioned your burglars, or, worse, some problem in the treatment that he doesn't want you to discover. Dear God, I hope not. You would have caught something like that, wouldn't you?'

She swallowed, her throat suddenly dry. 'I ... I don't know. Brain research is very specialized: I really don't know very much more about it than a layman. The treatment *was* approved for clinical trial, though. He would've had to submit evidence that it was safe, to get that approval, and if there was a real problem with it I don't think he would've been able to get it through. Unless there was something that came up on the animal trials that he suppressed.' She remembered David's smug satisfaction when she signed the consent form and the waiver, and felt cold all over. 'We're going to have to sort this out at once!' she exclaimed in horror.

'Probably it's nothing but a scam to collect funds,' Michael told her soothingly, 'but I agree. What time is it?'

It was ten minutes past three. 'Too late to do anything today,' Michael concluded. 'Tomorrow – damn! I have a meeting tomorrow morning. Tomorrow afternoon? I could meet you in the car park at the pub where we had lunch, and we could go on to Somers Synaptic together.'

'I could phone him right now. On this phone, not the one at home.'

'No. No, it would be better to confront him in person. Harder for him to bluff and lie his way out of it.'

'What if he's not in tomorrow afternoon?'

'Well ... phone him tomorrow morning. Tell him you'd like to see him, to check a few details or something. Don't tell him that I'm coming too.'

She contemplated the image of David surprised by Michael Shahid. It was surprisingly satisfactory. She realized that, for all his diffident politeness, Michael was not a man who could be brushed aside: there was a stubborn toughness there that she had sensed from the first, and which she was certain David had sensed as well. 'OK,' she agreed. 'I'll phone tomorrow. If it's on, I'll meet you – when? Two? And if he's going to be out, I'll phone and let you know.'

'Yes. Thank you. And ... don't worry. I think it really is likely that all he's doing is a spot of embezzling.'

Four

David was in on Tuesday morning and agreed to see her on Tuesday afternoon to 'discuss some concerns' she had, though he was irritable and resentful about it, and asked why she couldn't just discuss them on the phone.

'I'd rather see you in person,' she told him, and he snapped, 'Oh, very *well*!' and hung up. She phoned Michael and confirmed that she would meet him at two, and then went to tell Madhab.

Madhab's school was closed for th summer holidays: that was one reason why he'd had the treatment when he had. This did not, however, mean that his schedule was empty until September. Janet had no money for a holiday, but that was all right: Madhab had never had a holiday in his life, and had no particular desire for one now. He did, however, consider his long-denied education an enormous opportunity and a privilege. In consequence, he was signed up for remedial reading classes on Monday, Wednesday, and Friday, a 'Maths for Fun' course on Tuesday and Thursday, and – due to start on Saturday and eagerly anticipated – a six-week course at a local technical college called 'Build a Robot'. All of these had been on hold since the operation, since Janet had wanted to keep him under observation until she was sure he was free of immediate danger from the treatment. He had, however, been planning to start at the maths course that afternoon, and when Janet informed him that she planned to go to Oxford, he frowned.

'Maths Fun,' he reminded her.

'Yeah, I know,' she conceded. 'But I think – David Somers – told lies. I want – to learn – "What is the truth".'

Madhab chewed his lip. 'Bad?' he asked anxiously. 'Help?'

She hesitated. It was no use lying to him, though. 'No,' she admitted. 'I don't need you to help. Michael Shahid will help.'

He frowned harder at that. 'Good man?'

'I think so, yes,' she said. 'At least for this.'

Madhab grimaced, then nodded. 'OK.' Then he frowned again and suggested, 'You, Oxford. Me, Maths Fun. House key.' He slapped his pocket.

She hesitated. She could see that, from his point of view, the trip to Oxford was nothing but a long, boring car ride and a meeting to which he could contribute nothing, while 'Maths for Fun' was something he'd been

94

looking forward to. It was, of course, designed not so much for the 'fun' it claimed as to help the bewildered offspring of pushy parents gain a valuable skill; but Madhab genuinely enjoyed it. He hadn't been to the summer course yet, it was true, but he'd regularly attended an evening group run by the same people. Moreover, he was fifteen. In Nepal he would have been considered practically an adult, and in most ways he was well able to look after himself, despite his disability. Ordinarily she wouldn't hesitate to leave him alone in the house. Ordinarily, however, he hadn't been undergoing an experimental brain treatment.

'How is your head?' she asked bluntly.

He rolled his eyes. 'Fine! Fine! Fine head. Good brain med' cine no hurt.'

'Well ... OK, then,' she said reluctantly, and he grinned.

She left him with her old mobile, the number for the new one, and a list of other numbers to call *immediately* in the event of *any of the following symptoms*, plus notes to give to the people once he'd called them. He rolled his eyes and muttered something under his breath.

'What did you say?' she demanded suspiciously.

'Mother fuss, fuss, fuss,' he admitted.

She laughed, brushed his remaining hair over the shaved patch with a sweep of the hand, and set out.

The drive was already familiar to the point of tediousness, and she found it difficult to keep her attention on the road. She found herself remembering the recognition and amusement in the secretary's voice when she had learned who was on the phone: *Oh, yes! He's been waiting for you to call* – and then the eagerness in Michael's *Janet?* Had she imagined it?

If she hadn't imagined it, was she pleased? She could tell herself that she wanted nothing to do with a *spy*, that probably the man she thought she'd seen during that lunch at the country pub did not exist. Driving back to that same pub to meet him again, however, she admitted to herself that the truth was more complicated. She had liked Michael Shahid: liked it that he'd been willing to stop David's experiment dead in its tracks to protect Madhab; liked his quiet manners, his intelligent questions, the way his eyes creased behind his spectacles when he smiled. On the other hand, his job was *not* irrelevant. What sort of person would have applied for a job with MI5? A geekish misfit who thought it would turn him into James Bond? A right-wing super-patriot, ready to defend British interests by fair means or foul? A control freak who just liked to spy on people? And there was ... there was *all that* to take into account, as well – all her own

96

failures. She had loved George to distraction, and still the marriage had failed: was it wise to try again? Was it worth risking the heart-crushing grief and guilt? The triumph of optimism over experience – wasn't that the famous description of second marriages? ... Not that she was even thinking about marriage, of course.

She was not, she reminded herself, a Desperate Divorcee. She had a profession that was challenging and fulfilling. She had friends – and if they had been squeezed into the margins of her life recently, it wasn't because she was a sad loser, but because she had so little time. She had Madhab. She did not need an involvement with a highly dubious character like Michael Shahid.

She was ten minutes late to the meeting, delayed by a traffic jam round Oxford. Michael was already waiting, in his car – a very ordinary silver-grey Peugeot, which she now found she recognized. She parked, and at once he climbed out of his car and came over.

'Hi,' he said, smiling at her through the window.

'Hi,' she replied. 'Um ... do we want to take both cars, or just one?'

They decided to take both cars: while Michael did intend to take Somers Synaptic by surprise, he felt that it would be more stealth than was warranted to emerge unexpectedly from Janet's Datsun.

In the event, the visit turned out not even to be much of a surprise. They arrived, were admitted through the gate, and found the car park once again nearly empty. Elena the secretary scowled furiously at the sight of Michael Shahid, but David, who met them in her office, seemed more irritated than alarmed.

'You as well?' he asked in disgust. 'Huh!' He gave Janet an accusing look. They were all standing in the front office, with Elena glaring at them, but he did not ask them to come in and sit down.

'I've, um, been in contact with Dr Morley about some of my concerns,' Michael said, with that faintly apologetic air. 'I asked if I could join her.'

'This is about the rest of the staff, isn't it?' David demanded. 'I could tell that neither of you were really satisfied about where they were. OK, I admit it: they're gone. I had a quarrel with Jeremy two weeks ago, and he left. The technicians went with him – they always did work for him more than for me. I didn't tell either of you because I didn't want to rock the boat right before we started the trial of the procedure. Satisfied?'

Michael put his hands in his pockets and gave David a long, dark stare.

'No!' exclaimed Janet angrily. Jeremy Firsby, David's molecular biologist associate, had been responsible for preparing the drugs Madhab had received. Janet had met him only a few times, and had found him terminally difficult to talk to – able to discuss molecular biology at great length, but tongue-tied about virtually everything else. She was aware, however, that he had a reputation for work that was solid, if never actually inspired, and his departure was a blow. 'What did you quarrel with him about?'

David flung both hands into the air disgustedly. 'He wanted to do more work with fucking *monkeys*, and if Shahid's been at you, you know why he couldn't! He's told you, hasn't he?' It was an accusation. 'He told you I lost my licence? Fucking do-gooders and their poor little monkeys! Did he tell you who *he* works for?'

'Yes, I did,' said Michael, stopping David short. 'There's been a breach of security, Dr Somers. Dr Morley's house was burgled last week, and has proved to be bugged. Now I find that your colleague and the staff whom we vetted have all left, suddenly and unexpectedly, and that you saw fit to suppress this information. I am appalled.'

Elena made a noise of protest. David's eyes had widened in surprise at the mention of the burglary, but at the finish he seemed to dismiss the matter, and sneered. 'So what are you going to do?' he asked, sounding almost gleeful. 'Cut off my funding – in the middle of the trial? The kid's been treated now; his brain's full of stem cells and growth hormones, all working away like mad. You're going to close down my company, stop his treatment, and *leave* him like that? Dismiss the only man who understands what's been done? Suppose something goes *wrong*? Who's going to correct it for you? If the procedure goes haywire, and sends that kid out of his head, I'll make sure *you* get the blame for it. "MI5 destroys brain of Nepalese child in aborted experiment" – doesn't sound good, does it?'

Even Elena the secretary was looking shocked. 'You *bastard*!' Janet exclaimed in disbelief.

'Oh, grow up!' David replied. 'God, Janet, I know you were a smarmy prig back in med school, but you'd think that fifteen years in the real world would've knocked some sense into you!'

'I underestimated you,' said Michael quietly. 'I thought this was probably a scam to claim your staff's salaries.'

'Oh no!' David leaned back against Elena's desk, crossing his legs. 'No, I'm paying them all their last month's salary. You have to give people a severance package, even if they quit without notice. I mean, shit, they would have gone running to you at once if I hadn't.'

'And if they had come running to us?'

asked Michael. 'They would've lost that money?'

David smirked.

'Where are Dr Firsby and the technicians now?'

David shrugged. 'At home, I imagine. Job-hunting, I expect. I don't suppose you need *me* to tell you their addresses.'

'What about *Madhab*?' Janet demanded furiously. 'What happens to *him*?'

'We continue the trial, obviously,' said David complacently. 'We don't really *need* Jeremy any more. He extracted plenty of the neural growth factors when we were planning the work on the monkeys – enough for another forty doses. If the treatment isn't working by then, it won't work at all. You can bring the kid down on Friday, like we agreed.'

'You *bastard*!' Janet exclaimed again; it was a weak and pointless thing to repeat, but she couldn't stop herself. She suspected that the reason David had felt free to quarrel with his fellow researcher now was *because* Firsby wasn't needed any more – and now that he'd gone, before the trial started, any research paper published would not have to carry his name. David, though, was neither a molecular biologist nor a chemist: if Madhab needed some specialized neural hormone that *hadn't* been prepared in advance, David couldn't provide it. 'Madhab doesn't matter

101

to you any more than the monkeys did, does he?' she shouted.

'For God's sake, why *should* I care about some brain damaged Nepalese kid? He's already got you to wipe his nose for him; he doesn't need me as well. I'm supposed to be repairing the damage to his brain. That's what you asked if I could do, and I'm trying to do it. What more do you want?'

Janet went white with rage.

'That's enough!' snapped Michael. 'What about the security breach?'

'I don't know anything about it,' said David. 'Go ask Firsby, if you're worried.'

'I intend to ask Dr Firsby. I am also asking you.'

'I heard you. Maybe you didn't hear me: I don't know anything about it. This is the first I know of it. There's been nothing suspicious here.'

'You're certain?'

David shrugged impatiently. 'Yes.'

'I am going to have to send a man here to check your lab for bugs. I would also like to send an agent to examine your records, especially your telephone records and your e-mail, to see if there have been any leaks.'

'David!' interrupted Elena the secretary. 'You can't expect me to work with ... with *these people* crawling all over the place!' She gave Michael another furious glare, as though he were a dog that had cocked a leg against her desk.

David scowled. 'What happens if I say no?'

'I will have to conclude that your establishment constitutes an unacceptable security risk,' Michael said composedly, 'and I will recommend to the MoD that they cease funding it at once. I will ask Dr Firsby to assist us, and get him to find another specialist to take over Madhab's treatment. I will authorize him to disclose to that specialist all the treatment you have administered to date.'

David's face went bright red. 'You can't do that! This procedure is *my* intellectual property!'

'As you have just pointed out,' Michael said evenly, 'if the treatment goes wrong it could threaten the well-being of your patient, a vulnerable boy. I think any court would agree that our need to protect him outweighs whatever claims you may assert under patent law.'

'Fuck!' said David, under his breath. He glared at Michael and Janet both. 'All right, you can send somebody to check our records.'

'David!' Elena objected again.

David glanced at her irritably. 'There's nothing there, anyway.'

'I don't want them here!' protested Elena, suddenly close to tears. 'First it was animal rights people over those *bloody* monkeys, and then those horrible spooks from the MoD asking everybody questions, and now it's just me and you want more horrible spooks to come examine—'

'I don't fucking *want* them!' David shouted at her. 'We've fucking *got* them, and we've got to put up with them, OK?'

'No, it's not OK!' screamed Elena. 'You—'

'Oh, shut up!'

Michael touched Janet's arm. 'I think we had better go.' He went to the door, then stopped. 'Dr Somers,' he said quietly, 'if you had come to me immediately after your quarrel with Dr Firsby, it would have been much better.'

They could hear the argument breaking out again as they crossed into the yard, Elena shrill and tearful and David snarling and short. Janet unlocked her car, then stood leaning against it, shaking. 'Shit!' she whispered angrily. 'I am not taking Madhab back to see that man *ever again*!' Even as she said it, she knew she was lying. She had no choice but to take him to see David again.

Michael stood a moment facing her, looking at her with great seriousness. 'Please,' he said abruptly, 'you're in no state to drive back to Leicester. Let's go back to that pub where we met, and we can sit down and have something to drink.'

She gave a gasping laugh. 'If I have something to drink, I'll still be in no state to drive back to Leicester.'

'Have a coffee, then. Or a cup of tea.'

They drove back to the pub in their separate cars. Presently they were sitting in the oak-beamed dining room again, Janet staring at her hands on the white linen tablecloth as Michael ordered tea for two.

'First of all,' said Michael, when the waiter had gone off, 'can you tell me why you approached David Somers in the first place?'

She wiped at her eyes. 'Well ... like I said before, I knew him from med school; I knew he was working on the neurology of language acquisition...'

'You kept track of what he was doing?'

'They send us a newsletter,' she informed him, 'once a year. David had a bit about his work in it, so I wrote to him.'

'Ah.' Michael nodded. 'When was this?'

'Earlier this year. I think it was in January. Why?'

He studied her seriously again. 'Because I think that you're kicking yourself about having approached him, and I'm trying to assess whether or not it's justified.'

She gave another gasping laugh. 'You're right I'm kicking myself! I *knew* he was a slimy bastard; I *knew* it, and yet I still signed Madhab up for his crackpot experimental...'

'Is it crackpot?'

She was silent for a long moment.

'Dr Somers has a reputation for brilliance,'

Michael informed her. 'That's what we were told, when we were trying to decide whether the MoD should fund him: that many other researchers disliked him and refused to work with him, but that he was exceptionally brilliant. The consensus was that, if we could put up with him, he'd deliver the goods.'

'Yes,' she agreed, reluctantly. 'He is brilliant. Everybody always knew that. And no, I suppose it isn't a crackpot experiment. I just ... it's just that first I find out that he's lost his licence because of animal cruelty, and now—'

'January,' he interrupted. 'Your newsletter comes at the beginning of the year, does it? Presumably it was about two years after Madhab had the operation on his ears.'

'Not quite two years, but yes, getting on for that. I don't know. Madhab thought at first that he could learn to speak properly, and I hoped he could. He had all these appointments with speech therapists and psychologists, but...'

'But you both found it was very much harder than you'd expected. He was very frustrated and unhappy, and you wanted to help him. Yes? And then you got a newsletter, and in it you read that the brilliant Dr David Somers was working on the neurology of language, and you decided to contact him to ask if anything could be done for Madhab. He replied very quickly saying that, as it happened, he was working on an experimental treatment to aid language acquisition, and he'd be willing to trial it on Madhab as soon as he had it ready. He promised you it was safe – or that it had been approved for a clinical trial, at least, and carried no more risk than any other procedure involving brain surgery.'

Janet stared at him hard. 'Did you open our letters?'

'No,' he replied, smiling a little. 'That was just a guess.'

The waiter returned to their table with a tray containing tea in a china pot, two willow-pattern teacups, two large scones on a doily-covered plate, a dish of strawberry jam, another of cream, and a saucer of butter. 'Oh, God!' exclaimed Janet, staring at it in consternation. 'I didn't mean to order *food!*'

'It looks very good,' said Michael. 'Don't you like cream teas?'

'Well, yes, but...'

'I'm paying. It was my idea to stop here. Have some tea.'

They helped themselves to tea and scones. Janet split the scone and smeared it with butter, jam and cream, feeling wicked. She shouldn't be enjoying a cream tea; she should be worrying about Madhab.

'I'm not a doctor,' Michael resumed. 'Is the procedure likely to be as risky as Dr

Somers was pretending today – or as safe as he pretended before?'

She was silent for a little, thinking about it. She had a bite of scone. Fresh clotted cream! Quite wrong to think of that now, quite wrong!

She hadn't had clotted cream since that time she went to Devon with George. Shouldn't think about that, either.

'I don't understand the neurochemistry very well,' she said at last. 'And stem-cell research is something I only know about from the journals. But ... but I guess I still don't think the procedure is a bad risk. My impression all along has been that the thing most likely to go wrong is that the whole thing will be for nothing – that Madhab's brain will stay just exactly the way it is now, the way his childhood shaped it. What David was implying today – that the procedure might go haywire and do real damage – I suppose it's *possible*, but I don't think it would have been approved for clinical trial if there was much danger of that. Neural hormones normally break down very quickly – that's why I have to keep delivering more of them to Madhab at home. Some of the experimental treatments for brain damage actually use implanted pumps to deliver growth factors *continuously*, because ordinarily an adult brain just doesn't pay much attention to them. David thinks his are better, but even so, if there was any problem, all I'd have to do would be to stop applying the drugs. Madhab would be clear of them within a couple of days, and whatever effect they were having would stop. I don't think there's ever been a case of stem cells growing too much, either: normally the problem is getting them to grow at all. As far as I know, the main risks involved in the procedure are to do with the brain surgery – infection and inflammation and cerebral haemorrhage and so on. The shunt is supposed to be sterile and hypoallergenic, but there's always the possibility that one of those tubelets will trap bacteria, and then...'

'But you're looking out for that.'

'Yes, of course.'

Michael was smiling at her. 'Did you explain those risks to Madhab?'

'Well, yes, as well as I could. But he's a teenager, *and* he's from a Third World country. He thinks Western doctors are all-powerful, and he doesn't really believe that accidents can happen to *him*. You don't, when you're fifteen. And he longs to fit in, to have a normal life; he wants...'

'He told me: "No word, all over, Madhab." He must have been desperate for this treatment from the moment he knew it existed. Probably he'd still want it, even if he knew it would kill him. Do you *really* think you made the wrong decision in accepting it for him?'

'But ... but David's such a ... such an obnoxious, slimy, smug, self-serving complacent *bastard!*'

Michael laughed. 'Yes. He is.' He sipped his tea, eyes creased in a smile behind the specs. 'It was fairly breathtaking that he should tell *you* to "grow up", when he's the one behaving like a spoiled adolescent.'

She laughed weakly and waved it away. 'I suppose I do need to grow up. I wanted to believe that David was really a decent human being because he was helping me. I suppose I ought to be more honest, and admit that we're using each other. But you're right, you're right. I shouldn't cancel the whole thing just because David's a son of a bitch. In a way, David's right, too. I didn't contact him because I liked him; I contacted him because I hoped he would be able to help Madhab. Maybe if I'd realized how dishonest and unreliable he is, I wouldn't have. But maybe I would've anyway, because I don't know any other way to help Madhab.' She looked across at Michael earnestly. 'I *did* appreciate it when you threatened to shut David's company down, but don't, please don't. This is such a new thing. David understands it; someone else might not. And ... and I've calmed down now. I'm sure that he really does want the treatment to succeed. It's the *Somers* Treatment, after all. It's his hope of profit and glory. If it fails, he'll lose out too.'

Michael nodded. 'That's what I think, too. In a way, I'm reassured. I'll check it, of course, but I do think that all he's after with this trick is academic glory.'

'I'm sure he quarrelled with Jeremy Firsby deliberately. He'd decided that he didn't need him any more, so he got rid of him before the trial actually started. That way he doesn't have to give him any of the credit.'

'You think so too? I was planning to ask Firsby what the quarrel was about. It could not have been just the licence. He would've left last year in that case.'

'You do that. God, David's such an *obnoxious son of a bitch!*'

Michael smiled again. 'I thought at one point you were going to slap him.'

'I wanted to. God!' She had another sip of tea, looked up to find Michael watching her, still with the smile on his face. She smiled back, a bit nervously, and asked suddenly, 'What made you decide to work for MI5?'

He winced and looked away. 'Please, not so loud! And it was a stupid reason. Well, no...' He looked back again, now rueful and embarrassed. 'It wasn't stupid. It's just that I feel an idiot saying it.'

'Why?' she asked, amused. 'You wanted to be James Bond or something?'

He shook his head. 'No, nothing like that at all. It's just that it sounds like something out of a third-rate television drama serial. A quality show would come up with something more original. My wife was murdered by terrorists.'

Her amusement vanished. 'Good God.'

'We'd been married two years,' Michael went on, looking at her face now. 'We went out to Egypt for a holiday. I have family there, of course – all my father's relatives live in Cairo, and I have some cousins on my mother's side in Alexandria. Lorraine didn't speak Arabic, and it was boring for her visiting my aunts and cousins, who don't speak any English: she wanted to see the tourist sights. So one day she went off on a coach trip to Luxor while I stayed in Cairo, and the Muslim Brotherhood blew up the coach. She was ... she died next day in hospital.'

'I'm so sorry,' said Janet weakly.

He shrugged. 'It was twelve years ago now. Anyway, there was a bit about it in the papers, back here in Britain, and when I got home, the service approached me and asked if I would be interested in coming to work for them.'

'They "approached" you?'

He nodded. 'Mmm.' He sighed. 'Actually, that's a pretty good illustration of why we're so interested in Dr Somers' work. James Bond and his kin have it all wrong: an ordinary intelligence agent can't pass as a native speaker of some randomly selected foreign language any more than you or I could go to France and pass for Parisians. We give ourselves away every time we open our mouths. What ordinary intelligence agents have to do is recruit local agents, who are – with a few honourable exceptions – only interested in money and in getting even with their enemies. They don't care about your country and its causes – and, after all, why should they? It's not *their* country. So intelligence services are generally very interested in people like me, even though we may be thoroughly unsuitable in every other way. I can pass for an Egyptian Arabic speaker, and the service figured – correctly – that I'd be keen to do anything I could to destroy Islamic terrorist groups.' He paused a moment, then added, in a shamefaced rush, 'I used to work as a manager for British Telecom. I have a degree in Business with Computing from the University of Warwick. Does that sound like international spy material? No, but I speak Arabic, so off I went! The terrorists kicked me out one week into basic training. It wasn't that they didn't believe my cover story: it was just that I couldn't completely hide what I thought of them, even though my life depended on it. I'm disastrously bad at lying. Luckily for me, they thought it was just that I was a coward.'

'Good God,' breathed Janet again. After a moment, she added, 'So you went to work for ... for "the service" back here instead?'

'Not immediately. I spent a while in the Middle East, running local agents. Then' – he began to smile again – 'my boss noticed that I had a degree in Business with Computing, and I was back to being a bureaucrat. I think it's my natural role in life.' He paused, then asked diffidently, 'What about you? Did you always want to be a doctor?'

She was quiet. Her own life seemed so petty and ordinary, after the deadly dramas outlined so matter-of-factly by Michael Shahid. 'Yes,' she admitted, answering his question uncomfortably late. 'I wanted to help people. One goes into these things with so much stupid adolescent idealism...'

'Why do you put it that way? You think you were wrong?'

'No, it's just...' She hesitated again, looking at him. They were telling each other important personal histories, she realized with a sinking heart. 'It's just that when you start off you think you can change things, important things, and you can't,' she told him, suddenly angry, with him and with herself. 'What's that poem?

'...the world, which seems
To lie before us like a land of dreams,
So various, so beautiful, so new,
Hath really neither joy, nor love, nor light,
Nor certitude, nor peace, nor help for pain;

114

And we are here as on a darkling plain
Swept with confused alarms of struggle
and flight,
Where ignorant armies clash by night.'

There was a silence. 'All right,' said Michael evenly, 'what *is* that poem? I'm sure I've heard it before, but I'm just an MBA.'

She had to smile at that. 'Matthew Arnold. "Dover Beach". And no, I can't recite much poetry off by heart like that, but I've looked that one up *lots* of times since things started to go wrong for me.'

'Ah.' Another silence, and then he said, very hesitantly, 'You mean your divorce? Sorry, but you mentioned it before...'

'Yeah. And ... I don't know, most of the time you *can't* help people – not the way you wanted to when you were young and foolish. You see so much *misery* as a GP. Old people suffering with arthritis, losing their mobility, going blind and deaf – things that aren't going to kill them, but which make their lives a misery for years and years; you keep seeing them, and you keep giving them pills, but there's nothing you can really do for them. And then people die, of Alzheimer's and cancer and strokes and heart disease, and you can't help them, either. And other people, with nothing much wrong with them, come in and complain at you, and tell you to give them antibiotics for their colds, which won't help, or else they have some crackpot treatment they found on the Internet and think you should provide, and they shout at you when you won't ... and then there's the *stupidity*, the people who smash themselves up drink-driving, or poison themselves with home remedies, and the drug-users who want you to give them their fix ... and I suppose I wasn't very good at shutting it all out, at coming home and having a life of my own.' She smiled weakly. 'When we married, George was inspired and passionate and volatile, and I was the patient supportive one; but I started putting in such long hours at work, and I suppose I stopped listening to him. I suppose I started expecting him to support *me*. I think he did try, but he wasn't really cut out for it, and it wasn't the job he'd signed up for. He was unhappy. Frustrated. And then he met another woman, and she thought he was God, and, well ... she got pregnant and that was it.' She had, she realized, said much more than she'd intended to.

Michael was quiet for a moment, taking it in. Then he said softly, 'I bet you *did* help a lot of other people.'

She could feel herself blushing. 'Yeah, well...' She picked up the teapot to cover her embarrassment, but the tea was all gone. She set it down again.

'If I'd been George, I think I would've

116

asked you to name one good thing you did every day when you came home. I bet there would've been at least one patient you helped, even on the worst days. Thinking of that would've kept you going.'

Her face went hotter still. She laughed nervously. 'Do you tell yourself one good thing *you've* done at the end of every day?'

He shook his head. 'Mostly there aren't single incidents. Sometimes I've had days where all I see is evil. Cruel and violent men doing cruel and violent things. But I tell myself it's part of the struggle – that I'm working against terror and violence and the subversion of law. If I didn't believe that, I couldn't go on with it.'

'You're not at all what I expected,' she said, and wondered if that was rude.

He smiled. 'Oh, some of the things you've heard are true. Some of the *bad* things, I mean: mad phone-tappers and flagrant disregard for the law. I'm stodgy and straightlaced and mostly they don't tell me about things like that, but I know it goes on. Less of it than there was, I hope.' He snorted. 'I'm one of the modernizers.'

'Business and computing,' she said, suddenly understanding a great deal about his position.

He smiled again. 'Business *with* computing,' he corrected her. 'There's a difference. *With* means I did an MBA with a bit of

117

computer science on the side.'

The waiter returned with the bill. Michael paid it, and they got to their feet. 'Well,' he said, looking at her – and stopped.

'Thank you very much,' she told him. 'I haven't had a cream tea for years.'

'My pleasure.'

They went back to the cars. 'Um,' Michael said, as she unlocked the Datsun. 'Um. Would you like to go out to dinner some time? Um. Friday, maybe?'

She straightened, hand on the car door. 'I'm bringing Madhab here on Friday,' she reminded him.

He nodded. 'I wondered if I could meet you afterwards. In Leicester, perhaps. I could tell you what progress I've made with Dr Firsby, and you could tell me how things are with Madhab.'

'I'd like that,' she told him. Even as she said it, she realized that he was evidently planning to drive all the way to Leicester – two hours in the car if he was lucky with the traffic – just to see her.

He grinned. He tossed his car keys into the air and caught them again. 'Great. I'll see you Friday then. About seven OK?'

'Thank you. That would be lovely.'

Driving home again, she wondered about that response. It had come out of her as though generated by some internal platitude machine – *Thank you, that would be lovely* –

and yet she knew exactly what she meant by it. It made a difference, knowing what he'd told her. It made a huge difference.

For a moment she thought to wonder whether he had been trying to manipulate her for some secret MI5 reason. Then she realized, with absolute certainty, that he had not – and it wasn't the story about his wife that made her so certain, but the detail that he'd been called back to work as 'a bureaucrat' because he had a degree in Business with Computing. Somehow that had taken the whole shadowy organization out of the realm of film and novel and placed it firmly in the real world. It was a government department; real people worked there. There were management problems, flow charts, computer systems which no doubt occasionally crashed, as computer systems will. She could not only see that, but she could see Michael Shahid's place in it. He was a modernizer, and – she was suddenly sure of this, though he'd never said anything about it – he was middle-management and on his way up. He was trying to change the organization, to shift it from its old-fashioned Cold War spy games towards a focus on the new war against terrorism. She could even guess that he'd been telling the truth when he'd told her that he had switched jobs only a few weeks before. She suspected now that he'd been promoted to *take charge* of MI5

'Training and Research' because there had been some trouble there and the organization wanted someone 'stodgy and straight-laced' to clean up.

She remembered Madhab's question, *Good man?* Yes, she thought now, *he is*.

Five

There was, once again, heavy traffic around Oxford, which, combined with a jam on the A46, meant that it was nearly seven by the time Janet pulled into the drive of her house in Leicester. Madhab was out of the house before she'd switched off the engine, an expression of relief on his face.

'You OK?' he asked as Janet got out of the car.

'I'm fine,' she told him. 'Is something the matter?'

He shrugged, frowning. 'You late.'

'I'm sorry. There was traffic, and I stopped for tea.'

He smiled. 'OK now.' He waved at the house. 'Supper. Me make.'

'Thank you!'

Supper was *dhal bhat*, the Nepalese staple dish of lentils and Madhab's invariable first recourse in the kitchen. It had dried out a little from sitting on the stove too long, but it was still pleasant to come home to.

'So,' Janet began, over the dinner table, 'was "Maths for Fun" fun?'

'Yes. Good puzzle. David Somers what?'

'David Somers is a shit. Excuse me: bad word. I shouldn't say it. You remember Jeremy Firsby?'

She explained what had happened in the appropriate 'little bits'. Madhab did not seem surprised – but then, he'd never liked David Somers, and probably wouldn't have been surprised to find him guilty of anything short of murder. Firsby's departure from Somers Synaptic evidently did not worry him; but the fact that Janet had had tea with Michael Shahid evidently did. He frowned to hear of it. When she informed him that she had arranged to see Michael on Friday for supper, the frown became a scowl.

'What's the matter?' Janet asked him.

'Michael Shahid,' replied Madhab, still scowling.

'He's all right, Madhab. Really he is. When you and I – met Michael – for the first time – at that time, Michael was worried – about *you*. He wanted to help you. He wants good things for you. He didn't know – I want to help you, too. Now it's OK.'

Madhab made a gesture of frustration. 'Understand! Me ... ah!' He caught his breath, then tried again: 'You like Michael Shahid.'

She began to get an idea what this was about, and her heart sank. She had never tried to explain her love life to Madhab. She

122

had never had to: there had been no men in her life since the divorce, and Madhab himself had been blithely incurious. 'Yes,' she agreed, 'I do. Madhab, are you worried because I like Michael Shahid?'

He sat very still for a moment, then made a face. 'He have woman?'

'No. That is, I don't think so. Madhab, I don't know whether...' She remembered that he'd have trouble with a complex sentence like *know* + *whether*, and rephrased it: 'Maybe I will love Michael Shahid. Maybe I will not love him. I definitely love *you*, and that will not change.'

He looked at her intently, his face now tight with something very like fear. 'You have baby, no want Madhab. Send Madhab away.'

'No!' she exclaimed, appalled that he could think it. *'Never!* Madhab, I *love* you. I would *never* send you away!'

'You man send Madhab away. Say, stupid kid, no talk good, go home, moron!'

'Who's been saying things like that to you?' she demanded indignantly.

He shrugged. 'Kid. In school. You man say.'

'No, no, no! I promise you, I would *never* marry a man like that. If I ever marry again' (he had trouble understanding 'if', too, but she ploughed on regardless) 'the man must agree to be like your father. If' (dammit, another one!) 'he didn't agree to treat you, Madhab, as his son, I would send *him* away!

I promise you that, Madhab. You come first. Probably I'm too old to have any babies, but if' (yet another of the damned things!) 'if I did have a baby, you would be that baby's brother. Does a mother send away her first son when she has a baby? Of course not! She loves *all* her children; she wants the older son to help the baby and show him what to do; she wants the baby to love his brother and listen to him. And you are *not* stupid! Never believe that, whatever they say to you. You are very brave and clever and I am very, very proud of you!'

Madhab looked at her a moment longer. Then he got up from his seat, came round the table, and hugged her. She got up, dropping her fork, and hugged him back fiercely. Her throat was tight.

Eventually she let him go, looked into his face, brushed his hair off his forehead.

'In Nepal,' Madhab said softly, 'everybody think, Madhab stupid. No hear, but me know. You–' he struck her very gently on the shoulder – 'you *make* me clever. Me think, me think, no Janet, what? No mother, no clever, no school no house, nothing. Scared.'

'You don't have to be scared,' she told him. 'I love you very much, and I wouldn't lose you for the whole world.'

It was only later, cleaning up the dishes, that she thought to wonder. He had been using complex sentences. Hadn't he? *In*

Nepal everybody think Madhab stupid. He *had* said that, hadn't he? It wasn't just another string of two-word phrases, was it? No, it had to be a real complex sentence! 'In Nepal' (locative) + 'everybody thinks' + (complementizer omitted) 'Madhab is stupid'. Was it only the intensity of his feelings that had forced that expressiveness, or was the treatment actually starting to work?

She said nothing to Madhab about her sudden, exhilarated hope. If it turned out to be unfounded, her own disappointment would be hard enough to cope with, without adding his as well. She had trouble sleeping that night, though, and yawned through an eight-hour stint of locum work next day. It was the day Madhab started his summer remedial reading class, and a minibus came to collect him at nine. He went without any of the enthusiasm that had carried him to 'Maths for Fun': he found reading a grim and exhausting struggle. That evening they were both quiet and exhausted, and they watched television together in silence.

On Thursday morning Madhab had the last of the ampoules David had provided the previous week. As usual, he was required to talk while the drug diffused. At first he struggled on in the normal way, trying to describe what he was expecting to do in 'Maths for Fun' that afternoon. Then he said, carefully and distinctly, 'Have right

125

number card, solve puzzle' – and stopped, looking at Janet, seeming almost afraid.

Complex sentence, she thought again, her heart beating hard; a condition using 'if', even though the 'if' itself had been omitted. *If you have the right number cards, then you can solve the puzzle.* And Madhab evidently *knew* it was a complex sentence. He had found the right two pieces of the jigsaw puzzle fitting together on his tongue.

Madhab reached up toward the micro-shunt. His hair, which had grown quickly into a thick black fuzz, almost hid the scars of the operation now, and the plug, with its gleaming ampoule attached, paradoxically looked more artificial than ever. His fingers curled over it protectively, not touching it. 'It work,' he whispered.

Janet swallowed. 'I think it is starting to work,' she whispered back. 'I only hope it keeps on working.'

Madhab grinned so widely that it looked almost as though he were screaming. His eyes glowed. He flung out his arms and stamped his feet in excitement. 'It work!' he shouted.

'Shh, shh!' she urged him. 'It may stop working. It may not do everything we hope. It may even reverse, God forbid. Don't trust it yet, love, it will break your heart if you do.'

'Heart fine!' Madhab replied joyfully. 'Head fine!' He laughed out loud, then tossed his head back and screamed with joyful excitement.

When she set out to do her day's work, he was sitting down with one of his reading primers and a tape cassette long abandoned as too difficult, as though the whole citadel of language would fall to him at once.

The following morning – Friday – they drove down to Oxford again.

David had commissioned an independent language assessment for Madhab during one of their early meetings, well before the operation. He had hired an Oxford psycholinguist for the purpose – a sour, shrivelled old woman who had spent the intervals between tests complaining bitterly about her department and her colleagues. When Janet escorted Madhab back into the soulless black-and-white lab, the same woman was sitting waiting, notebook in hand.

'What's that on his head?' asked the psycholinguist, staring suspiciously at the microshunt. She had been told something of Madhab's history, but little of David's plans for him.

David gave his self-satisfied smile. 'It's for the treatment,' he informed her. 'It delivers the drugs to the appropriate areas.'

The old woman gave him a disgusted look. It had been plain from her comments the last time that one of her disagreements with the rest of her department was that she did not believe there were 'appropriate areas' for language. 'I think you're wasting my time, Dr Somers,' she sniffed, 'but you're paying. Well, let's get started!'

Madhab gave her a wide smile. 'Le's go!' he agreed.

The tests were of a fairly simple nature, involving spoken, rather than written, language. Most of them involved describing what was happening in sets of pictures; some required plurals for invented words, or a correct form for an invented verb. Madhab had struggled with them before, and he struggled again; but it was almost instantly apparent that he was struggling at a higher level. Before, he had looked at a sequence of drawings that showed a girl climbing into a tree to pick an apple and falling, and described it in gestures and two-word phrases: 'Girl. Want apple. Up, up! Ouch! Down.' This time, faced with a cartoon of a boy falling off a bicycle as he tried to impress his friends by a cycling trick, Madhab said, 'Boy have bike. He say, "Look, look!" Kid look. He go, fast, fast, ups hands, no hold bike. Crash! Stupid boy.'

The psycholinguist blinked at that 'ups hands', and made a note. Janet, with two bitter years' experience behind her, was certain that what was being noted was not that 'to up' was being used as a transitive verb, but the fact that Madhab had used a third-person singular verb form and a plural correctly.

After half an hour of testing the woman turned to Janet with a glare. 'You've coached him,' she said accusingly.

'I've coached him as much as I could,' Janet agreed, 'but I couldn't know what pictures you'd show him, could I?' The woman scowled.

After an hour the psycholinguist put away her notebook. 'Well, obviously the boy has made progress,' she admitted reluctantly. 'He seems to have gone from the level of a normal twenty-month-old to that of a child of about two and a half. If the facts of the case are as they were represented to me, that's surprising. However, if he's as bright as his guardian says, perhaps this is natural progress. With normal children, the explosion in language learning generally occurs between two and two and a half, so it could be natural. Or perhaps there was an element of deceit – which I don't rule out!' She glared at David and Janet both.

David smirked.

When the linguist had departed, he was openly gleeful. 'It's working!' he exclaimed, and grinned almost as widely as Madhab.

'It's working,' Janet agreed; and, despite everything, felt compelled to add, 'Thank you. You're a genius.'

David wanted to administer another dose

129

of growth factors, and had another rack of the drugs waiting in the fridge. Madhab was willing – indeed, eager – to have it. Janet, however, was cautious. 'It's working,' she said. 'Can we just see first how well it goes on working before we go pumping more drugs into his brain? I mean, he's been exposed to language ever since he got his ears fixed. That should mean that he already has a lot of information which he simply has to slot into place, shouldn't it? It seems to me that he must be getting an awful lot of natural stimulus as it is and I'd really prefer it if we could keep the artificial stimuli to a minimum.'

'What do you know about it?' David demanded contemptuously – but agreed to wait and see how things progressed over the next week.

Madhab was silent as they started the drive home. Janet was more aware of his frustration than if he had shouted about it.

'I'm sorry, love,' she told him, after a few miles on the road. 'I just don't think we should push it too hard. It's working now; let's see how well it keeps on working before we do anything more, OK? The treatment is planned to last for *months*, and the drugs will keep.'

Madhab made a face, then nodded resignedly. *Fuss, fuss, fuss*, she thought, wryly. Maybe I am a mother, after all.

All through the week she had been aware of Friday evening, when she would see Michael again; even the intense excitement over the treatment had been unable to obscure that. Now, however, she found herself wondering whether she should go. It seemed wrong to leave Madhab alone, on this of all nights: she ought to be taking him out to celebrate. By the time they arrived back in Leicester she had managed to convince herself that she should cancel the dinner date. She stopped at a public phone box before she reached home and telephoned Michael, hoping that she'd catch him before he left London.

'Janet!' he exclaimed when he picked up the phone and, at the pleasure in his voice, her resolution began to crumble.

'M-Michael,' she stammered. 'I, uh, was wondering about tonight.'

'Is something the matter?' he asked, abruptly concerned.

'No, it's just that ... well, the fact is that the treatment seems to be *working*.' Her discomfort with the call was suddenly swamped by the exhilaration that had kept her sleepless. 'Madhab's had some more tests, and his language has progressed up to the level of a normal two-and-a-half year-old – just in the last couple of weeks! He's using complex sentences and plurals, Michael; he's really starting to be able to *talk!*'

'That's wonderful!'

'It's fantastic! Anyway ... anyway, you see, he's very excited about it, and I can't just leave him alone in the house to fix his own supper, and...'

'Bring him along.'

Somehow that possibility hadn't occurred to her. She stood in the phone box, the receiver clutched hard against her chin.

'Is that a problem?'

'N-no,' she stammered. 'That is ... that is, he's very anxious about you...'

'I noticed,' said Michael, with a touch of amusement. 'That's another reason for him to come along.' There was another moment of silence, and then he said, 'Janet, I know he's included in the package. I understand that. We might as well see if we get on with each other.'

Her own words echoed back at her: *If I ever marry again, the man must agree to be like your father. If he didn't agree to treat you, Madhab, as his son, I would send him away.*

This is moving too fast, she thought – but had no idea how to slow it down, and was not even sure she wanted to.

What the hell had she done that had so impressed a man like Michael Shahid?

'Oh ... well then,' she faltered. 'If ... if that's really OK with you.'

'Great! See you at seven, then.'

She went back to the car, where Madhab

132

was waiting for her. 'Michael asks you to come to dinner as well,' she told him.

Madhab was surprised, then sullen.

'He wants to get to know you,' she said. 'He knows you are my son. He knows that I am *never* going to send you away.'

The sullenness lifted a little.

'Madhab,' she said earnestly, 'I told you, you come first. If you hate Michael, then I must tell him, "Go away, Michael." But I like Michael. I want to get to know him better. I think you *might* like him, if you knew him better. I know, I said "might" and "if"; those are hard words to understand, but – do you understand them?'

Madhab looked at her intently in silence, frowning a little. Then he nodded. 'Understand,' he whispered. 'Good. Want Janet happy.'

'I want you to be happy, too, Madhab,' she told him, and touched his hand.

When the doorbell rang, promptly at seven, Madhab went to open it before Janet could reach it. From halfway down the stairs she watched him admit Michael and shake hands with him. His air of resolute politeness touched her deeply.

'Janet told me that the treatment is working,' Michael said to him, smiling widely. 'I'm very happy for you. You must be very excited.'

At that, Madhab smiled back. 'Yes.'

Janet started on down the stairs, and Michael glanced up, saw her, and smiled. She could feel herself blushing. She had put on a good skirt and her best blue-silk blouse, and with Michael looking at her she felt beautiful for the first time in years.

They went out to a local Indian restaurant. Janet ordered starters extravagantly, and offered to split the bill.

'No, no!' murmured Michael. 'My treat.'

'I can't let you *keep on* paying for everything!'

His eyes creased behind the spectacles. 'Why not? I'm sure I get paid more than you do, and I haven't spent much for years.'

She would have queried that, if Madhab hadn't been present. The territory seemed too delicate, however, to explore before a witness, so she merely made dissenting noises.

Over the starters, Michael asked about the treatment, and they told him. Madhab seemed to have temporarily overcome his anxiety about the visitor, probably because he was so full of joy and excitement that it was hard for him to concentrate on anything else.

'It's fantastic,' Michael concluded warmly. 'A real miracle treatment.'

'It is!' Janet agreed.

The main-course curries arrived, and for a few minutes they were all busy spooning aromatic mixtures over rice and sampling them. Then Michael cleared his throat. 'I was, uh, supposed to tell you how I got on with Jeremy Firsby.'

'Oh! Yes.' She had almost forgotten about that.

'I phoned him Tuesday, asked him if he would see me. He was reluctant.' Michael smiled. 'He's never been happy with our involvement: in his view, we're trying to steal a medical treatment designed for victims of brain damage and use it for the nefarious purposes of the MoD – I, uh, never told him I don't actually work for the MoD. I think he was also worried that he might lose his month's severance pay, though he didn't actually say so. However, he did eventually agree to see me.' He took a mouthful of lamb dhansak, swallowed, and went on, 'As we suspected, David Somers did pick that quarrel. Firsby hadn't wanted to resign at all – he expects the Somers Treatment to be a major success story, and he really wanted his name associated with it. However, Somers started in on a brutal critique of his lab work, and Firsby eventually hit back by blaming Somers for the loss of the animal licence, and I gather there was a lot of shouting. In the end, things went so far that Firsby had to choose between walking out and crawling to Somers with an apology – which he felt he couldn't do. He's bitter and very angry: he's worked for Somers Synaptic for the last two and a half years, contributed a lot of hard work, put up with a lot of unreasonable behaviour from his boss – and now he'll get no credit for any of it. He feels that Somers has stolen years of his life.'

'Poor man,' said Janet; but her feelings were mixed. It sounded as though Firsby's departure had everything to do with David's ambitions, and nothing to do with any dirty secrets in the treatment itself. That was good news.

Michael nodded. 'I felt sorry for him, too. I told him that when Somers asks me when he can publish, I'll make it clear that it'll happen a whole lot sooner if he credits Firsby.'

Janet laughed, and Michael grinned and sketched a bow. 'Firsby liked me better, after that. Anyway, the main news is that Firsby wasn't aware of any problems with the treatment: on the contrary, he expects it to be a great success. However, one thing he said does worry me. Apparently one of the issues that came up in the quarrel was that there's a monkey missing. Somers blamed Firsby for it, but Firsby vehemently denies that he was responsible.'

She frowned. 'An experimental monkey?'

'Mmm. One of the last three used to test the procedure. It was either stolen or escaped – with Somers' special microshunt still in its head. *That* is another thing Somers should have told us when he first approached the MoD.'

'Monkey?' asked Madhab. 'Have this?' He touched the microshunt.

'Exactly,' agreed Michael, nodding. 'The missing monkey had a shunt exactly like that.'

'Monkey talk?'

Michael shook his head. 'No. Monkeys can't talk, even with Dr Somers' treatment. The shunt and drugs were being tested, to see if they were safe and if they worked.'

Madhab nodded thoughtfully. 'Monkey gone?'

'Yes. Apparently, it was locked up in its cage one night, but in the morning the cage was open and empty.'

Madhab frowned.

'When was this?' asked Janet.

'September last year,' Michael replied at once. 'Before we were involved, and before Somers lost his licence – in fact, he lost the licence partly *because* of it. He phoned the company that had supplied the monkeys and the cages, complained, and threatened to sue. The suppliers, to defend themselves, objected that Somers Synaptic hadn't been looking after the monkeys properly and filed an animal welfare complaint. The inspectors came, saw, and shut them down.'

'It must've just got out,' said Janet. 'The

137

security on that place is ferocious. Nobody could've got in without triggering an alarm. What sort of monkey was it?'

'An African squirrel monkey,' replied Michael. 'You may be right: it may just have got its cage open and escaped. From what Firsby said, they're bright and dexterous and pretty tough, and Somers' treatment may have improved its ability to solve puzzles. But it's odd that it hasn't turned up again. Apparently they can survive in the wild in Britain – there are a couple of safari parks where they keep them outdoors all year, with just a few shelters for them to retreat to in the middle of winter. You'd think, though, that if a squirrel monkey was living wild in Oxfordshire, raiding bird feeders and barns and the like, somebody would've remarked on it.'

'This ... this monkey...' Janet began uncomfortably. She supported the use of animals in medical research – she was well aware of how many advances were owed to it – but at the same time she hated animal suffering; as a result she felt guilty and uncomfortable whenever the subject came up. 'What effect did the treatment have on it? You said it could solve puzzles?'

'That was Firsby's suggestion,' Michael said, 'his explanation for how it might have got out of the cage. Apparently squirrel monkey brains aren't complicated enough to allow them to develop the kind of symbolic logic you need for speech, but the treatment did produce some growth in its left cerebral hemisphere in an area which, according to Firsby – who was citing Somers, who doesn't really know much about monkeys – it would use to perceive patterns and solve puzzles. Maybe that helped it to escape. And maybe I'm worried about nothing, and it hasn't turned up because it was caught by a fox or a buzzard and eaten. On the other hand, I have to consider the possibility that somebody working on the project stole it.'

'You think it may have been your spies again,' said Janet resignedly.

Michael frowned. 'It went missing *before* Somers turned to the MoD,' he pointed out. 'I wouldn't've thought there were any spies interested in it then – ours or the other side's.' He had another mouthful of curry, looking thoughtful, then said, 'The thing that I *really* don't like about it is that it raises another possibility: that the people who commissioned your burglary aren't spies at all. Not *political* ones, that is. It could've been industrial espionage.'

Janet thought about that. It sounded plausible. The Somers Treatment had dozens of potential applications: besides its use to treat brain damage, it could be sold to those who desperately wanted to learn a second language. There could be a lot of money in it –

139

and some pharmaceutical companies were notoriously unscrupulous.

'You know, that sounds much more likely than the KGB,' she said slowly.

Michael let out a long breath through his nose. 'It does, doesn't it? Damn!'

'Damn?'

'I haven't been able to find whoever hired your burglars, and I've run all the usual checks. I did include the possibility that it was industrial, but way down the list, and that skews the results. I should have put that possibility first. Damn, that was stupid! I'm sorry.'

'But worrying about industrial espionage isn't your *job*, is it?'

He looked embarrassed. 'We keep, um, telling the government that we could help counter it. Another of our new post-Cold War roles that hasn't actually taken off yet.' He sighed. 'I'll run the checks again, and I'll talk to Somers' technicians. I've spoken to one of them already: he confirmed Firsby's account of the quarrel, but didn't have anything to add about the monkey. I was planning to see the other two next week. I should do it sooner, shouldn't I? If we're right, and the monkey was stolen and sold to a multinational, it was probably one of the technicians who took it.'

'If we're right,' she said slowly, 'then whoever took it *doesn't* have what he wants yet. I mean, yes, he'd have a microshunt, but he wouldn't know what drugs to use. *I* don't know that, except in the most general terms. David's been keeping that as close as possible. Firsby must know, but I doubt anyone else does.'

He nodded. 'Yes. That makes sense. It makes sense of the burglary, too. If the technician they bought couldn't tell them, they *would* try to find out from you. Damn. I should've seen this at once!'

'What?' asked Madhab, breaking a long excluded silence.

Janet and Michael both looked at him.

'One more problem with Somers Synaptic,' David said. 'But we should not be talking about it tonight, Madhab.' He picked up his glass of Cobra beer. 'Tonight we should celebrate. Madhab, here's to you, and to all the words you will ever say!'

'To you!' Janet echoed, picking up her own glass.

Madhab lifted his glass of fizzy orange, smiling again. 'To word!'

They did not speak of Somers Synaptic again that evening. Instead, they talked about Nepal and Egypt and England, about Leicester and London, Cairo and Kathmandu. They left the restaurant late and cheerful, and drove back in the Datsun – Michael's car had been left at Janet's house because of his lack of familiarity with the

Leicester roads.

When they got back to the house, it seemed natural to Janet to say, 'You don't want to drive back to London tonight. It's too late. You're welcome to stay the night.'

Michael looked at her, surprised and hopeful.

'On a folding bed!' she added hastily. Did he think she was the sort of woman who went to bed with a man on the first date? 'I could set it up for you in my office. Or in the lounge, if you prefer.'

His eyes creased. 'I think I'd prefer the lounge, if it's no trouble. Thank you. I really would prefer to do the drive back tomorrow.'

She set up the folding bed in the lounge, then fetched sheets and pillows and a blanket. Michael stood about watching, occasionally taking his hands out of his pockets and trying rather ineffectually to help. Madhab was looking worried and suspicious again. She regretted her hospitable impulse.

'Any chance of coffee?' asked Michael.

She made instant coffee for two. Madhab, who didn't drink it, hovered anxiously at the foot of the stairs.

'Go to bed,' she advised him. ' "Build a Robot" starts tomorrow, remember? All I'm going to do is drink my coffee and go to bed, too.'

At this Madhab went off upstairs. Janet

took her coffee mug into the lounge and sat down on the sofa. Michael sat in the lounge chair. She was uncomfortably aware of the folding bed, in front of her to her left. Michael stirred a spoonful of sugar into his coffee and glanced around the room. She noticed his gaze lingering on a watercolour of Glencoe.

'George painted that,' she informed him, mock-casual. 'My ex.'

'Ah.' He got up, carrying his coffee, and went to inspect it. 'It's very good. Amateur, but talented amateur.'

She nodded. 'He is good. It's his hobby – one of his hobbies, I mean. He has several: watercolour painting, motorbikes, and jazz guitar.' She shrugged. 'He was good at all of them – and at his job. He's a television company manager; people who worked with him were always telling me how good he was.'

He looked back at her, his face giving nothing away. 'And you? What are your hobbies?'

'Walking,' she said, without hesitation. 'Mountains in particular. Not mountain climbing – just walking in the mountains, enjoying the scenery. I suppose that's one reason why I was so tempted by Nepal. I haven't had much time for it the last couple of years, though.'

He smiled. 'I like art. And opera. And archaeology, probably because of being

143

Anglo-Egyptian.'

'I like archaeology,' she admitted. 'And opera.'

He came over and sat on the sofa beside her. 'In case you were wondering,' he said, after a moment of silence, 'there aren't any other women. There've been four, since Lorraine died, but with two of them it only lasted for a couple of months, and the last one was over a year ago.'

She felt her face heating. 'There hasn't been anybody since George,' she told him, in a whisper. She was aware, suddenly and painfully, that it had been more than three years since she'd made love. She hadn't felt the sharp physical lack of it for a couple of years. The first year after the divorce had been agonizing, but after that, she'd grown accustomed to celibacy. Now she felt the warmth in her genitals, the tingling in her breasts, as though no time had passed since the first aching months of her solitude.

He nodded, unsurprised. 'I didn't think you were the sort to be casual about it. And I...' He blinked at her from behind the specs. 'And I just want you to know, I'm not either. I don't want to scare you off, God forbid, but you ought to know: I'm deadly serious, so if you want to get rid of me, tell me now. I'd much, much rather write it off now than later.'

'I don't want to get rid of you right now,'

she whispered. She forced a smile. 'I hardly know you.'

'Just so you don't hate the idea,' he conceded. He gulped the coffee, then set the empty mug down, looking at her, uncertain. She found herself aware of the pounding of blood in her ears and swallowed uncomfortably. Neither of them moved.

'I was so surprised when I first saw you,' Michael told her. 'I'd expected a kind of female counterpart to Dr Somers – some cold, self-satisfied medic with immaculate make-up wearing a white coat over a suit. Instead...' He reached out, very hesitantly, and brushed a wisp of her untidy hair away from her face. 'You're one of the most utterly natural and least self-interested women I've ever met.'

She laughed nervously. 'I *thought* you looked surprised.'

'Oh, I was astonished. I began to suspect I'd got it wrong right away, though I wasn't sure until I saw the way Madhab was ready to hit me for insulting you. I don't suppose you're even aware that he adores you?'

She looked away. 'Nobody beside me ever ... ever *bothered* about him much.' She hesitated, looking back, then asked abruptly, 'Do you have children?'

'No,' he replied at once. 'Lorraine and I were thinking about starting a family when it happened. She was a primary school teacher. She loved young children.' His voice was wistful and affectionate more than grieved.

'Madhab's relatives thought I wanted Madhab because I didn't have any children of my own,' she admitted. 'I think that, at heart, Madhab believes that as well.'

'But you would have tried to help him even if you'd had twins in tow.'

She looked into the dark eyes behind the spectacles. 'Yes. I'm sure I would have. It's what *he* is that counted.'

'Did you want children?' he asked, very softly.

'I wanted a baby,' she confessed. 'I suggested to George that we try for one, several times. But George never thought the time was right ... and then things started to go wrong, and I thought it would be the last straw. I thought I could put it off just another year or two. But...' She broke off, thinking of when George told her about Fran, about how Fran was pregnant. The child must be three now. Maybe Fran was pregnant again, with another of George's babies.

Thirty-six wasn't too old to have a baby, something inside her insisted.

Not *necessarily*, she answered herself; but often there are problems, and they escalate sharply with every year after thirty-five. She really didn't know Michael Shahid very well;

146

she didn't know yet whether she was even willing to go to bed with him, let alone marry him and have his baby. Even if she decided that she was, it might only be to discover that it was too late for it. Only the morning before, she'd warned Madhab not to hope for too much, because disappointment can break the heart. Resolutely she put aside the thought that Social Services would be much more willing to grant an adoption order to a couple than to a woman on her own. Desperate Divorcee, she reminded herself: what a pathetic creature!

She set her empty coffee mug down. 'Well,' she said decidedly, 'goodnight.'

Her resolute gaze met a look of hopeful determination. 'May I kiss you goodnight?'

She went upstairs with the kiss hot on her lips and her heart beating hard. She was not really surprised to find Madhab sitting on the landing. She brushed his hair off his face and over the fuzzy scarred patch, then bent to kiss his forehead. 'It's OK,' she told him gently. 'See? I drank my coffee and said goodnight.'

He smiled back at her, relieved. 'OK,' he agreed. 'Goodnight.'

Six

She was woken by the sound of voices.

She rolled over and looked at the alarm clock: 3.13, it read, in glowing figures – so who was up, and whom was he talking to?

She got up, tossed on her dressing gown, and went out on to the landing to find Madhab already there, standing at the top of the stairs and staring down, naked apart from a pair of boxer shorts. The plug of the microshunt gleamed in his rumpled hair. The voices rumbled from the lounge, low and unexcited. Perhaps Michael was watching television?

At three o'clock in the morning?

Janet silently gestured to Madhab to wait, then pulled the dressing gown more tightly round her waist and stalked down the stairs.

There were three people in the lounge: Michael, in his shirtsleeves, and a middle-aged couple she did not know. They all looked up as the door opened, the strangers with an oddly coordinated nervous start. The folding bed had been pushed up against the window, out of the way.

148

'Oh,' said Michael, getting politely to his feet. 'Janet. These are Otto und Liese Bleicken. They, um, were trying to break into your house again.'

'No!' protested Liese Bleicken instantly. 'We did not break in. Mr Shahid *invited* us in.'

She was a stout woman a few years older than Janet, her bouffant hair an unnatural shade of red and her nails painted to match. She looked the sort of woman one would expect to see cruising a shopping mall in garish too-tight clothes, though she currently wore black jogging trousers and a baggy black sweatshirt. She was no one's idea of a German spy.

Shahid regarded her with a smile, but behind the black framed spectacles his eyes were cold. 'They were outside your back door,' he informed Janet, 'with a large holdall, a roll of electrical tape and a hammer. I did invite them in.'

Janet stared at him, then at the Germans. *Why* had he invited them in? Were they armed? There were no guns visible, and the holdall Michael had mentioned was nowhere in evidence – but perhaps one or the other of the pair had a weapon hidden under their sweatshirt.

She prayed fervently that Madhab would stay upstairs, out of the way.

'Ve haff not broken any laws,' Otto

149

Bleicken pointed out coolly. He was a balding man with bloodshot eyes and a beer gut, dressed identically to his wife. While her accent had been noticeable but unobtrusive, his was pronounced.

'You stole my great-grandmother's opal necklace,' said Janet, beginning to be angry as well as stunned and afraid. 'You stole my computer.'

'There is no evidence for that.' Otto Bleicken held up empty hands. 'None. There is no evidence we were ever here before. And tonight we were out jogging very late – ja? – because we drank too much; and Mr Shahid invited us in.'

'You usually take a hammer with you when you go jogging?' asked Michael mildly. 'Never mind. I agree that we have no evidence that you have been involved in any criminal activity in the United Kingdom – none, at least, that would stand up in court.'

Herr Bleicken relaxed, but Frau Bleicken remained perched aggressively on the edge of the worn lounge chair. 'Why did you invite us in, Mr Shahid?'

'I've already told you that,' said Michael calmly, 'though I'm sure you guessed it anyway as soon as I spoke to you.'

So he hadn't been threatened?

Liese Bleicken gave him a sly smile. 'Our clients expect us to be discreet, Mr Shahid.'

'Your clients,' returned Michael, 'need

know nothing about this conversation.'

The German woman shook her head doubtfully.

'You can hardly expect to continue in your current employment anyway,' Michael pointed out reasonably. 'If you tell your clients what happened tonight, they'll know you're compromised. They'll dismiss you at once. If you don't tell them, however, they'll expect you to deliver the goods they asked for.' He paused. 'I don't think I need to point out that those will now be impossible to obtain.'

What goods? wondered Janet – then remembered that, if the treatment hadn't been working so well, she would have had another week's supply of drugs sitting in the refrigerator.

'It is true,' agreed Frau Bleicken, 'whatever happens, we will have to look for a new job.' She looked at him keenly. 'So we need money, *ja*?'

Michael leaned back in his seat and crossed his ankles. 'No. You've been spying on classified British research; you cannot expect us to reward you for it.'

'The MoD has lots of money,' Herr Bleicken pointed out.

Michael raised his eyebrows.

'You work for the MoD, *ja*?' said Herr Bleicken, less confidently.

Michael shook his head.

The two Germans froze, staring at him. Then the man swore.

'I don't know you,' said the woman nervously.

'*Er kennt unsere Namen*,' said the man. '*Er müsst MI5 sein.*'

'*Shahid ist keiner Englischer Name*,' objected the woman unhappily. '*Vielleicht...*'

Michael gave her a sour half-smile, fished out his wallet, extracted his ID card and set it down on the coffee table. The man and the woman both looked, then sat back, glumly resigned. Janet realized that they were, to some extent, *reassured* to know that they were dealing with an established intelligence service, and not some wild-card body that might not follow the rules.

'It's true,' Michael said quietly, 'that we would find it difficult to prove anything against you in court. However, I'm sure you're aware that there are other ways we could make your lives very, very difficult. I believe you had one escapade in Russia that did not turn out well.' He picked up his ID card and put it back into his wallet. 'The details of that incident could stay in our computer. On the other hand, I could arrange it so that everyone who thinks of hiring you finds out about it.'

Otto Bleicken swore again, glaring at Michael with a swollen, red-eyed malevolence that Janet found very frightening.

Michael seemed entirely unmoved by it.

'Tao Pharmaceuticals,' said Liese Bleicken sharply. 'That is the name you want.'

Michael looked surprised and doubtful. 'Dow *Chemical*, isn't it? It isn't even their line, and surely they're more likely to be spied upon than to spy.'

'Not them! *Tao*. Like the Chinese philosophy. Named after it, to represent balance and health, ha!'

'Never heard of them.'

'They're new.' The German woman wrinkled her nose in disgust. 'The new entrepreneurial China, out to show the world that they can match the biomedical skills of the decadent West.'

'Your contact there?'

'He gave his name as Bobbie Wong,' replied Liese Bleicken, with a shrug that made it clear she didn't believe that was his real name and didn't care. 'He hired us in May. He said he'd heard we did private detective work.' She used the description without the slightest trace of irony. Janet suspected that it was the one she used for herself, and wondered, with a stab of anger, how she reconciled it with stealing jewellery.

'How did you contact him?' asked Michael.

The woman looked at him with narrowed eyes.

'If he is any good,' Michael said evenly, 'he

153

will already know that we're aware there's a leak, and that we've been trying to track it. In that case he'll probably assume we traced him through Somers Synaptic. If he isn't any good, he'll never know he's been traced at all. Either way, he won't know about this conversation, unless *you* plan to tell him.'

Liese Bleicken let out her breath with a small noise of disgust.

'Perhaps you think we're incompetent,' Michael added composedly. 'Maybe you're telling yourself that you placed two devices on Dr Morley's telephone, and we didn't spot them, so we can't be trusted to keep your part in this quiet. Think again.'

She blinked in surprise. There was another obscenity from her husband.

'I want to know how you got in contact with this "Bobbie Wong",' Michael insisted.

Liese grimaced, then glanced resentfully around the room. 'I will give you the number!' she said.

Michael got up, fetched his jacket from the bed, and took out a pen and a pocket diary. He ripped a page out of the back of the diary and gave it to her with the pen, keeping the diary itself securely in his own hands. She wrote something down, and he took it, read it, and folded it carefully.

'Do they have the backing of their government for this?' he asked, putting the paper back into his diary.

Liese laughed contemptuously. 'How would I know? But no, I think not, though they may have bought a government minister or two. What is certain is that, if you accuse this company of industrial espionage, the Chinese government will say it is a monstrous slander, and dismiss any evidence you present as fabricated.'

Michael made a face. 'Very well. Who was your contact at Somers Synaptic?'

The German woman shook her head. 'We never had one. They handled that.'

Michael raised his eyebrows.

'Obviously, there is someone!' snapped Liese. 'We can see that as well as you. But we were only hired in May, for a specific task, and they didn't tell us everything.'

'They did not even tell us that the MoD was funding this research,' agreed Otto, with venomous resentment. 'We discovered that for ourselfs. If we had known it when they hired us, we would never have touched this.'

Oddly, Janet found that completely convincing. Otto and Liese Bleicken called themselves 'private detectives' and practised industrial espionage, freelance bugging and petty theft; when they'd realized that they'd run up against MI5, they'd recoiled and capitulated at once. If they'd known that the job was going to be so tough, they wouldn't have taken it.

Michael evidently believed it as well,

because he sighed. 'One more question, then: what did you do with Dr Morley's jewellery?'

There was a silence. The Bleickens both looked from Michael to Janet and then back again, and Janet saw the surprise in their faces. Until that moment they must have believed that Michael was there for purely professional reasons – that he'd been waiting here to trap them. They were not sure whether to be relieved (because he hadn't known quite as much as they'd feared) or alarmed (because they'd burgled an MI5 agent's girlfriend). Then both faces became sullen with suspicion.

'Take it as a request for *advice*, then,' said Michael equably. 'You have ... professional contacts who might know where thieves would be likely to dispose of such items. What you might tell me is not evidence that you yourselves are guilty of any crime.'

Liese glanced warily at her husband. 'On such a basis,' she said, 'there is a pawnshop here in Leicester that I believe thieves might use.' The 'second-hand store' she named was one of the ones the police had advised Janet about. She hadn't visited it; she'd found the whole business too depressing.

'Thank you,' said Michael politely. 'Goodnight.'

The two Germans took their cue and got up. 'We have been helpful,' Liese Bleicken reminded him.

'You've been helpful tonight,' Michael agreed. 'I expect you to remain helpful by leaving the country. I do not want to see you again.'

'Hah!' exclaimed Otto bitterly. 'Not if we can help it!' He started through the lounge door, then recoiled with an improbable screech of *'Himmlischer Gott!'*

'Was ist los?' demanded his wife, pushing forward as her husband staggered back – then stopping.

Madhab came forward into the room, still naked apart from the boxer shorts. He was carrying a *kukri*, the traditional curved knife of the Gurkhas. He did not look like a linguistically impaired fifteen-year-old: he looked lithe and strong and quite terrifyingly uncivilized.

'You!' he spat at the Germans. 'You *thief.*'

'Madhab, Madhab!' cried Janet, thrusting past the pair. 'It's OK. Let them go.' She caught his bare shoulder, and found it tense, damp with sweat and hard as stone. 'It's OK,' she told him again. 'Put the knife down.'

Madhab did not lower the knife. 'Get out!' he ordered the Germans. 'You come back...' He jerked the blade sideways – not a teenage play-acting slash, but a movement controlled, precise and chillingly knowledgeable. Used properly, a *kukri* could take a man's head off. The Germans, from their expressions, were aware of that notorious fact.

'*Du lieber Gott!*' whispered Liese. She edged past Madhab and fled. Her husband followed her.

Michael went after them, presumably to ensure that they went. Janet turned to Madhab and took the *kukri* from his now-unresisting hand. He smiled at her. Unsteadily, she set the knife down on the coffee table. She knew exactly where it came from. It had belonged to Madhab's father, who'd been a soldier in a Gurkha regiment of the Indian army, and who'd died in Kashmir when Madhab was three. The knife had come back to his widow with his ashes, and Madhab had been given it on her death a year later. It was almost the only thing he had from his father, so of course he had brought it to England. She'd never realized that he actually knew how to use it.

Of course he did, she told herself now. He was a Gurkha from a village of Gurkhas. There'd been lots of other knives about, and the men did practise with them sometimes: she'd seen them herself. Of course he'd copied them.

'You mustn't do things like that,' Janet said urgently.

'No hurt,' Madhab pointed out. He seemed quite calm now.

'That's not the point! Madhab, you could get into trouble for threatening people with a knife. And ... and there were *two* of them! You *scared* them. People can be dangerous when they're scared. If they'd had a gun...'

Michael came back in as she said this. 'No,' he declared confidently. 'They wouldn't carry a gun here in Britain. Too much risk.' He grinned at Madhab. 'God, you did scare them, though!'

Madhab grinned back at him fiercely. 'Thief,' he said, with contempt. 'Take Janet thing.'

'They didn't like me,' Michael told him, still grinning, 'but they knew what I was. They didn't have a clue about you.' He laughed. 'Wild boy with a knife! God, you scared them! They won't come near this house again for any money!' Then he went on, reluctantly, 'Janet is right, though. You should not threaten people with knives.'

'Bad people,' Madhab told him.

'Even bad people,' said Michael, shaking his head. 'Listen to me. Janet's right. When someone is scared, he may fight. Then someone will get hurt, you or him. If you hurt someone – even if you hurt a bad man – you could be punished. Worse, they might send you back to Nepal. I know, it's unfair; but the world *is* unfair. How long were you listening?'

Madhab shrugged.

159

'The whole time?' suggested Michael, and the boy nodded.

'I never heard you,' said Michael admiringly.

Madhab shrugged again. 'Think, maybe Janet need help. Get me father soldier knife. Wait, me, listen.' He studied Michael a moment, with wary respect, then continued, 'Want them no come back. Want them know, me here, have knife.'

Michael looked so entirely approving that Janet wanted to scream. *Men!*

Michael turned to her, as though he'd heard that furious thought. 'I'm sorry about the disturbance,' he said formally.

'Did you expect it?' she asked bluntly. She remembered the Germans' obvious belief that they'd walked into Michael's trap.

He was taken aback, both by the question and by the anger in her voice. 'No!' he protested. He stared at her face. 'Do you think I came up here tonight because of *that*?'

'I don't know what to think!' she shouted, and sat down. She found that she was shaking and fighting an impulse to burst into tears. Like any doctor, she was used to midnight alarms, but this had not been the sort of struggle that normally roused her. She saw again Michael's quiet ruthlessness, Otto Bleicken's useless hate, and Madhab's set face behind the knife.

'Janet!' Michael protested. He made a

move towards her, and she waved him back furiously.

Madhab came over and began rubbing her shoulders. 'OK,' he told her. 'No hurt.' She caught his wrist and held it, but found nothing to say.

'I'm sorry,' said Michael again, after a silence. 'It wasn't a nice thing to wake up and find in your living room.'

'It wasn't your fault,' she replied, and tried to swallow the anger tightening her throat. It *wasn't* his fault. She had grave misgivings about the world he inhabited; she had fresh doubts about whether she could tolerate it – but this was not his fault. The Bleickens would have invaded her house whether or not she'd even met him, and it certainly wasn't anything he'd ever supported or approved.

After another moment of silence, Michael asked, 'Was there any reason the Bleickens would expect there to be more of the drugs for the treatment here tonight?'

'Yes,' Janet agreed listlessly. 'If the treatment hadn't been going so well, there would have been.' Then she picked her head up and asked, 'That's significant, is it?'

He hesitated. 'Maybe. I'm sure I saw an insulated freezer bag in that holdall of theirs. Did the drugs have to be kept cold?' When she nodded, he asked, more eagerly, 'Did you use the phone to tell anyone you'd be going to Somers Synaptic yesterday?'

She tried to remember. The arrangements with David had been made in person. She had told the primary care group that she couldn't accept a locum placement for the Friday because her ward had a medical appointment; but that had been by e-mail. The phone tap wouldn't work on e-mail – would it? No, surely not: the server had insisted on changing the password when she'd hooked up her new computer. On Thursday she'd thought about phoning her parents and telling them that Madhab's treatment seemed to be working; but she'd decided not to do so. For one thing, it had seemed too soon to count on it; for another, her parents didn't really care. They were pleasant enough to Madhab when they met him, but they were dismayed by the way their daughter was ruining her career for the sake of a disabled Nepalese boy.

'I don't think I did,' she concluded at last, 'unless the phone tap works on e-mails.'

He smiled tightly, and she looked a question.

'Firsby and the technicians left Somers Synaptic before Madhab's operation,' he explained, 'nearly three weeks ago now. *Maybe* they were aware of the planned schedule for the treatment, but I don't think it's likely. And the phone tap the Bleickens were using wouldn't work on e-mail.'

'Oh!' she exclaimed, understanding. The Bleickens had obviously expected to find the drugs in the house, but if they couldn't have found out from their phone tap, and if the technicans couldn't have told them, then they must have heard from Elena Simonson or from David himself. 'I don't see why David would tell them,' she said, out loud. 'As he said, it's *his* intellectual property.'

'No,' agreed Michael. He smiled again. 'The woman I sent to check Somers' records *thought* they'd been tampered with, and Ms Simonson was certainly very unhappy about the fact that we were looking.' He stood up, stretching. 'I think I need to talk to Dr Somers – and to his secretary.' He glanced at the clock on the mantelpiece: it was now quarter past four. Already the dawn was showing grey through the windows. 'I don't think I'm going to be able to go back to sleep,' he said apologetically. 'Would you mind if I used your computer? I need to send some e-mails.'

Janet shook her head. 'Go ahead. I *know* I'm not going to be able to go back to sleep. I'll make some breakfast.'

After such an early rising it was bound to be a very long morning; that Janet expected. What she did not expect was that it would improve rapidly from its grim beginning. She made fruit scones for breakfast – an exceptional indulgence, since ordinarily she ate toast or nothing while Madhab glutted himself on cold cereal. The three of them ate the scones together, sitting in the early morning sunshine with the window open. Afterwards they went for a walk by the river. Ducks quacked and fluttered on the calm water, and birds sang in the willow trees. The visit of the Germans began to seem unreal.

'What will the Bleickens do?' she asked Michael uneasily.

'Oh, they'll leave the country,' he said confidently; 'go home to Berlin and trawl for another job.' He glanced at her and added, 'They'll probably tell their client here that they were inspecting the house when they realized that I was here, and they suspected that it was a trap. Then they will say that they did some investigating and discovered that I was MI5. That will give them an excuse to pull out and go home. They have a lot of experience in the business: they know how to keep themselves whole.' He said the last with contempt.

There were repercussions, of course. Michael was determined that the house should be equipped with a proper system of alarms, and kept under guard until this was installed. Several of his e-mails had been to arrange this. 'We can pay for it,' he assured her. 'It's a completely justifiable expense.'

'But ... a *guard*!' she protested helplessly. 'You said yourself that the Bleickens were never going to come near the house again. And we don't even *have* any of David's special drugs in the house!'

'Tao Pharmaceuticals don't know that,' Michael replied at once. 'They may have other contacts they could use to burgle you, or they might even risk trying it themselves. The Bleickens probably supplied them with all the details of your house and your schedule.'

'I don't have a regular schedule,' she objected. 'I have placements, and they change all the time.'

Michael only shrugged. 'All the more reason to take precautions. If they broke in while you were at home, there might be violence. I've contacted a reputable and reliable firm. If you don't want the guard to stay in the house, they can arrange a van. It can park outside; you'll scarcely know it's there.'

'Neighbourhood Watch will call the police!'

'Oh, the police will be notified. Neighbourhood Watch would find out it's OK. But if you don't want the disturbance, you can let the guard stay in the house. It would only be for a couple of days, until the security system's installed.'

'I don't *want* a burglar alarm! They're always going off for nothing and annoying the neighbours!'

Michael shook his head. 'This would be a *good* system.' When Janet glared, he coaxed, 'It would actually enhance the value of the house. And they're required to redo any paintwork they damage installing it, so you could probably get them to touch up all the window frames while they're at it.'

She wasn't sure whether to be angry or to laugh.

'If you won't accept this,' Michael said hesitantly, 'then I have to recommend that you and Madhab move to a safe house.'

'That's ludicrous!'

He shrugged. 'A foreign company has burgled the home of a British subject in an effort to obtain classified information about a Defence-funded British research project. I don't think it's at all ludicrous for us to take steps to protect the research and you.'

Put like that, it didn't sound ludicrous. 'How the *hell* did I get into this?' she asked no one in particular.

He had the grace to look embarrassed. 'I'm sorry. I know you didn't bargain on any of this, um, *spy business*. But it's going on, and probably it started even before you contacted David Somers. It's too late for you to avoid it. Given that, I really do think you should accept as much protection and support as you can get. After all, we're on your side.'

She looked at him in frustration, and he

added, low voiced, *'I'm on your side, anyway.'*

She remembered again the quiet, composed ruthlessness with which he'd confronted the Germans. He must have heard them out there in the dark, risen and dressed, gone to the back door and called them by name – all without raising his voice. A formidable man, one nobody would want to have on the *opposing* side. She wondered if she should be afraid of him. 'Why are you on my side?' she demanded bluntly.

He was silent a moment, just looking at her. 'Because I want to go back to believing that Good can triumph in this world, if it really works hard at it,' he said at last. 'Evil has its own way so much of the time – natural evil, and then human evil on top of it. A child gets born with the bones in his ears fused; he could be cured, but he belongs to a poor family in a poor country, so he isn't. Then his parents die, of the sort of things people die of all the time in poor countries. He's a bright, brave boy, but basically he's thrown on to life's scrap heap. That's the natural order of the world. You're trying to overcome it. I'm on your side, Janet.'

'Oh,' she said, and felt her face burning. 'Oh.' She thought of saying, *No, you've got it all wrong: I'm not this saintly person you're making me out to be; I'm a middle-aged childless*

167

divorcee who's trying to atone for her failures –
but the words sounded too feeble to utter.
Anyway, it was true that she was trying to
win Madhab a justice that the world had
denied him. Beside that, her own failures
were almost irrelevant. 'Oh,' she said again.

'Besides,' added Michael, more lightly,
'when you go stern like that, it makes me
weak at the knees.'

I think I love you, she thought, but she
didn't dare say that, either. Instead she only
blushed harder.

Madhab's 'Build a Robot' course started at
half past nine. In the long wait for the hour
he told Michael about it, and Michael
seemed very interested. It turned out that
he, too, was a fan of the popular television
series that had inspired the course – he, too,
enjoyed watching home-made robots
attempting to smash one another before an
enthusiastic audience. In the end – to Janet's
surprise and discomfort – Michael offered to
accompany Madhab to the first session, to
help him understand the instructions.

'You don't have to,' she told him.

'I'd *like* to,' he replied. 'It sounds *fun*.'

Full of doubt, she watched them depart in
Michael's car for the technical college where
the course would take place. She herself
went to the second-hand shop where the
Bleickens had sold her jewellery.

She spotted one pair of earrings at once,

168

and when she told the shopkeeper that she was looking for 'something antique as a present for my sister', he took her great-grandmother's opal necklace out of a drawer. She pretended to inspect it, put down a deposit on it, then went back to her car and phoned the police.

The shopkeeper, of course, claimed that he'd bought the jewellery in good faith. He demanded that Janet prove that it was stolen. That was not difficult, since she'd reported the theft, and had already sorted out several pictures of herself wearing the necklace for the insurance company. Confronted with these, the shopkeeper admitted that it must have been stolen, though still insisting that he'd bought it in good faith. 'They were a foreign couple,' he told the police. 'German, I think: they said they were on holiday and had found a car they wanted to buy, so they were selling some of her stuff to pay for it.'

The police obviously didn't believe this story for a moment, though they took down the details. There was then more fuss and argument, and eventually Janet was given the earrings and the necklace. She drove off triumphant, and did the shopping on the way home.

Michael and Madhab returned at a quarter to one, also looking triumphant, and full of plans for 'their' robot. It seemed that

Michael had done much more than simply interpret for Madhab: he was designing the electronics for the machine while Madhab concentrated on the mechanics. Michael described the control system he was planning with so much enthusiasm that she finally had to accept that he was not just being polite: he really was having fun.

'Are you planning to come back next week for it?' she asked him.

He looked up at her, eyes startled, then eager. 'Would that be OK?'

'Yes,' she told him. 'That is ... Madhab? It's your robot.'

'Is good, is good!' Madhab exclaimed instantly. 'Michael come, build control. Great!'

'You could come up again Friday evening,' Janet said, feeling both exhilarated and afraid. 'I could make dinner. Pay you back for the meals you've bought us.'

After Michael left, Madhab was very thoughtful. At supper that night he said suddenly, 'Janet. You say good. Me know Michael, me like.'

'I think he likes you, too,' she told him.

He gave her a huge smile. 'Everything good!' He gestured hugely at the world around him. 'Shunt give word, Michael good man, good everything!'

'I just hope it doesn't all go bad,' she said in a low voice. The natural order of the world, she thought, with a tremor of dread, would be for Michael to cry off suddenly without any explanation, for the treatment to stop working ... and for the shunt to collect some bacteria and start an infection that blasted Madhab's brain. But there was nothing she could do to prevent any of it, except to be on her guard and hope.

The arrival, shortly after supper, of the guard from the firm Michael had contacted was oddly reassuring. The reminder that some things had indeed gone wrong already somehow made it seem more likely that the rest might work out – like that old Greek king, Janet thought, who threw the ring that was his most prized possession into the sea, so that the gods would content themselves with that loss and not demolish all the rest of his good fortune.

She wondered if she should sacrifice the necklace.

Seven

The weekend passed, and the new week began with bewildering normality. On Monday a trio of workmen arrived and began to install the alarm system, as matter-of fact about it as if she'd ordered it herself. They agreed to repaint all the window frames while they were about it, for a very minimal extra fee.

The telephone company also arrived on Monday – in response to another of Michael's e-mails – to investigate the 'fault' on the line. They found the two bugs, expressed their astonishment, horror, and bewilderment, removed them, and told her they would order an investigation at once. Madhab went off to his remedial reading class; in the afternoon she started a new locum placement.

The alarm was fully installed by lunchtime on Tuesday. It was fully computerized, had a hook-up to the phone line, and was supplied with cameras and lights as well as alarms. The workmen told her proudly that it was state-of-the-art. They showed her how to set it and switch it off, and went over an instruction manual with her. It wasn't as complicated as she'd feared, and the workmen assured her that it was unlikely to go off by accident, though if it did, there was a number that she must ring within one minute or the police would be despatched to check. There was also a card to put in her wallet, with instructions on how to reset the system by phone – which apparently could be done once the police gave the all-clear. No, there was nothing to pay: the company would send an invoice to the billing address: 'Thames House, Millbank, London SW1 – Department of Training and Research. Is that right?'

'Yes,' she said. 'Thank you.'

She also sent an e-mail to the security company that had provided the guard, telling them that the young man didn't need to come any more and asking them to thank him, though in fact, she was relieved that he wouldn't be coming again: he'd been so shy that it was impossible to talk to him, and the sound of him watching television downstairs at night had kept her awake.

Madhab set the alarm off on Tuesday evening, Wednesday morning, and Thursday lunchtime while trying to figure out how the infrared sensors worked, but on each occasion they managed to phone and cancel in time. The rest of the week was uneventful.

On Friday morning they once again set off on the drive down to Oxford. It was the end of July now, and another hot day. The air was full of insects that died messily against the windscreen, and the thick weeds on the verges of the motorways were beginning to bleach. Madhab had brought along a notebook and his copy of *The Way Things Work*. He sat beside her, frowning at the drawings of gears and wheels and levers, occasionally making a little drawing of his own in the notebook – for his robot, she was certain. The patch of his scalp that had been shaved for the operation was now covered with his thick black hair. One more haircut, thought Janet, and it would be impossible to tell that he'd had surgery at all – except for the telltale of the microshunt, gleaming above his left ear.

They had not discussed his treatment at all recently, partly because of the events of the weekend, and partly because they knew that they disagreed about what should be done next. Janet was keenly aware that Madhab wanted more of the growth stimulants. He'd wanted more last time, and he would certainly want more now; but did he need them yet? It was true, his linguistic ability hadn't made any more dramatic leaps, but his confidence and fluency with what he'd gained had been increasing steadily. She felt, instinctively and perhaps irrationally, that his mind must need time to consolidate its new linguistic structures, and she was afraid to do anything that might damage the delicate new growth.

'Madhab,' she said hesitantly, as they joined the M40 near Stratford, 'I think we should wait at least another week before getting any more of the drugs.'

Madhab set his book down in his lap and scowled at her. 'Good brain-med' cine,' he told her. 'Works fine.'

'Yes, it does! It works so well that I really don't think you need any more.'

Madhab shook his head vigorously. 'No talk good, now. In school, teacher say, "Madhab, you understand?" Kid laugh. Want talk *good!*'

'Yes, but I think you will soon talk better, even without any more of the brain medicine. David always expected the treatment to take months. Why hurry now?'

'*Good* brain-medicine!' declared Madhab emphatically. 'Bigs talk place Madhab brain. No hurt.'

She grimaced. 'Madhab, you remember in Nepal, you used to put manure on the garden?'

'Man-yure?'

'From the animals. The smelly droppings from the animals. You used to dig it into the garden, remember?'

His face cleared. 'Oh, yes! Manure. Yes.

175

Grows plants good.'

'What happened when you put too much manure on just one plant?'

He was silent. 'Brain-med' cine –' He used his *sort*-of hand gesture – 'manure?' he asked at last.

'I don't know.' She stared ahead of her at the road, the traffic. 'I don't know, Madhab. Brains aren't like plants. Brains aren't like anything else in the world. But ... but maybe *growing* is the same. Plants grow; your brain is growing. Put too much manure on just one plant, and it dies, doesn't it? It can't get enough air and sunlight and it chokes, or else too much other stuff grows in that manure, and the plant rots. The brain-medicine is good – now. But maybe too much would be bad. It must be strong: it works better than anyone expected it would work. I don't know, but it makes me worry.' She glanced over at him, saw his frown, and added, 'I know, I worry too much! Fuss, fuss, fuss, you said, and you're right. But I love you, and I really, really want this to work. Right now it *is* working. So I'm afraid to change anything.'

His frown deepened. 'David Somers know brain.'

She grimaced again. 'Yes, he knows a lot more about brains than I do. And yes, I know he wanted to give you more of the medicine last time. But – Madhab, darling –

he doesn't care about *you*, and I do.'

'Kill monkey,' said Madhab, and touched the microshunt.

The matter-of-fact calmness of that chilled her. 'Yes,' she agreed, in a whisper; 'but you're not a monkey.'

Again he was silent for a long time. Finally he said, 'No more med' cine this time. *Next* time.'

She was relieved that he'd agreed – and still anxious, because she might have got it wrong. What if the delay in giving more of the growth stimulants meant that his language remained permanently impaired? 'We can always give you *more* of the medicine,' she said, to encourage them both. 'We can always phone up David in the middle of the week and ask for another dose. But once it's in your brain we can't take it out again.'

Madhab nodded resignedly.

They left the M40 north of Oxford, swung round to the south of the city, and arrived at Somers Synaptic at five past eleven. Pulling up beside the intercom panel at the gate, Janet wondered apprehensively if Elena was still there. She assumed that Michael had spoken to both David and Elena by now, and that some conclusion had been reached. Probably there'd been a terrible scene during the course of the week – accusations

177

of treachery, rage and tears.

She suddenly wished that she'd phoned David to confirm their appointment. She hadn't wanted to: since the events of the weekend her aversion to the man had been reinforced by her wish to stay well away from a confrontational mess. Now, however, she wished that she'd at least checked whether the meeting was still on.

She told herself that if David had wanted to cancel, he would have phoned *her*. Probably he didn't want to cancel. Madhab's treatment was his only remaining project, his source of funding and his hope of glory. He had no other research contracts, and all his staff had gone. He wasn't going to cancel his last chance. Feeling guilty, she rang the bell.

There was no answer. She rang again, then switched the engine off and got out of the car.

It was quiet, apart from the song of a bird from the bushes beside the road. The air was hot, close and damp, heavy with the scent of meadowsweet. Gnats danced in a cloud above the drive. She peered through the fence into the gravel yard. David's Mercedes was there, but no other cars. She rang the bell a third time, but there was still no answer. Perhaps, she thought, it only registered at the receptionist's desk. David must be in – why else would his car be there? – but if Elena had indeed gone, and he was working in his lab, he wouldn't know they'd arrived. She went forward to inspect the gate.

It moved at her tentative tug: the electronic lock had been left open. She pulled harder, and it dragged open perhaps an inch in its bed, then stuck. Madhab climbed out of the car and came to help her. Together they managed to open the gate enough for themselves, but it was impossible to force it wide enough to admit the car. Janet looked at Madhab; he smiled and shrugged.

They left the car in the drive and trudged across the yard to the house. When they were within a few paces of the door she realized that it was ajar, and stopped, struck by a sudden cold doubt. Something about this was *wrong*.

'Janet?' said Madhab.

She waved a hand at the inch-wide opening of the door. Her heart had started pounding, and her mouth was dry. She told herself that all this spy business was destroying her commonsense: most likely David had left the gate unlocked and the door a crack open so that they could get in without help from the receptionist. She found, nonetheless, that she could not make herself go forward to open the door and see what lay behind it.

'I'm going to try phoning,' she said abruptly. She took out the mobile Michael had given her, fished her address book out of her handbook, and dialled the number of Somers Synaptic. In the office behind the door the phone rang, very loud in the stillness of the empty yard. It blended with the signal from the phone at her ear, again and again and again. There was no answer. She saw Madhab looking at her, his eyes worried.

Janet switched off the phone, put the address book back in her bag, turned around, and started back toward the car.

Somewhere nearby a door banged, and suddenly she found herself running in blind panic. She pelted back through the gate, tore open the door of the Datsun and flung herself into the driver's seat. She started the engine just as Madhab dropped into the passenger seat beside her. She rammed the gear lever into reverse and they jolted backward along the drive into the lane, which was, fortunately, empty.

'Two mans,' said Madhab quietly, waving toward the house.

She didn't even look; she slid the car into gear and drove off along the road with a screech of tyres.

She didn't stop until she reached the pub where she'd met Michael. There she pulled in and parked, then sat, clutching the steering wheel and breathing in great hot gasps. Her heart was still pounding, and she was shivering and drenched with sweat.

'Stupid,' she whispered. 'Stupid!' There

was no reason to think that whoever had been at the house was doing anything wrong. Probably the 'two men' had been David and a colleague, or a pair of workmen come to mow the lawn.

She made herself let go of the steering wheel, noting with disgust that she'd been gripping it so hard her fingers had gone white. *I've never been so frightened*, she thought, and for what? An empty yard, a phone ringing in an empty office and a door banging. 'You saw two men?' she asked Madhab.

He nodded, his eyes very wide. 'Two mens,' he said. 'Nepal.'

'What?' she asked, startled.

He made a face. 'Nepal mans. Black clothe. Come out back house, stop, look. Janet and Madhab in car, go down road, vroom!' He hesitated. 'Bad mans?'

'I ... I don't know.' She took out her phone again. 'I was just scared, Madhab. Suddenly I was just ... scared.' She dialled Michael's number.

'Training and Research,' said the secretary; and she said, 'Janet Morley for Michael Shahid, please. It's urgent' – and wondered if it really was.

'Janet!' said Michael.

'Michael,' she faltered. 'I...'

'Is something the matter?'

'I don't know,' she told him. 'Probably not.

181

Only I was just going to Somers Synaptic for Madhab's appointment, and nobody answered when I rang, but the gate was unlocked, and the front door was ajar. I don't know why, it worried me, and I tried to phone them. The phone rang and rang, but nobody answered. Then I heard a door shut and I got scared – it was just a stupid panic – and I ran back to the car. Madhab says two men came out of the back of the house while we were driving off. He said they looked Nepalese.'

'Where are you?' Michael's voice was suddenly sharp and hard.

'That pub. Probably it's nothing, but—'

'Would Madhab say a Chinese person looked Nepalese?'

'Probably,' she said. 'I mean, he'd know the difference, obviously, but it'd be the closest word he knows. The area he's from is hill country. There are a lot of vaguely Chinese looking types there. He said they had black clothes.'

'Stay right where you are. I'm going to phone the police.'

'Oh, no! You really think that's ... I mean, well, if anybody phones the police, it ought to be me, and—'

'No, they'll pay much more attention if I do it. I'll phone you back in a minute and tell you the name of the officer they're sending. I'll come up myself as soon as I can, but I think it may be important to get somebody on the spot immediately. What's your number?'

She had to check it on the leaflet that had come with the phone. Michael thanked her and hung up.

A couple of minutes later, the phone buzzed. 'They're sending a PC Sean Hobson,' Michael told her. 'I gather he isn't very senior, but he is nearby, and will be there in a few minutes. He'll meet you in the car park at the pub, and you can tell him what happened.'

'Don't you think we may be overreacting?' Janet asked. Now that she'd had time to calm down, she was beginning to feel very foolish. 'I mean, *nothing* happened. Those men were probably just workmen come to fix the fence or something, and if we come screaming up to Somers Synaptic with the police to arrest them...'

'If that's all they are, we apologize. I hope that's what we end up doing. Don't worry: the police will blame me, not you.'

She was silent for a moment, registering that hope. 'What ... what happened about Elena?'

He sighed. 'I'll tell you later. Please be careful. I'll be up as soon as I can.'

About five minutes later, a police car pulled into the car park, siren howling and lights flashing. Janet reluctantly climbed out of the Datsun and waved to it. She now felt acutely ridiculous – though, beneath that feeling, the sick panic she'd felt in the empty yard still shifted uneasily.

The police car jerked to a stop and an officer got out. He was a young man – barely out of his teens, by the look of him – with ginger hair and a self-important expression. 'Dr Janet Morley?' he asked, coming over. 'I'm Police Constable Sean Hobson. You reported something suspicious at a research company near here – is that right?'

'Yes,' she confessed apologetically. 'Probably it isn't anything to worry about, but...'

'We got an urgent request to investigate from *MI5!*' PC Sean Hobson told her proudly. Probably he'd impress his girlfriend with that detail that evening.

'Yes,' Janet admitted guiltily. 'Probably it's nothing, but ... well, the MoD is funding the research.'

The young man frowned anxiously. 'It's not some sort of place where they do, like, chemical or biological weapons research, is it?'

'No, no, no! Nothing like that.' She thought about saying, 'My ward has been having an experimental treatment for language impairment there,' but how could she explain why a treatment for language impairment was classified and needed special police attention? Instead she smiled appeasingly and said, 'It's a medical research establishment. It doesn't handle anything dangerous. Madhab – in the car there, my ward – had an appointment for some treatment from the guy who runs it, but it looked like ... well, it looked like it might have been broken into. And nobody would answer the buzzer or the phone, even though David – the doctor we were going to see – was supposed to be there. So I phoned a friend at MI5 to ask what I should do, and he phoned you. He said probably we'd end up apologizing for wasting your time.'

'Better show me where it is,' said Sean Hobson importantly. 'I'll check it out.'

She drove carefully back to Somers Synaptic and pulled into the drive with the police car close on her tail. The gate, which she'd left ajar, was wide open. David's Mercedes was no longer in the yard.

She stopped the car in the drive again, and got out. PC Sean Hobson, who'd stopped immediately behind her, got out in turn and came over. 'What's the matter?' he asked, glancing in puzzlement at the open gate.

'When I was here just now the gate wouldn't open properly,' she said numbly. 'And David's car was ... that is, David Somers, who owns this place ... his car was parked there, in the yard. Now it's gone.'

Sean Hobson frowned impressively. He

stalked through the gate and across the yard to the door. Janet and Madhab trailed shamefacedly after him. He knocked emphatically, then flung the door open – and froze.

Elena the secretary was lying across her desk, her face hidden against its black-stained panels. The back of her skull was a ruin of blood and shattered bone.

'Oh, shit,' whispered Sean Hobson, in a tone of absolute horror. Despite the uniform, he suddenly looked like any young adult confronted with a violent death.

Janet pushed past him to the young woman's side. Even as her fingers felt for a pulse she knew there was nothing she could do. No one survived a wound like that.

'I gotta ... I gotta...' faltered Hobson, fumbling his phone out of his pocket. His face had gone white, making his freckles look dark. 'I gotta phone.'

He began dialling his headquarters. Janet stayed for a moment, bent over the body, her fingers pressed against Elena's still-warm flesh. The young woman's face was lying in a puddle of blood, she noticed numbly. Blood was beginning to congeal in the black hair, and mixed in with it were flecks of brain tissue. She abruptly remembered Madhab.

He was standing in the doorway, almost as pale as the policeman. She straightened, drew her fingers away from the dead woman,

186

and hurried over to him.

He clutched her arm hard. 'David Somers,' he said, in a low voice. 'Where?' He let go suddenly and ran into the lab.

'Madhab, stop!' she shouted, afraid of what he might find there – then ran after him.

The computer that had processed Madhab's scans was torn open, its circuit boards broken on the floor, but the room seemed otherwise untouched. Madhab rattled at the door to the biology lab, then shot across into the chemistry section. He came out again in a moment and rattled the door to biology again. 'Lock,' he said, looking back at her with a hopeless, frightened face.

Sean Hobson trailed through after them. 'This is a *murder scene!*' he told them shrilly. 'You mustn't *touch* anything!'

'Somebody may be in there!' Janet shouted at him. 'Somebody may be *hurt* in there!' Afterwards she was sorry that she had shouted, but at the time she could do nothing else. She went over to the door and called, 'David? David, are you in there?'

Hobson blinked at it as though he hadn't registered before that the door was even there. Then he came over and tried the handle himself.

'Other door,' suggested Madhab. 'Back, behind house.' He always remembered the physical layout of a building.

Janet remembered the door she'd heard bang shut while she stood in the empty yard, remembered that Madhab had said the men had come from *behind* the house. She knew, with a sudden sick certainty, what they would find in the biology lab.

She was not wrong. The back door of the house was unlocked, and it opened into the biology lab. A body was lying in a bloody heap in front of the fridge where the drugs had been kept. The fridge was open and empty.

She went over. The body was a man, face-down with his arms folded up under his body and his chin tucked in, his back covered in blood. Fair-haired and stout – yes, oh God, it was David. She knelt beside him and felt for a pulse: there wasn't one. She caught her breath, then began examining him, hoping that somehow she could fix what had been so brutally broken, knowing that she could not.

She found the wound in his left side – a fist-sized hole under his shoulder blade, fringed with fragments of bone. *An exit wound*, she thought, in sick numbness, *like the one in the back of Elena's head*. She turned him over, and found the smaller entrance wound on the right side of the chest.

She sat back on her heels, pressing her blood-stained hands together.

'He's dead, too?' asked PC Hobson in a

choked voice.

She nodded. 'The bullet must have gone straight through his heart,' she said faintly. 'He must have died instantly.'

'Oh, God!' the young man cried miserably. She looked up at him, and saw that he was now more grey than white, and covered with a sheen of cold sweat. She got hurriedly to her feet.

'Come outside,' she ordered. She took him firmly by the elbow.

Madhab was standing by the door and staring numbly at the body. Janet jerked her head at him to tell him to get out, and escorted Hobson out into the fresh air. He stumbled on the step. She made him sit down and put his head between his knees, and closed the door behind them.

Her hands were covered in blood. She went over to the overgrown lawn behind the house and began wiping them on the long grass.

'I'm not used to *murder*!' PC Hobson told her wretchedly. 'I just do burglaries, noise abatement orders, things like that. I don't do *murders*.'

'It's all right,' she told him soothingly. 'You've already done what you should. You phoned your headquarters, didn't you? They'll be here soon.'

'I'm sure there's *other* things I'm supposed to be doing!' Hobson protested, pressing his

189

forehead against his forearm. 'But I can't go back in there, I can't face it!'

'Janet,' said Madhab in a low voice.

'It's all right, darling,' she told him. She wanted to touch him, for comfort, but her hands were still bloody, and she didn't want to get blood on him. She couldn't seem to wipe it all off. 'It's all right. They've gone.' Even as she said it, she wondered how she could be so sure.

Madhab shuddered, then sat down on the pavement behind the house, wrapping his arms around his knees. 'Them took brain-med' cine,' he whispered. 'When we come, them here. Kill David Somers, take brain-med' cine away. All gone.'

'Yes,' she agreed. 'Oh, darling...'

She couldn't finish. The same selfish grief was in her own mind, crouched shamefully beside her horror at the two deaths: this ended Madhab's treatment. She remembered his scream of joy when he had realized that the treatment was working, that he was finally acquiring the power of speech and becoming fully human. She could not imagine what he must feel now. 'Maybe you didn't need any more of the medicine anyway,' she suggested weakly.

He just looked at her blankly. She could think of nothing more to say, and so went and tried to wipe the blood off her hands again. As she did, she thought of one of the

190

things Hobson was supposed to be doing. 'They must have taken David's car!' she exclaimed. 'It was a '57-reg Mercedes. You'd better phone your headquarters and tell them.'

Hobson made the phone call, though she heard nothing about the outcome of it for some time. The Oxfordshire police arrived in force shortly afterwards, and Janet spent the afternoon being interrogated.

She realized afterwards that they had never seriously considered her a suspect: it just felt that way. She had been at the lab at approximately the time the murders were committed; she had found the bodies; she had, by her own admission, known David and not liked him much. The police questioned her at length, first at Somers Synaptic, then back at their headquarters in Didcot. They questioned Madhab, too – separately. That horrified her, and she protested furiously: Madhab was a minor, was naturally shocked and distressed by what he'd seen, had trouble understanding and communicating, hadn't grasped what they were doing or what they wanted, wasn't even a UK citizen. It did no good: Madhab was led off by a beefy constable and an Asian WPC, and Janet was interrogated exhaustively by a Detective Inspector Bailey.

At about quarter past four, Michael Shahid interrupted. She had rarely been so glad to see anyone; she would have jumped up and hugged him, if she hadn't been sure that she would break down in tears if she did any such thing.

'Janet,' said Michael seriously, and she replied weakly, 'Hi.'

Michael turned to Detective Inspector Bailey, introduced himself, and offered his ID. The inspector took it, examined it with a mixture of suspicion and pleasure, and handed it back. 'So,' he said. 'MI5. Are you going to tell us what was going on here, or is it all classified?'

'I can tell you quite a lot about it,' Michael said quietly. 'Let me, um, speak to my friend Dr Morley a moment first, though. Janet, are you OK?'

'They took Madhab away,' Janet told him, her voice sharp. 'I don't know where he is. They shouldn't have done it – they really shouldn't've. He gets very frustrated and confused when he can't understand what's going on, and he saw the bodies – he was really shaken. They should've let me stay with him. I tried to explain...'

'The boy is *fine*!' said the detective impatiently. 'He's being seen by an officer who's trained in how to question children. I told you that.'

She glared at him. 'Where *is* he?'

The detective sighed in exasperation. 'We're pretty much done anyway. I'll get someone to take you to him.' He went to the door.

'Are you all right?' Michael asked again.

'I'm worried sick about Madhab!' she snapped.

Michael crossed the room and caught both her hands. 'Listen to me,' he ordered. 'This is true and important. You're all right, and so is Madhab. You almost walked right into the middle of a murder, but you felt that there was something wrong, and you got him away and kept both him and yourself safe. Listen to me: you *did* look after him. You did absolutely everything right. Madhab is OK – and you know perfectly well that the police never had any intention of hurting him, and that if they'd thought he needed you, they would have sent for you. So you can stop blaming yourself and *stop worrying.*'

She was not quite sure how she ended up sobbing on Michael's shoulder, but when she finally managed to get control of herself, she was clutching him tightly, her face pressed against his shirt collar. She picked her head up, and he kissed her, brushed damp hair out of her face, and kissed her again. She wondered what had happened to the detective inspector, and let go.

Detective Inspector Bailey seemed to have abandoned his office. Janet wiped ineffectually at her nose. 'Sorry,' she said vaguely.

Michael shook his head. 'You don't need to

193

be sorry for anything. Did that stupid inspector even give you a cup of tea?'

She found her handbag and dug in it for a travel pack of Kleenex. She blew her nose. 'Tea, yes; lunch, no. Michael, probably you're right and I'm worrying too much after the event, but I still really do want to see Madhab.'

'Yes. Of course. I have to brief this guy. Can I talk to you later?'

It turned out that Detective Inspector Bailey had been waiting outside his office for her to calm down. When Janet emerged, he gave Michael an uneasy look. 'I didn't realize she was upset,' he said defensively.

Janet blew her nose again. 'I'm a doctor. We have to be able to look like we're coping, even when we're not.'

'Ah,' said Inspector Bailey, with some embarrassment. He indicated a young policewoman beside him: 'This is WPC Willoughby. She'll take you to see your ward.'

WPC Willoughby escorted Janet off into the maze of Didcot police headquarters. 'Are you with MI5?' she asked, after a few minutes of silence.

'Me?' asked Janet, taken aback. 'No. I'm a GP. I'm only here because my ward, Madhab Limbu, was having treatment from David Somers – from the man who was murdered.'

WPC Willoughby was unconvinced. 'They're saying that the security services are mixed up in this – that this David Somers character was doing top secret research for the MoD, and that's why he was murdered.'

'I don't know why he was murdered,' Janet said heavily. 'I really don't. It's true David was doing research for the MoD, but it wasn't top secret. It wasn't even middling secret. And yes, there were people spying on him, but they were with a pharmaceutical company and wanted industrial patents. I wouldn't have thought there was anything going on that was likely to end in *murder*.'

Saying it seemed to crystallize an awareness she'd had for hours: it shouldn't have ended in murder. Ambitious researchers and greedy pharmaceutical companies were to be found all over the world, and relations between them, while frequently strident and angry, did not usually end in *murder*.

So why were there two bodies at the converted farmhouse? Because MI5 and the MoD were involved, and that upped the stakes? Or had the industrial spies intended a simple burglary and panicked because David and Elena came in unexpectedly and they were caught in the act?

Or had David been up to something else, some other piece of dishonesty greater than the small secrets they'd discovered already?

She didn't know, and, to tell the truth, she

didn't want to know. She followed WPC Willoughby up a flight of steps, pondering the only really important question: what was going to happen now?

She remembered David's high-pitched, self-satisfied voice saying, *The kid's been treated now: his brain's full of stem cells and growth hormones, all working away like mad. You're going to ... stop his treatment, and leave him like that? Dismiss the only man who understands what's been done? Suppose something goes wrong? Who's going to correct it for you?*

She had to hope that Jeremy Firsby would be able to 'correct it' – though she strongly suspected that David had intended to get rid of his associate all along, and had deliberately kept him in the dark. Well, she told herself, trying to be optimistic, the treatment did seem to be working. Perhaps nothing more would be needed. Perhaps nothing *would* go wrong.

Perhaps the natural order of the world would not apply.

Eight

Madhab was very relieved to see Janet, though not for the reasons she'd expected. It turned out that *he* had been very worried about *her*. Apart from that, he was fine. The blank grief that had afflicted him at Somers Synaptic seemed to have gone, and he was soberly self-controlled. He seemed, as well, to have had an easier time of the interrogation than she had. The charming young policewoman who'd taken a statement from him shook Janet's hand warmly and informed her that Madhab was a very observant young man. She did hope, she said earnestly, that this language treatment thing he was having worked out. Janet thanked her.

A few enquiries garnered the information that the police had no further need of them that evening, though they were obliged to sign out with 'the investigation' and to make themselves available again whenever they were required. They duly found the office where they could sign out, then located the car and started for home.

'Janet,' said Madhab, after a long silence

on the motorway, 'what we do? Brain-med' cine all gone.'

She winced. 'We'll talk to Jeremy Firsby. Maybe he'll be able to make some more.' She glanced over at him, then continued resolutely, 'Madhab, even if we can't get any more, the *biggest* part of the treatment is already done. The *big* part of the treatment was the stem cells. You've had those, and they obviously *are* growing and working in your brain. Your language is much better than it was and it's going to get even better whether or not you have any more of the medicine. It's entirely possible that the treatment is finished *anyway*.'

He was silent. Another glance showed that he was unconvinced. He knew, better than anyone, how huge an expanse of human speech lay untouched before him. He had struggled to conquer it before, without the help of the Somers Treatment, and he had failed. He did not believe he would conquer now.

He did not say anything more about it, however. After a few more miles he instead declared, abruptly, 'Poor David Somers. Poor man, all blood. Sorry me say bad man, sonovha bitch. He help me. He give me words. Sorry now.'

'I feel exactly the same way,' she told him, with feeling. 'He helped us when no one else could, and I'm ashamed of the way I talked about him.' In fact, she decided, she was ashamed of more than that. A brilliant man whom she'd known for many years, and who had helped her freely, was dead – and her chief regret was that he wouldn't be around to complete Madhab's treatment. That was shameful.

They stopped for supper at a Little Chef near Warwick, and arrived back in Leicester at about seven. The house was quiet, and the new alarm system indicated that it had been undisturbed during their absence. Janet went upstairs and had a shower, then washed her hands repeatedly and anointed them with a scented hand cream, to remove the last lingering traces of David's blood. She'd had blood on her hands often enough before, but the blood of surgery and first aid had never seemed as sticky or as hot. She cursed herself for being irrational, but she couldn't stop herself.

The doorbell rang at about nine, and Janet opened it to find Michael, looking tense and very tired. 'I'm sorry,' he said, without even waiting for a greeting. 'I know that probably you don't want to see anyone tonight. But – can I come in? Please?'

She let him in and made coffee, and they sat on the sofa to drink it. Madhab came and sat in the lounge chair, watching them intently.

Michael sipped his coffee, then set the mug

down with a deep sigh. 'You don't know how glad I am to see you,' he said, looking from one of them to the other. 'When I think about what might have happened today ... I suppose that's the reason I had to come up here tonight: to see you both.'

'P'lice talk Janet long time,' Madhab said accusingly.

Michael nodded. 'Yes. They were hard on you both, and I'm sorry. I can understand why they did it, though. You were both witnesses. They wanted to know everything you saw.'

Madhab shrugged. 'Catch bad mens?'

Michael hesitated. 'That's what they're *trying* to do, obviously.'

'And you don't think they can?' asked Janet.

'Well, I *hope* they can. But it's not like a ... like a domestic murder. In many ways the whole business is much more our line than theirs – and I don't have a clue why it happened. We'll help as much as we can, but...'

'But MI5 has trouble cooperating with the police?' she asked sourly.

He winced. 'In a nutshell, yes. You could say that the police find it hard to cooperate with us on our terms, but it amounts to the same thing. I am trying. I did brief Detective Inspector Bailey pretty thoroughly. But at some point the police always want us to

200

testify or produce evidence in court, and that's very difficult for us.' He sighed. 'I don't know – maybe in this case, since it's industrial not political...' He trailed off disconsolately, then picked up his coffee again.

'You said earlier you were going to tell me about what happened with Elena,' Janet prompted.

Michael sighed. 'Yes. Well. It turned out to be more complicated than I expected.'

'What, she was sleeping with David or something?'

He gave her a startled look. 'You *knew* about that?'

'No, of course not! You mean, she was?'

'For the past couple of years, from what I can make out. Pretty much from the time Somers hired her.' He paused, frowning, then added, 'Even if it is news to you, it obviously isn't a surprise.'

'Well, David always was...' Janet shrugged. 'Look, any group of med students, there're always a couple of stupid young men competing over who can get the most girls into bed. David was one of them. Fellow students, nurses, cleaning staff, townie girls in bars – if it was female and not actually hideous, he tried it on. Elena was young and pretty. So I'm not surprised he was sleeping with her, though I suppose I am surprised she put up with him for two years.' She stopped, remembering David as she'd seen him that morning, and felt her face burn. 'I shouldn't have said that,' she confessed guiltily. 'He probably just saw himself as full of vitality and animal life.'

Michael's eyebrows were up. 'Did he ever make a pass at you?'

'Yes, of course! I told you – he used to try it on with anything female. I told him he was disgusting. He was so ... so *tacky*, such a pathetic self-satisfied tabloid Lothario.' Again she remembered the bloody corpse and blushed in shame.

'Do you know,' murmured Michael, 'I suddenly understand a great deal.' At her look of eager surprise, he added hastily, 'Not about the case. Just about your attitude towards him and his towards you.' He had a swig of coffee, then went on: 'Be that as it may, he had a long-running affair with Elena Simonson. She used to come stay at his house most weekends. All her friends knew who he was, and most of them disliked him.'

'How did you find all this out?' asked Janet with distaste.

'I sent one of our people to ask around, of course. Among other stratagems, she pretended she worked for a company interested in hiring Ms Simonson. Most of Ms Simonson's friends said they wished she would leave her "swine of a boss" – from which I gathered that Ms Simonson had complained to them about him – but most warned my agent that she probably wouldn't, because she was going to marry him.'

'*Marry* him?' repeated Janet incredulously.

'That, apparently, is what her friends believed.'

Janet shook her head. 'I don't believe that. He would never marry his *secretary* – and he never acted like she was anything special. She must have been kidding herself.' She frowned. 'Maybe she pushed him to marry her, and he laughed at her, so she agreed to spy for Tao Pharmaceuticals to get even with him?'

'Maybe,' said Michael. 'But, as I said, it got complicated. He was outraged at the very suggestion that she'd do any such thing. He said that she loved him and he had complete confidence in her loyalty.'

'Oh!' exclaimed Janet, taken aback.

Michael nodded, stretched, then said hopefully, 'Could I possibly have a sandwich or something? I missed supper.'

They went into the kitchen. There wasn't much to put in a sandwich, apart from some elderly cheese and a little mango chutney. She hefted them at Michael with an enquiring lift of the eyebrows. 'Fine!' he said hastily, and she began to butter some bread. 'Do you still think Elena was working for Tao Pharmaceuticals?' she asked, opening the chutney.

'Oh yes,' he agreed at once. He leaned

wearily against the kitchen counter, watching her. 'Obviously, I've also had someone enquiring about Tao. It is a registered company – new, as the Bleickens told us, and beginning to make inroads in the pharmaceuticals market in South-East Asia. Several of the established pharmaceutical giants have complained that it's selling generic medicines and infringing their patents.'

Janet sliced cheese and grunted. She had no sympathy for the way pharmaceutical giants charged people in Third World countries: they made obscene profits, and poor people who couldn't pay died. She was aware of all their arguments about development costs and the need for investment, and those arguments all collapsed in the presence of a dying child. When she'd dispensed drugs in Nepal, she'd been happy to cheat Bayer and its ilk as much as she could. If Tao Pharmaceuticals was selling generic medicines in South-East Asia, then good luck to it!

'It doesn't trade in the United Kingdom,' Michael went on, 'but it's affiliated to a Chinese trade association with offices in London. At present Tao Pharmaceuticals has two registered representatives in this country. They've been here for some time – three years in one case, eighteen months in the other. Since the company doesn't actually trade in Europe at all, one has to wonder what they're doing here.'

'Do you wonder?'

'Not really,' admitted Michael.

Janet put the cheese sandwich on a plate and handed it to him. They went back into the lounge and sat down, Michael with the sandwich on his knees.

'Anyway,' he continued, taking a bite, 'we're looking into both of these people. One of the big medical research companies is convinced that Tao is spying on their research. They were very pleased when they understood that we're taking an interest, and sent us a dossier they've been compiling themselves. There's nothing conclusive in it – nothing that would stand up in court – but some of it is suggestive. You know the sort of thing: a break-in at a research establishment, or a research assistant reporting to his superior that he was offered a bribe – which implies others who might not have reported it – followed by a new drug being released by Tao Pharmaceuticals.' He had another bite of sandwich, then added, 'The company in question was funding some of Dr Somers' research before he lost his licence.'

'Oh,' she said, 'that figures. So did this company have any evidence that Tao had hired Elena?'

'No. Though that isn't conclusive: as I said, they don't have hard evidence for anything. Anyway, on Thursday I met with Dr Somers and presented him with the evidence that there was a plot to steal his precious intellectual property. He was very angry and immediately accused Firsby.'

'Firsby?' Janet repeated in bewilderment.

'Firsby. I put it to him that Firsby hadn't known when your appointments were and couldn't have told the Bleickens when the drugs would be at your house; that if the spies had access to Firsby they wouldn't *need* to steal drugs from your house; and that our people think that some of Somers Synaptic's records have been tampered with. He had an answer for everything. He said that Firsby could guess that the appointments would be on Fridays; that security at the lab meant that Firsby couldn't take the drugs home, and that the exact composition of the mixtures was secret; furthermore, that if the records *had* been tampered with, Firsby had had access to them. He said he'd had suspicions of Firsby for a long time, and that that was one reason why he'd got rid of him. I asked why he hadn't mentioned it before, and he said it was because he had no evidence. I told him that I suspected Elena, and he flew into a rage, as I said. He insisted that she was completely innocent. He called her in and told her what I'd said. They both screamed at me for half an hour.'

'Oh, dear!' said Janet, unsure whether to be sympathetic or to laugh.

'In the end I retreated with my tail between my legs, planning to try again another day, when they were cooler. Only...' Michael stopped, as though he, too, had become aware of the ghastly double meaning: David and Elena were certainly cooler now. 'I wish ... I don't know,' he resumed quietly. 'Maybe my accusation was what prompted the murder. Maybe if I'd been wiser it wouldn't have happened. But I still don't understand *why* they were murdered. To tell the truth, I can imagine Somers and Firsby having an almighty row, and one of them shooting the other in the course of it. But the police said Elena was shot sitting at her desk, and I can't see either of them doing that.'

'If we were wise, it would be a different world,' said Janet.

Michael sighed unhappily. 'Yes. Anyway, when I left Didcot, the police had sent out a car to pick up Firsby for questioning. I'm telling you this because I'm sure you were hoping to consult him about Madhab's treatment.'

'Yes,' agreed Janet, her heart sinking. 'You don't think he *could* have done it, do you? Madhab saw two men there, and he didn't recognize either of them. He *knows* Firsby.'

'Firsby had motive,' Michael pointed out. 'He also knew the lab, and he still had his key card for the gate. Somers Synaptic had a very good security system, and the police checked it: it hadn't been compromised. It had all been switched off, which can only be done from inside the receptionist's office.'

'But the men Madhab saw...'

'...might have been waiting to meet Firsby after he removed the drugs from the lab. Perhaps they went to look for him because he failed to turn up, and when they found the gate unlocked, they went in to see what had happened. That was the sort of scenario Detective Inspector Bailey was imagining. Whether it's right...' Michael put down the remains of his sandwich and spread his hands in expressive ignorance. 'For what it's worth, I agree with you that Firsby didn't do it. I just can't imagine him shooting Elena Simonson at her desk. But I'm not a police detective. Who knows? It could turn out that he had a motive to hate her, too.'

Another point struck Janet. 'You're saying now that you don't have a clue about why David and Elena were killed,' she said slowly, 'and yet ... you suspected that something terrible had happened the minute I phoned you. It was in your voice.'

He did not attempt to deny it. Instead he said quietly, 'I spent a long time in the Middle East. Probably if I'd spent that time in England, I wouldn't have suspected anything.'

She'd forgotten that. She wondered again what sort of terrible world he had inhabited, that an unlocked gate created in him the terror of imminent death. 'Oh. Yes.'

Michael picked up his cheese and chutney and took another bite. 'Anyway,' he said, more briskly, when he'd swallowed it, 'it's Detective Inspector Bailey's business to find the murderer, thank God, not mine.' He looked at Madhab with grave concern. 'My business, I suppose, is to see how much of Dr Somers' research can be salvaged – and yours is to find someone to help Madhab, if he needs more help. Firsby may be too shocked or too busy to be able and willing to help, even if he's cleared.'

There was a long silence. Michael finished his sandwich.

'I suppose we should contact Dr Bhattacharya,' Janet said at last. 'He's a neurological consultant at the Radcliffe in Oxford; Madhab was assigned to him in hospital. I had the impression that he's an associate of David's, and that David had told him at least some of what he was doing.' Even as she said it, she was struck by doubt. David had said that Dr Bhattacharya 'knew what was going on' – but that could have meant only that the consultant knew about the brain surgery, not that he'd been informed about the treatment. Still, Dr Bhattacharya was a respected neurologist, and at the very least he'd be able to protect Madhab from the worst disasters.

'We'll do that, then. Tomorrow.' Michael

yawned, stretched, then looked at her hopefully. 'Do you want me to leave tonight?'

'No,' she told him. 'Stay.'

Madhab got to his feet. 'Me fetch fold bed,' he announced, and went off to do so.

Michael looked at Janet again.

'Probably best,' she told him. 'I don't want to upset him. He's starting to like you.'

Michael smiled slowly, and she realized that she'd admitted that if she hadn't been worried about upsetting Madhab, she would have shared her own bed. When had she made *that* decision? She cursed herself silently, swept up the empty plate and the coffee cups, and went off to fetch some sheets.

She thought about Michael when she was lying in bed that night – about what it would be like to have him there beside her. He had a thin body, angular; probably he had knobbly knees. She imagined running her fingers over him, trying to count his ribs. (Was he ticklish? Would he laugh and gasp, or tickle her back, or wrestle with her and pretend to pin her down?) She thought about his hands touching her, imagined what his smile would look like without the spectacles. She rolled over and pulled up the covers impatiently. *Not yet*, she told herself, *not yet. I don't know him well enough. What if he cries off next week, with no explanation?*

Going to bed with a man had never been

the sort of romp you saw on television – not for her, anyway. Going to bed with a man meant you gave him power over you. When George had regarded her as beautiful and sexy and intelligent, part of her had believed it; when he had left her, part of her had been convinced she did not deserve to be loved. So probably, if the man thought you were an easy lay, part of you would believe that, too.

He had said that he was not the sort to be casual, that he was deadly serious about her. Words, though, were cheap. To everyone except Madhab they flowed smoothly from the tongue, sweet half-meant lies mingled indistinguishably with truth. If Michael was really deadly serious, he would show it by staying around. If he wasn't serious, it would be better if he left. It would certainly be phenomenally stupid for her to go down-stairs right now.

She wondered if he was a Muslim. That was not in itself a problem – she'd had a Muslim colleague when she was a member of a practice, she'd had Muslim patients and a couple of Muslim friends, and she had nothing but respect for their religion. On the other hand, what if he wanted her to convert? A good Muslim man would certain-ly want to convert a woman he loved: he couldn't have a religiously valid marriage with an unbeliever. She'd been brought up Christian, though, and her religious con-

211

victions, such as they were, were bound up in that faith. All her lifelong yearning to be *good*, her belief in the primacy of love and the necessity of sacrifice and the rest of the sentimental and improbable imaginings she still at heart adhered to – it was all shaped by Christianity. She'd been an occasional church-goer before the divorce.

Guiltily, she told herself she was being unfair to Muslims. She remembered her colleague Ahmed earnestly explaining to her that *jihad*, holy war, properly referred to the believer's struggle against evil in himself and in the world, and that the young men with bombs were even more abhorrent to true Muslims than they were to Christians. She was well aware of the fact that Islam was bound up in his own desire to be *good*, just as Christianity was involved in hers.

Yes, but Muslims believed in that struggle *differently*. The sensibility and the imagery were foreign to her, and she could not be comfortable with them. She didn't like the Islamic attitude to women, either, however much Muslim women insisted it respected them. She couldn't convert just to please a man. She couldn't adapt to his terms, and would probably end up losing her own. It would be a betrayal of her self. She was a little shocked to find herself thinking that. She had never thought of herself as more than vaguely Christian; would she really give up a man for a faith she only half-believed? The point, though, wasn't what she half-believed: it was what she didn't believe, and what he did.

Maybe Michael wasn't a Muslim. Probably his father was at least a nominal Muslim, but he'd once said he ate pork – hadn't he? – so maybe he was a lapsed Muslim or an agnostic. Michael wasn't an Islamic name, either ... or was it? It was the name of an angel – of an archangel – and she rather thought that Muslims had the same archangels as Christians and Jews. It was the archangel Gabriel who was supposed to have appeared to Mohammed, wasn't it? – as he had to Mary. So maybe Michael *was* an Islamic name, just an uncommon one. Or maybe Michael's mother was responsible for the name. He'd never really talked about her ... but then, there were lots of things he hadn't talked about. Lots of things she hadn't talked about, either – her own parents, for example.

She wondered if her parents would like Michael.

Damn, damn, *damn*! David Somers murdered that morning, and all she could think about was the man sleeping downstairs. Disgusting. She got up, drank a glass of water, washed her hands and put more cream on them, then went resolutely back to bed alone.

In the morning Michael looked as though he hadn't slept much more than she had, but he seemed more relaxed than he had the night before. Rather to her surprise, he took it for granted that he and Madhab would attend the 'Build a Robot' session at the technical college.

Madhab frowned at that. 'David Somers dead,' he pointed out.

'That's why we need to go,' Michael replied. 'We need something to take our minds off it.'

In fact, it did seem to take their minds off it, because they returned from the session much more cheerful than they had been when they'd departed for it.

Janet had spent part of the morning trying to get hold of Dr S. Bhattacharya. The Radcliffe's website had provided phone numbers and e-mail addresses for every department and for every consultant. None of them provided immediate access to the man, though she sent e-mails and left messages on answering machines. She doubted, though, that he would check any of them during the weekend, and his home phone number wasn't in the directory. She resigned herself to receiving no reply until Monday.

She cooked for Saturday lunch the meal she'd planned for Friday evening, and the three of them sat down to eat it together – like a family, she thought, with a tremor of dread that the thought itself might bring bad luck. Afterwards they went for a walk by the river and talked – first about Dr Bhattacharya, and then about Leicester and London. Michael had a flat in Thamesmead and he invited them both to come and stay for a weekend and see some of the sights of London – after 'Build a Robot' was finished, of course. It was a sweet, sunny, green afternoon, and Janet was sorry when the evening came, and Michael drove home.

David's obituary was prominent in the Sunday-morning paper – more prominent, really, than the coverage of his death. There was a photo, probably from a scientific conference, showing him confident and excited and several years younger. He was described as 'one of the world's leading authorities on the neurological foundations of language' and his death was, predictably, called 'a tragedy'. There was no mention of the loss of his licence to experiment on animals. Janet stared at the article for a long time, trying to make herself grieve. It was hard: she was, she found, very angry with David, not only for his lies, but also for getting himself killed. She told herself again that he was a brilliant man, still quite young, with tremendous – yes – 'animal vitality' and tremendous intellectual vitality as well. He'd died violently and terribly. His family must be devastated. In the end she succeeded in feeling real grief

215

for him.

There was no obituary for Elena, but Janet had no trouble feeling sorrow for her. The violent death of a pretty young woman was, in and of itself, enough to move anyone to sorrow and pity.

Dr Bhattacharya did not phone back on Monday morning, and Janet tried again to contact him, even though she had work and it meant sacrificing her lunch break. The Neurology Clinic of the Radcliffe Hospital informed her that Dr Bhattacharya was away on leave – had been away since the end of June, and wouldn't be back until the third of September.

She remembered the smooth way David had assured her, early in July, that Bhattacharya could cope with any difficulties Madhab had at the Radcliffe, but that it was unlikely she'd ever need to speak with him. She thanked the receptionist, put the phone down, and cursed.

That evening she was trying to work out who would be the next-best person to approach when Michael phoned. He, too, had contacted the Radcliffe during the course of the day and discovered Dr Bhattacharya's absence.

'So I, uh, phoned around a few medical research establishments that work in neurology – the same people my colleagues talked to before we started funding the

216

research, actually, when we wanted to know if it was worth doing. The consensus seems to be that there's a Professor Ian Clark, at the Institute of Neurology of University College here in London, who's done some work in the same field as David Somers and who would be the best man to take over from him – though I've been warned he and Somers are at opposite extremes of some neurological debate. You ever heard of this guy?'

'Only vaguely,' she admitted. 'But that doesn't mean anything. All I know about brain research is what I picked up trying to help Madhab.' After a moment, she added, 'The Institute of Neurology at UCL is supposed to be top-notch.'

'Well, I'm trying to get hold of him,' he informed her. 'If I can get him, I'll arrange for him to see Madhab.'

She was silent a moment. She had been prepared to do this task herself. She was *accustomed* to doing all such jobs herself, fitting them in around the edges of her work or taking time off. To find that it had been done already, by somebody else, left her off balance, vaguely put out, and with a lingering feeling that it couldn't have been done *right*.

She told herself that her reaction was stupid. Michael, with all the resources of his office, could probably do a *better* job of

217

finding the right person to consult than she could from her three-bedroom semi in Leicester: the Institute of Neurology would pay much more attention to him than to a mere GP. Moreover, he had *not* been thrusting himself in by doing this unasked: it was quite legitimately part of his job. The correct response, she told herself severely, was gratitude. 'Thank you!' she said gratefully.

On Tuesday Michael phoned to say that he had succeeded with the professor, and that the man was willing to see Madhab on Saturday at three thirty.

'If you like,' he suggested diffidently, 'I'll drive up to Leicester on Friday. Madhab and I can go to the Robots thing Saturday morning, and then I can drive us down to London for the appointment. Afterwards you could stay the night at my place – folding bed and sleeping bag, if Madhab doesn't mind that – and on Sunday we could do some sight-seeing before you go back to Leicester.'

She noted, with amusement, that he had carefully ring fenced 'Build a Robot'. She wondered if that was because it was a way for him to win over Madhab, or whether he simply enjoyed it so much that he didn't want to miss it unless he absolutely had to. She made a mental note to come and admire their marvellous machine as soon as possible. 'Thank you!' she exclaimed. 'That sounds wonderful.' *Another rote response*, she thought, hanging up, generated from some polite-phrase conversational subroutine – but freighted with so much hope.

She remembered him telling her: *If you want to get rid of me, tell me now. I'd much, much rather write it off now than later.* It was going to be very difficult if she had to write him off.

On Wednesday the Oxfordshire police sent a detective up to Leicester to go over the statement she'd given them. It seemed in order, and she signed it. She asked the detective what was happening in the investigation, but he was wary, and would not tell her.

On Thursday there was a bolt from the blue. She returned from work to find a strange car in the drive, and entered the house to find Madhab and his tutor from 'Maths for Fun' drinking tea and waiting for her in the lounge.

The tutor was an enthusiastic young black woman in a T-shirt and corn-row braids. Janet knew her slightly, since the same woman had been involved in running 'Maths for Fun' as an evening class during the school term: her name was Jeri, and she was a trainee teacher earning what she could from the part-time work. When Janet arrived, she jumped up, braids swinging. 'Dr Morley!' she exclaimed in relief. 'I need to talk to you about Madhab.'

Janet shot Madhab a mystified look; he shrugged and smiled a don't-blame-me smile.

'What's he done?' she asked, heart sinking.

'He's *brilliant*!' exclaimed Jeri enthusiastically. 'He's *incredible*! He's been working out a version of *non Euclidean geometry* on his *own*! We want to get him into a programme for gifted children.'

Janet had no idea what to say. She looked at Madhab again; again, he smiled. This time she recognized the smile for what it was: an expression of satisfaction and delight. 'He's been working out what?' she asked feebly.

'Non-Euclidean geometry!' supplied the tutor, beaming. 'We've been setting the kids some problems – y'know, puzzles? – and we had some that were about triangles. Madhab was trying to work out what would happen if you projected the triangles on to a curved solid. Just for fun! That's very high-powered, very advanced stuff! He's never been taught it, has he?'

'No,' said Janet, stunned. 'He ... he never had any education at all, until the last couple of years. He grew up in Nepal, and he was deaf.'

'Yeah!' agreed Jeri, beaming even more widely. 'You told us that before, didn't you? Well, he's certainly making up for lost time! Anyway, what I came about was this programme they're going to have for mathematically gifted children. It's going to be at the University of Warwick, starting in September, and entry is by recommendation from a maths teacher. It's free. It's what they call an enrichment programme – stuff outside the regular curriculum, that's more challenging and more interesting than the ordinary problems the kids get set in school. John and I – you 'member my colleague, John Ridgewood? – we think Madhab could cope with it and that he'd get a lot out of it. We'd like to recommend him for it. It's going to run on Saturday mornings during the school term. His school hasn't recommended him, has it?'

'No,' whispered Janet.

'Didn't think so. He goes to a special school, doesn't he? Because of the problems he has with language.'

'Yes,' agreed Janet. 'He was deaf for a lon̩ time.'

'That's right. Though recently he's been doing much better, hasn't he? It's really noticeable. He was telling us it's because of that thing he has in his head. I never heard of anything like that before: I think it's terrific! Course, Madhab never seemed to have any trouble understanding maths concepts anyway. Well, we need parental consent before our recommendation can go forward, and you're his guardian, aren't you?'

'Yes,' said Janet, completely and happily

stunned. 'I ... I'm very glad. *I* always knew he was something special, but it's terrific to hear it from somebody else. Uh, you need my consent. Madhab, you want to do this?'

He nodded emphatically. 'I want. Sounds fun.'

'Great!' said Janet, beaming, and wrote out the note at Jeri's direction.

When the young woman had driven off, Janet turned to Madhab. He grinned at her.

'I always *knew* you were brilliant!' she told him joyfully. 'Let me take you out to dinner!'

She was still bursting with pride when Michael arrived the following evening. She told him about it over supper, and he congratulated Madhab warmly – though he also seemed subdued.

'Is something the matter?' she asked, when the meal was nearly finished.

He sighed. 'The police investigation ... they're charging Firsby, and I can't help it, I think they've got the wrong man.'

'Oh, God!' She stared at him shocked. 'What—'

He lifted a hand in a silent request for space. 'I'll see if I can set it all out straight for you.'

There was a moment of silence. Madhab pushed his plate aside, then picked up the other plates and set them on top of it, but he did not take them through into the kitchen.

'Right, then,' Michael began at last.

'Apparently Somers went to Firsby's house on Thursday, the evening after I spoke to him, and accused Firsby of spying for Tao Pharmaceuticals. There was a huge shouting match, and Firsby's wife called the police. Somers left before they arrived, but as he was leaving he shouted a threat to "ruin" Firsby, which all the neighbours heard. Early Friday morning Firsby drove off from his house after telling his wife that he was going to take all of his own equipment from Somers' lab. Yes, I know! You wouldn't think the equipment was his anyway: you'd think that lab equipment came out of grant money; but apparently there were a few bits and bobs that Firsby had put in himself to make his own work space more comfortable – a chair, and some shelves and a bulletin board and so on. He hadn't bothered to remove them before, he says, because he didn't need them at home; but after the quarrel he decided to take them anyway. He claims that he arrived at Somers Synaptic before anyone else got there – and, in fact, the security cameras record him arriving there at a quarter to eight: it's the last thing they do show, because once he was in he apparently switched off the whole system. He said Elena Simonson came in as he was putting the last of the equipment into his car, which would make it about nine o'clock – it's entirely credible that it took him that

223

long to collect the things, incidentally: the shelves were fitted to the wall on brackets. There's no question that he did take them down at some point, but there is a question about when. Anyway, he said that when Ms Simonson found him at the lab she shouted at him, but he ignored her. He says that when he drove out of the gate she was yelling at him to return his keys, so he threw the keys and his key card out of the window. However, if Simonson was there, she didn't pick them up, because the police found them in the grass beside the drive.

'He didn't arrive home until about noon. He says that after he left the lab he stopped in the countryside near Abingdon and went on a long walk to cool down.'

Michael grimaced and went on, 'Of course, from the police point of view, Firsby had a ferocious quarrel with Somers the evening before the murder, went out to Somers Synaptic the following morning on an errand likely to lead to another quarrel, and has no alibi for the time between nine and eleven, when they believe the murder occurred.'

'His car wasn't there,' Janet pointed out. 'The only car there was David's.' She suddenly thought to wonder how Elena had got there.

'David Somers' car has now turned up, abandoned, in a station car park at Appleford, between Didcot and Oxford,' Michael told her wearily. 'There are, unfortunately, no fingerprints or bloodstains or any other convenient clues as to who left it. The police scenario runs roughly as follows: Firsby was indeed spying for Tao Pharmaceuticals. After Somers threatened to "ruin" him, he decided on a pre-emptive strike and promised to get them samples of the drugs they were interested in. He went to Somers Synaptic at a quarter to eight on Friday, not to collect his things – which, they say, he'd removed before – but hoping that he could steal the drugs before anyone else arrived. The drugs were kept in a fridge, which was locked; only Somers had the key to it. The police suggest that it took him longer to break into it than he'd anticipated. Somers and the secretary came in unexpectedly. There was a row, and he shot them. Then he drove off in a panic. The spies were waiting somewhere nearby to take receipt of the drugs. When he didn't show up, they eventually went to see what was the matter, and found the gate unlocked. They were stealing the drugs when you arrived. They knew that they'd been seen, panicked, and stole Somers' car to get themselves back to the nearest rail station.'

'You said you knew who the spies were,' Janet said, watching him. 'You said you had people looking into them.'

He nodded. 'But, unfortunately, nobody

tailing them. Still, I was able to tell Detective Inspector Bailey that the two men – Wong Xinpei and Tan Yiji – were away from their office in London on the Friday in question. Wong Xinpei, incidentally, seems to be the senior and superior in the party. He's undoubtedly the "Bobbie Wong" who hired the Bleickens.'

Janet was frowning. 'But if you *know* who these people are...'

'Oh, the inspector sent someone to question them, all right. The trouble is, they simply denied *everything*. They have never engaged in industrial espionage, and have no idea why they should be accused of it – unless it's a malicious smear by a rival pharmaceutical company unable to compete with them fairly. They've never been to Oxfordshire, and they spent the whole of the relevant Friday in London. An associate at the Chinese Trade Association has vouched for them.' He grimaced. 'We know they're lying. On Thursday evening our phone tap picked up two phone calls from Wong Xinpei and one from Tan Yiji cancelling meetings on Friday, and our camera caught Wong arriving at the Trade Association office at quarter to seven on Friday morning and coming out again with a briefcase. He didn't go back that day, and Tan Yiji never went into the office at all. The trouble is, our phone tap and our camera were illegal. I *did* apply for a surveillance order, but they always take a while to come through, and we only got it yesterday. So – unfortunately – our evidence is not admissible in court. We can't even mention it without exposing ourselves to prosecution.'

'Oh,' Janet said blankly.

'Oh, indeed,' agreed Michael. 'I used to be a liberal. I used to believe that rules of evidence were put there to protect citizens from being abused by the police. Now I tend to think of them as put there by lawyers to protect their clients from the justice they deserve.'

'But ... but you're saying that poor Dr Firsby's been arrested for murder, and *nothing* is going to happen to the spies?'

'That's what I'm saying. Detective Inspector Bailey, to give him credit, is working on it, trying to turn up evidence. I was able to give him a description of the car they were probably using. If they went home by train, the car may have been sitting around somewhere long enough to provide a lead. On the other hand, if they simply abandoned Somers' car at the station, collected their own from wherever it had been waiting, and went home...' He shrugged.

'You said Firsby had a wife,' Janet said, after a silence. She hadn't known that – found it, in fact, rather difficult to imagine the shy, balding, silent man managing to acquire one.

'A wife and two children,' agreed Michael unhappily. 'All very distressed.'

'Oh, God!' She found that she suddenly had a clear image of the wife and children: a shy, mousy woman and two plump, anxious kids who were bullied at school. She pictured them clinging to one another in tears, anguished and bewildered by the monstrous event that had engulfed husband and father.

She told herself impatiently that she didn't know anything about that wife and those children: the woman might be as talkative as her husband was silent, and the kids might be giggly and loud. They existed, though, and the fact of their distress was suddenly inescapable.

After another silence she asked, 'What about the gun?' Even as she said it, she realized that she was now casting wildly about for some way to prove that Firsby was innocent.

'It hasn't been found,' Michael replied promptly, 'and none of the people involved has a gun licence. The police ballistics lab thinks it was a Colt revolver. That's an antique, a collector's piece: it could well have been in somebody's attic for fifty years – in which case, we're not going to be able to trace it.'

'God.' After a moment she tried again: 'What about Elena's car? She normally went to work by car. Somers Synaptic is miles from the nearest village and you can't get to it by public transport.'

'Now *that* is an interesting question.' Michael said thoughtfully. 'I'll put that to Detective Inspector Bailey next time I see him – though probably he's already thought of it himself. He's not stupid – obstinate and callous, maybe, but not stupid.' He was quiet a moment, then said determinedly, 'We should stop talking about this. We're not going to get anywhere with it, and it isn't our responsibility. We will simply have to trust the police. Madhab, would you show me some of the famous maths puzzles? I want to see if I can do them.'

Nine

Professor Ian Clark turned out to be a nervous little man of about forty, thin, wiry and restless, with nondescript brown hair and intense brown eyes. He was waiting in the entrance to the UCL Institute of Neurology in Queen Square when Michael, Janet and Madhab arrived, and he ushered them up to a common room and offered them coffee.

They sat in the common room drinking coffee – or tea, in Madhab's case. Janet told Clark as much about the details of 'the Somers Treatment' as she could, and Clark asked probing questions, many of which she could not answer. Michael said very little, and Madhab sat in his usual attentive silence – struggling, Janet knew, to follow as much of the conversation as he could.

After about an hour and a half, Clark ran out of questions and sat silent, fidgeting with a pen and chewing his lower lip.

'Well?' asked Michael.

'Well,' said Clark. He sighed. 'Well, David Somers was clearly a genius and his death is a great loss to neuroscience, but ... God!

God. I don't know whether I'm more impressed or horrified. I wish he'd published more.' He shook his head. 'I have to say first off that I would *never* have done what he did. Maybe that's partly because I *couldn't* have done it, but I think it's mostly because I would never be so reckless. Nobody I know would be. Here at the Institute, what Somers did would never have been allowed.'

'The treatment was approved for clinical trial!' Janet pointed out, shocked.

Clark began fidgeting with his pen again. 'I know. But...' He made a face. 'Well, OK, Somers was a modularist, I'm a globalist; each of us obviously thought the other's approach was all wrong. So maybe I'm all wrong; modularists would tell you so. But...'

'I'm afraid I'm not clear what a, umm, modularist is,' said Michael, with that disarming apologetic air.

'Oh. Right. Well, one of the big debates in modern neuroscience is whether or not to think of the brain as basically modular – that is, as something that has lots of separate modules adapted for specific tasks, such as vision, hearing, language and so on, all acting pretty much independently of one another. Somers was a modularist. He thought you could treat areas of the brain like circuit cards in a computer – just isolate the faulty module that does language, plug in a repair, and *voilà*! your brain is fixed. I don't think it works like that: I think you have to consider the entire brain as an integrated system. I don't deny that specific areas are devoted to specific tasks, but I think you also have to consider all the communication between them, the endless feedback and feedforward loops. Ultimately, what affects one area affects everything. Lenneberg, the great biologist of language, once said that "any modification on the brain is a modification on the entire brain", and there's an awful lot of evidence to support that. I'd expect that anything that affected the language centres would have effects on the function of the brain as a whole, and for that reason I wouldn't have given this trial the go-ahead. What's more, there are enough people who agree with me for me to be very surprised that *anybody* gave it the go-ahead. Do you know who *did* approve it? I wonder if they really understood what was involved. There are lots of other people trying to use stem cells to repair brain damage; I bet whoever OK'd this thought it was more of the same.'

'Well, it is, isn't it?' asked Janet defensively.

'No! It's *completely* different!' Clark suddenly put the pen down and straightened, eyes flashing. 'Somers may have called what he was doing "repairing" your ward's "brain damage", but in actual fact your ward's brain wasn't "damaged" at all. His language centres weren't blasted by some trauma: they just never got the chance to develop the way they should have. A growing brain *certainly* isn't modular: neurons compete with one another, and if the language centres aren't growing, other bits will grow *more* at their expense, and make lots of connections to still other bits of the brain that the language centres would normally monopolize. Somers stuck a completely new set of wiring into the middle of a huge, complicated, fully integrated system. There was a very real danger of damaging the whole left hemisphere!'

'Are you saying the treatment has hurt Madhab?' asked Janet sickly.

'I'm saying it was dangerous and it *could* have hurt him!' Clark took a deep breath and began nervously running his hands along the surface of the coffee table. 'Fortunately, it doesn't seem to have done so. I think if it had, you would've seen it before now. Well, brains do *adapt*. Even when they're damaged, they try to rewire themselves so that they *work*, and I suppose that this was within the limit of what Madhab's brain could accommodate without disruption. From what you've told me, he had about two years of exposure to language before this treatment, so probably he did have a lot of the neurological structures for dealing with language already in place, even if they weren't strong enough to support the complexity of adult language. That meant his brain had somewhere for the new growth to go. Somers may have caught it at exactly the right moment, too – there's normally an explosive development of language at about the age of two, and your ward's brain may have been neurologically primed to adapt to that – but I'm horrified that Somers wanted to keep on applying the growth factors even after it was clear that the treatment was having an effect. You were absolutely right to resist that. The risks...'

'I want talk,' Madhab declared, suddenly and loudly. 'I know risk. Want words.'

Clark blinked several times. 'You risked damage to your entire brain,' he told Madhab, directly and seriously.

Madhab dismissed that with an expressive shrug. 'No words, better dead.'

A true Gurkha, Janet thought, with the mixture of admiration and exasperation the attitude always provoked in her: *It is better to die than to live as a coward.*

'Well,' Clark said, after a silence, 'there is that. Yes. Well, maybe Somers was justified, after all, in starting the treatment. But he should have been a *lot* more careful!' He picked up the pen again and looked at Janet. 'I definitely, *definitely*, think that you two shouldn't even *consider* any more of this treatment. You've been lucky so far, but your

234

luck could run out at any time. I think, too, that you should have that microshunt out as soon as possible. As long as it's in there's a danger of bacterial infection or blood-clotting and stroke.'

So it was all over.

'Could you recommend somebody who could take it out?' Janet asked faintly. 'I was expecting David to do it.'

'I can get somebody for you,' agreed Clark. 'The best place in the country for it is right next door.' He hesitated, then looked uneasily at Michael. 'I understand that you're a civil servant, and you're here representing the MoD, who were funding Somers' research. I've never had anything to do with this sort of thing. What was it you wanted it for?'

'Somers told us it could be used to help us learn to speak any given language like a native speaker, without an accent,' Michael replied evenly.

Clark considered that. His misgivings were obvious. 'It might do that,' he conceded; 'on the other hand, it might damage your understanding of your own language. I would never recommend such an invasive treatment without real clinical need. The risks are just too great.' He shrugged. 'I would've thought the greatest potential for this treatment is as a therapy for linguistic impairment after strokes or other trauma to the brain.' He chewed his lip some more. 'It *might* be possible to get some of what you want through a variation on the treatment, though ... a restricted part of the drugs regime, maybe, combined with intensive language tuition ... it'd need more work, though. In fact, it would need a *lot* more work before I personally would feel happy recommending it even as a therapy, and what you want is probably only deliverable a couple of years after that, if it's deliverable at all.' He bit the pen, then put it down again, meeting Michael's eyes. 'OK, I admit, I'm interested – I'm very, very interested. This is a terrifically bold and exciting piece of research. I'm probably going to be up all night thinking about it. You were proposing that I see how much of the research Somers did could be salvaged, weren't you?'

'That was our idea,' agreed Michael. 'We'd be prepared to continue funding, if there was some hope of getting the desired result.'

Clark made a small, wary grunt. 'When we spoke on the phone, you told me that this research was classified.'

Michael hesitated. 'It was. That might be negotiable. It was never a very high classification, and it's probably been compromised already.' He spread his hands. 'There's also the point that if the research isn't likely to give us anything we want in the foreseeable future, but might provide a useful form of therapy for stroke victims, we might do better to step aside and allow more conventional sources of funding to move in. I haven't discussed this with my superiors, incidentally, though I do have a remit from them to try to sort things out.'

Clark gave another grunt, this one encouraged.

'I hope you appreciate,' Michael continued pointedly, 'that, so far, we've been supplying you with all the information we have freely and without preconditions.'

'Yes, I do appreciate that,' said Clark. Then he raised his eyebrows and added, 'Though I could point out that you wanted my help, and if you hadn't supplied that information, you wouldn't have got it. And I think I also appreciate that if you and the MoD do bow out, you'll undoubtedly keep an eye on what's going on, in case you decide to bow back in again.'

Michael shrugged. 'Professor Clark,' he said softly, 'we're interested in this technology because we think it might improve our effectiveness against terrorist organizations. Would you *mind* if we used it for that purpose?'

The two men regarded one another a moment. Then Clark said, 'No. If that's what you want it for, you're welcome to it.'

Michael nodded and sat back in his chair with a satisfied air. Janet sensed that a deal had been done, and only the details remained to be settled.

'Well,' Clark resumed briskly, 'I'm certainly willing to try to see if I can work out what Somers actually did, and we can talk about the rest. I'll need to talk to this man Firsby.'

'He's in custody,' Michael admitted unhappily. 'He's going to be charged with Somers' murder.'

'Oh!' exclaimed Clark. 'God. What a horrible business!' After a moment, however, he shook his head and went on: 'Maybe I can talk to Firsby anyway. He must have put a lot of work into this, he can't be eager to see it all go down the plughole. Where is he?'

Michael told him, and Clark wrote it down, then told Janet he would talk to a friend about the operation to remove the microshunt. She thanked him. Michael thanked him. He thanked them both and escorted them back out of the building.

They trudged along the leafy Bloomsbury street back to Michael's car, which had been left in an underground car park under the square. Janet had left the Datsun in Leicester, since she planned to go home again by train; she had never liked driving in London.

'I'll take us back to my place,' Michael said, unlocking the car.

'Thanks,' said Janet automatically, and

wiped at her face.

Michael paused, hand on the door handle. Then he grimaced. 'Madhab,' he said softly.

'What?' asked Madhab at once.

'Janet is worrying,' Michael told him. 'She thinks she did a bad thing. She thinks she should not have asked David Somers to help you. She thinks the treatment was too dangerous.'

'Janet!' exclaimed Madhab, with so much reproof and affection in his voice that she nearly burst into tears on the spot.

'Well it's *true!*' she protested. 'Did you understand what that man was saying? The treatment could have seriously injured you! I should never—'

'I *want* brain-med' cine,' Madhab interrupted. 'I want *much.*'

'There are three other points you should consider before you start kicking yourself,' Michael put in quietly. 'First point: David Somers, who knew far more about brains than you do, never mentioned any of these risks, and you respected his assessment. Second point: for whatever reason, the treatment wias approved for clinical trial. Third point: Ian Clark, by his own admission, is at the other end of this modular–global spectrum from David Somers, and probably sees more risk than most other experts would. I don't say that Somers was right and he's wrong, but probably the truth is somewhere

239

in the middle.'

Janet wiped at her face again, then gave up and took out a Kleenex. 'I'm sorry,' she said, blowing her nose, 'but I just keep thinking I should have known better. I always *knew* I couldn't trust David, but I did; I was a complete fool and I did, because I *wanted* to so badly, and I should've realized, he was in mad-scientist territory, off by himself in the country like that; I should've remembered that *respectable* research happens in a big place like this, with lots of—'

'Janet,' said Michael firmly, 'darling – stop kicking yourself. You did the very best you could, and it's turned out perfectly OK. And southern Oxfordshire is not in the least mad-scientist territory. There are plenty of reputable people there.'

Madhab patted her on the back. Standing there in the car park Janet had an over-powering awareness of their little group as a unit, a working arrangement of cooperating individuals – a *family*. *They know me*, she thought, *they know I'm a compulsive worrier, they understand that, and they still care for me.* She was suddenly explosively happy, and she wanted to cry. Human beings, she thought, blowing her nose again, *human beings really are extraordinarily odd.*

Michael's flat in Thamesmead was part of a 'luxury development' by the river – an elegant cluster of buildings in stone-trimmed brick, arranged about an immaculate green. He parked the car in front of one of these, between a glossy BMW and a Rover 350, and led them to the third floor, apologizing that he hadn't bought one of the flats with a view of the river – 'It would've cost fifteen thousand more, and, while it is a fine view, I didn't think it was *that* fine.'

The flat behind the varnished-oak door was a surprise. She had expected it to be orderly and tidy, but – despite the fact that he'd told her he liked art – hadn't expected it to be full of colour. It was, though: oriental-style carpets in burgundy and gold; curtains in gold and green, and prints and paintings everywhere. There were reproductions of Egyptian funerary paintings, Arab calligraphy, copies of a Turner and a Constable, with a few original line drawings and landscapes in various styles scattered among them. On one wall, by itself, hung a wooden panel with a Byzantine icon: a dark-skinned madonna holding a solemnly regal child.

'That's a copy, too,' Michael said diffidently, when he saw her looking at it. 'The original is in the church in Cairo where my father's family worship.'

She looked at him sharply, startled. 'I thought they were Muslims!' Then she blushed, because he had never said they were anything of the sort.

241

He shook his head quickly, with a sour smile. 'No. My family are Copts – Egyptian Orthodox, Egypt's oldest minority; under-counted in every census, disadvantaged in every public forum, and sporadically perse-cuted. My mother's parents, and my own father, got fed up with it and eventually managed to emigrate to England – where, of course, they've been disadvantaged and abused as Arabs.' He shrugged. 'The Arab world thinks all Arabs ought to be Muslims; the West assumes we all are.'

She hesitated, wondering what to say, then admitted honestly, 'I'm sorry. I'm also reliev-ed, though. I would've accepted it if you were a Muslim, but I don't think I could convert.'

His smile became more genuine. 'When I was in the Middle East, I lost two girls be-cause *I* couldn't convert. I actually thought about it once, but it would've killed my father. Have you ever been to an Eastern Orthodox service?'

'No,' she admitted.

'Bells and smells,' he said succinctly. 'And lots of chanting in archaic languages. You'd probably find the service at a mosque more intelligible. There's a Coptic church here in London: St Mark's in Kensington. I go along most Sundays if I'm in town. The whole Coptic community turns up then.' He waved one hand in vague dismissal. 'I'm not suggesting that we go tomorrow. I'm just mentioning it in case we get pounced on in the street by prune-faced little Egyptian ladies.'

She laughed, though she was slightly staggered by the realization that Michael Shahid, Warwick MBA and MI5 middle-manager, was part of an 'ethnic community'. Not only that: he was an Arab Christian, a minority's minority. She thought of his sudden transitions from apologetic diffidence to steely resolution and wondered what sort of time he'd had at school.

Madhab had walked over to look at the icon. He frowned at it, then glanced back at Janet. 'Who?'

'It's a picture of the Christian God and his mother,' Janet told him.

Madhab hesitated, then *namaste*'d to the icon respectfully, the way he'd been taught to before images of the Hindu gods. Janet felt a momentary stab of shame that she'd never tried to reintroduce him to the faith he'd been brought up in. She was certain that he understood almost nothing of the tenets of Hinduism: nobody had been able to explain them to him when he was deaf. She should have brought him along to the temple in Leicester – only she wasn't a Hindu herself, and it had been hard to find the time for something he'd never asked about.

They talked about temples and churches

and mosques over a takeaway supper at the flat. Madhab said that he'd always understood that the Hindu images in his village represented gods, even though he hadn't understood any of the stories about them. Michael was intrigued, and asked about religious life in Nepal, then compared it with growing up Coptic in London. Janet admitted that she, too, had been through Sunday school, a traditional woolly Anglican one, and they compared notes on Sunday-school teachers and confirmation classes and laughed a lot.

'Did you stop going when you left home?' Michael asked her.

'No,' she told him, 'when I got divorced.'

There was a silence, and she regretted the admission. Michael frowned, then asked softly, 'You couldn't believe in God after that?'

'No,' she said – and found herself telling him something she had barely admitted even to herself. 'I couldn't believe in *me* after that. If George didn't love me, then I wasn't lovable. I felt like an empty plastic bottle rolling about at the side of the road. What's eternal salvation to an empty bottle? It didn't matter what I did any more. I was so empty.'

Something kindled in the eyes behind the specs, something so warm that she had to look away. She saw Madhab's face, puzzled, and touched his hand lightly. 'You helped me,' she told him, finding relief in that truth. 'I knew *you* mattered.'

He smiled, but his eyes were still puzzled.

Later that night, lying on the folding bed in Michael's lounge with Madhab in the sleeping bag beside her, she thought about what she had said: *I was so empty.*

She wondered what had really gone wrong between George and herself, and when it had begun. She had loved him so desperately – the handsome, multi-talented, impetuous young media student, successful in a crowded field where most failed; and he had loved her: she was sure of that. Sometimes she'd thought that he still loved her, even at the end – after Fran, after his announcement that he wanted a divorce. She had seen in his eyes the same sadness and guilt she glimpsed in her own mirror. So *why* had it happened, that terrible bitter breaking of their lives? Could it really be as simple as that she worried all the time, and he didn't know how to stop her or to tolerate it?

Michael knew how to do both. Deliberately, she turned her mind from a vision of the future in which she was married to Michael, accompanying him to his exotic Coptic church, while Madhab celebrated the gods he had conceived of in his prison of silence. *If it comes*, she told herself, *I will be happy, but chase happiness and it recedes for ever. I must try to be happy with what I have right now.*

'Janet?' came Madhab's voice out of the darkness beside her.

She wasn't surprised that he was still awake: he was in a sleeping bag on the floor of a strange room, and the treatment that he had hoped would give him speech was over for good; they would take the shunt out as soon as possible. 'Yes, love?' she asked gently.

'Tonight. You say you are empty. When you come to Nepal, you are empty?'

She *was* surprised that he returned to that. 'That was what I meant, yes.' She swallowed, uncertain whether to say more. He was aware that George existed: there were plenty of tokens of her husband's long presence in the house, and George and Madhab had met once briefly, when George turned up at the house after she got back from Nepal to settle some legal matters. 'Because of George,' she explained, deciding on honesty. 'Because I loved him, and he left me.'

That didn't seem to be what had puzzled Madhab. 'In Nepal,' he said carefully. 'You help sick people, hurt people. Help many people. I see. People know, this important woman, this good foreign woman, come help. You are empty in Nepal?'

'I did not feel as empty when I helped,' she conceded. Then, perhaps because they'd

246

talked about Sunday schools earlier, she found herself adding, 'But sometimes even then I felt empty. There's a saying in our Christian holy book: "Though I give all my goods to feed the poor, if I do not have love, it profits me nothing." I only stopped feeling so empty after I met you.'

Madhab sat up suddenly. Light through the curtains showed the gleam of his eyes. 'Why you love *me*?' he demanded. 'Stupid no-talk no-hear nobody?'

'You weren't stupid!' she protested, also sitting up in bed. 'I saw that. I could see what you were. That you had so much inside you, and it wanted so much to come out, and it couldn't. I thought you were so brave, the way you fought the silence and refused to give up – and so *good*, the way you weren't angry with the world, even though it had been so unfair and so cruel to you. And, I don't know, I just *did* love you. I wanted so much to help. I know it hasn't worked out. I know I—'

'It work *fine*,' Madhab interrupted her. 'Why you say not?'

He sounded angry. Janet hesitated, afraid that this midnight conversation might now proceed to truths she'd prefer not to know.

Madhab reached across and caught her wrist, his face fiercely intent. 'You say, many time, you say, "Madhab, you want go to Nepal?" I say, no. You nod' – he nodded,

247

imitating her own earnest gesture – 'but you say again, other time, "Madhab, you want go?" Now you say, "It not work out." You want me go?'

'No!' she protested. 'Of course not! You know I love you, that I want to adopt you.'

'So why you say, "It not work out"?'

'Because I know it's been so hard for you!' she protested, ashamed at the wobble in her voice. 'I thought when we fixed your ears everything would be fine, but it wasn't. I know the school is hard for you, that sometimes the other children are cruel. You're so brave, and you work so hard, and you just can't do what they ask you to do, and it hurts; I see it hurting. Every time we heard about a new therapy I would think, "If we just tried *that*, maybe everything would be OK" – but it never was. And then I let David try his treatment, and it was dangerous – we're very lucky that it didn't damage your brain! I'm a rotten mother. In Nepal you have family; people there are kinder – they didn't tease you. Sometimes I think you'd surely be happier there. That's why I keep asking you if you want to go home: because I want you to be happy. For me – no, I don't want you to leave! It would be as bad as when George left. I would be empty again.'

He squeezed her hand so hard it was painful. 'Home,' he said, in a low voice. 'Nepal not home. In Nepal...' He swallowed, and she could feel his struggle for words. 'In Nepal I have no mother, no father. Nobody love me. I fix other pump, you know? Before you come, I fix pumps. Nobody say, "Madhab is clever." Nobody say, "Madhab, go to school, learn maths, learn clever people thing." Other childrens go to school; I dig garden, clean other people house. Stupid Madhab!' He touched the microshunt. 'I want words. I want talk good, learn good, yes, I want *much*. But I want my own home, my own mother *more*. And I *have*. So I say, it work *fine*, Janet. I never talk good, still, it work *fine*.'

'Oh, my baby!' she exclaimed, choking on tears, and hugged him. He threw his teenage dignity to the winds and hugged her back, fiercely.

'Not "rotten mother",' he told her. 'Good mother.'

They sat locked together for a long minute, as though they could force their separate flesh and blood into a unity by mere pressure. At last Janet let go, and fumbled around for a tissue. 'Not a mother who worries too much?' she asked, and wiped her nose.

He patted her arm and laughed. 'Yes, worry too much!' he told her. 'Good mothers worry. Fuss, fuss, fuss.'

When they were still again, trying once more to sleep, she listened to the dark beside her, noticing when the quick breathing of wakeful excitement slowed, and grew even and steady with sleep. She turned his words over in her mind, treasuring them. Other words surfaced, from the Sunday school passage she had quoted part of earlier: 'Though I speak with the tongues of men and angels, and have not love, I am a sounding brass or a tinkling cymbal.' It seemed almost too apt. I will have to show him that passage some time, she thought, and settled into sleep.

Ten

The operation to remove the microshunt took place the following Sunday at Clark's next-door 'best place in the country': the National Hospital for Neurology and Neurosurgery, which, as Clark had pointed out, was also on Queen Square, London WC1. The operation to take the shunt out was far less complicated than the one that had inserted the device: it used key-hole surgery, and did not reopen the skull. Madhab was home again the following day, with a new, much smaller shaved patch on his scalp and a neatly stitched circle of red in the middle of it. There was another plate on the bone underneath. Professor Clark kept the shunt.

Madhab endured the pain and disappointment with the silent courage Janet expected of him. He took paracetamol for the headaches, did not complain, and resumed his summer classes the day after he came home. If he stared at his face in the bathroom mirror sometimes and fingered the stitches where the shunt had been, he said nothing about what he thought of the loss.

It was the middle of August now, and his summer classes were drawing towards an end. The Saturday after the operation was the next-to-last session of 'Build a Robot' – the last session, apparently, was to be devoted to a tournament among the roboteers, in imitation of the popular television programme. Michael made his now-familiar drive to Leicester on Friday evening.

For supper Janet cooked a casserole of lamb and brown beans that she'd found on the Internet labelled as Egyptian. Rather to her surprise, Michael recognized it at once, and ate it with such enthusiasm that it wasn't until the coffee and ice cream that he got round to telling her the news.

'Clark's spoken to Firsby a couple of times,' he informed her. 'He says Firsby is helpful and cooperative.' Then he frowned. 'He's told me that he's sure Firsby is innocent. I still think that, as well, but the police are still working hard on the case against him.'

'Have they found any evidence to use against the spies?' Janet asked, pouring the coffee.

He shook his head glumly. 'Detective Inspector Bailey has been pushing Firsby to implicate them, but Firsby emphatically denies that he ever knew they existed. I think he's telling the truth, but I don't have any way to convince Bailey.' He took his cup with a nod of thanks and added a spoonful of sugar.

'Did you ask about Elena's car?'

Michael nodded. 'And Bailey *had* already looked into it. Elena's car is at Elena's house in Didcot. Bailey's suggestion is that David Somers picked her up in his car after he quarrelled with Firsby, and that she stayed the night at his place in Abingdon and went into work with him the next morning. Nobody actually saw them together that night, but it seems reasonable enough. They normally spent the weekends together.'

'Firsby said he saw Elena on Friday morning,' Janet pointed out. 'He never said anything about seeing David.'

'But the police think he's lying about the whole thing anyway.' Michael sighed. 'I keep hoping that our surveillance on the spies will turn something up, but they obviously know they're being watched. To be honest, they would have to be stupid not to have realized that, after the Bleickens warned them and the police arrived on their doorstep. Even the trick I set up with the number the Bleickens gave me ... well, never mind: I'm not supposed to talk about it. At any rate, they're not saying anything compromising where we can hear it, and I'm going to have to end the surveillance soon.' He made a face. 'Half their calls are in Chinese, and our translators have more urgent things to monitor than a

253

minor case of industrial espionage. If this hadn't involved murder, I doubt that I'd have got a translator at all.'

'There's one other thing that's been bothering me,' Janet said slowly: 'the neural growth factors. David said he had another forty doses. Probably most of that was deep-frozen in tubes, not packed in racks like those ten-mil prepared doses – but probably there were a whole lot of different tubes, because he was using several different things. Most of them couldn't be kept at room temperature, so you'd have to transport them in an insulated case. So if you wanted to steal them, you'd need to take handfuls of deep-frozen test tubes out of the bottom half of the fridge, fit them into a rack in a bulky insulated case, and ... and David's body was lying right in front of the fridge. There was blood everywhere. If you took the hormones after shooting him, you'd be sure to get blood all over the case, and your shoes and hands. It would be certain to get on the car. You said, though, that the police didn't find any traces in the car.'

Michael blinked at her. 'You know,' he said slowly, 'that is a very good point.' He pushed aside his empty ice-cream plate. 'Well then, Dr Morley, what do you think happened?'

'Me? I don't know!'

'You know something about packing medications,' Michael pointed out. 'If you

254

were trying to steal those drugs, what would you have done?'

'Moved the body out of the way first,' she said. Then she stopped, thinking about it. 'You know, they would almost have *had* to do that. Nobody would have unpacked the fridge with the body where it was.'

There was a silence. They were both aware that the police scenario had Firsby fleeing in panic after the shooting, and the industrial spies stealing the drugs after he left. Then Michael sighed and shook his head. 'Inspector Bailey will just say, "So? Firsby stole the drugs, and then shot Somers and Simonson."'

'Then where are the neural hormones now?'

'Ditched in the countryside somewhere, along with the gun.'

'I don't like this at all!' Janet protested angrily. 'We *know* Tao Pharmaceuticals was up to all sorts of illegal things. They commissioned the Bleickens to burgle me—'

'We can't prove that!' Michael objected. 'The Bleickens are not going to testify in court.'

Janet waved that irritably aside. 'My point is, we know that these guys, Wong and ... what was the other one's name?'

'Tan. Tan Yiji.'

'We know that Wong and Tan were up to things. Poor Firsby doesn't seem to have

255

been up to anything in his entire life, apart from molecular biology, and the only real link between him and Tao Pharmaceuticals is David's accusations. We know Wong and Tan were at Somers Synaptic when Madhab and I arrived – well, all right, we don't *know* that, but we *strongly suspect* that they were the ones Madhab saw. If Firsby was around then, we certainly didn't see him; and yet, if the police view is right, then the spies are almost irrelevant. They just happen to have turned up, practically by coincidence, after Firsby had committed all the crimes. I don't believe that!'

'I agree it seems very unlikely, but—'

'You know what I think? I think Inspector Bailey is going after Firsby simply because he needs somebody to prosecute for the murders, and he knows he can't get Wong and Tan.'

There was a brief silence, and then Michael said tactfully, 'Leaving that aside, the point you made about the only link between Firsby and Tao being David Somers' accusations – that's true. I hadn't thought about it, but it is. And that worries me, because when Somers made those accusations I thought they were far-fetched. As a matter of fact, I suspected he was only accusing Firsby because he wanted to distract my attention from Elena Simonson.'

'Well, yes!' agreed Janet. 'You said he told

you that Firsby couldn't have removed the drugs from the lab because of the security. But that's rubbish: it's *clearly* rubbish. Firsby had a key and a key card: he could have taken them any time he liked. As for getting into the locked fridge – before he was sacked he must have been putting things *away* in that fridge all the time. He could've taken samples of the mixtures at any time, topped the test tubes up with water, and waltzed home without anybody even noticing. Why would he wait until after the quarrel – and then come in at a stupid time like eight o'clock in the morning, when the middle of the night would be much safer?'

'I've never seen why Firsby would need to steal the drugs at all,' said Michael warmly. 'He was the one who prepared them: he *knew* what they were, and, even more important, he knew how to extract them – which Clark says is the complicated bit. True, he didn't know the exact composition of the different mixtures Somers was using at the different stages of the treatment, but according to Clark that's something you could play around with anyway.' He paused, frowning. 'I should have told Bailey flatly that the accusation didn't make any sense.'

'Bailey should be able to work that out for himself!' exclaimed Janet.

'Bailey's bound to take the accusations seriously,' Michael told her reprovingly.

'Somers was making them loudly and publicly immediately before he was murdered. And Bailey never met David Somers.'

There was a silence, and they looked at one another.

'David Somers bad man?' asked Madhab – who, as usual, had been listening in silence.

Michael looked at him grimly. 'Yes, he was. I wonder if he really was trying to protect Elena Simonson – or if he had some other game that he didn't want me to find out about. A game that went wrong.'

'I wondered that,' said Janet. 'Even on the day he was shot, I wondered that.'

'What would he gain by it, though?' asked Michael. 'The treatment was his own intellectual property! If he sold it to the Chinese, he'd be stealing from himself.'

'What if what he sold them wasn't really the treatment?' suggested Janet. 'Suppose he was feeding them false information? The other week you were saying that you were probably going to declassify the research because it had been compromised. David *wanted* to publish. If he could publish sooner by making you think the research was compromised – then that's what he'd do, isn't it? And ... and maybe the spies started to suspect that he was lying to them. That would explain why they'd hire somebody to spy on *me* – because they knew Madhab was getting the real treatment, and they wanted to compare it with the information they'd been given.'

Michael shook his head. 'That doesn't work. The monkey was stolen before the research was classified.'

'Oh. That's right.'

'But...' He drew in a long breath. 'I don't know. This still feels right. Would there've been any reason for David Somers to want to claim that his research was compromised last October?'

She considered that. 'You know,' she said slowly, 'there might be. You remember what Professor Clark said – that he didn't think the treatment should've been approved for clinical trial, and he didn't know how David managed to get approval?'

'God!' exclaimed Michael. 'Yes. If he'd gone to whoever approves these things and said "There's a foreign pharmaceutical company that's been spying on me, and some of my material has been stolen. I need to proceed to the trial stage fast if I want to claim it as my own British discovery, so please could you expedite this" – it would have had an effect, yes?'

'Yes,' said Janet, stunned. 'I never thought of it – but it was really very suspicious that it was the *last* monkey that was stolen, and that David had permission to do a clinical trial at all, when the people who'd been funding him obviously expected that he wouldn't be able to continue his research without using animals. I mean, that *is* why they cut off his funding and he went to the MoD, isn't it? If they'd expected him to get permission to do a clinical trial right away, they would've gone on signing the cheques.'

'But why would Somers complain about the monkey to the suppliers, then?' asked Michael, mystified. 'If he was telling the medical board that it had been stolen by industrial spies, why would he tell the suppliers that it had escaped because the cages they'd provided were inadequate?'

Janet shrugged. 'It's just the way he was. Maybe he started making a fuss about the cages because it was what the staff expected him to do. He always half-believed his lies once he got going on them.' She shook her head. 'He must really have regretted that one.'

'I want to check this,' said Michael, with determination. 'Or rather – I suppose I'm going to ask Detective Inspector Bailey to check it. If the monkey disappeared immediately before Somers applied for permission to do a clinical trial, I would find that extremely suspicious. Can I use your computer?'

He sent a long e-mail to Detective Inspector Bailey, and they spent the rest of the weekend trying not to think about it.

Detective Inspector Bailey, whatever his faults, was evidently a hard worker. On Monday evening, when she returned home from work, she found a message from him on her answering machine, asking her to phone back and giving his home phone number to use if it was after five p.m.

'I've had an e-mail from your friend in MI5,' he told her when she dialled it, 'suggesting a couple of new angles for our investigation, which I've been looking into. I need to check a couple of points with you.'

'That's fine,' Janet told him vaguely.

'Right,' said Bailey briskly. 'First, in your statement, you say that when you found Somers' body you checked it for signs of life. Did you move it?'

'No,' Janet said, seeing the point at once. 'I'm sure that's in my statement already. I felt for a pulse and then examined the body for wounds. I did not move it away from its position in front of the fridge.'

There was a pause. 'You know what this is about,' Detective Inspector Bailey said disapprovingly.

'Yes,' agreed Janet. 'Michael and I were talking about the case together. Is there something wrong with that?'

'A sharp barrister would say he coached the witness, and use it to disqualify your testimony,' replied Bailey. 'On the other hand, it doesn't look like your friend Shahid is going to exist at all, as far as the court's concerned, so I suppose it's OK.' He sighed. 'Huh. First time the disappearance of the Security Service at the crunch has ever been convenient. Next question, then: when and how did you contact Dr Somers about treatment for your ward?'

Janet gave him the details. She could hear Bailey grunting as he made a note of dates. 'Can I just ask you a question?' she said, then went on at once before he could say no: '*Was* the monkey stolen immediately before David applied for permission to do a clinical trial?'

There was a silence, and then Bailey said shortly, 'Yes.' There was another silence, a longer one, and suddenly the inspector announced angrily, 'And yes, he did ask the referees to expedite their approval, because he'd had some of his research material stolen by industrial spies. What's more, there've been substantial payments made to Ms Simonson's bank account that her family and her relatives can't explain. One of them was made the week the monkey disappeared. When was it your house was burgled?'

She told him about the burglary, and about the bugs. He was pleased with the latter: their removal by the telephone company constituted the only concrete evidence of industrial espionage he had. 'So, can you just tell me,' he went on, 'this discovery by Dr

Somers – this "Somers Treatment" – how much would you say it's worth?'

'I don't know,' she answered. 'Nobody does. I know David was hoping to promote it as something anybody could use to help with learning a second language. That would be a huge market. On the other hand, Professor Clark – the man who's helping Madhab now – says it's quite dangerous, shouldn't have been approved for a clinical trial yet, and may never be safe enough to use except in cases of acute clinical need. It would still be valuable even then, of course – there are an awful lot of stroke victims and accident victims who'd benefit from it – but it would be a lot *less* valuable than David thought it could be.'

'So he stood to gain a lot if he could get approval and a successful trial without anybody doing any careful scrutiny of the method,' Bailey said thoughtfully. 'He could form a company to market his treatment for widespread use and watch its stock soar; and later on, if it turned out the treatment was too dangerous for widespread use, he'd be the first to know, so he could sell before the bubble burst. Clever.'

Janet hadn't even thought of that aspect of things – but she bet that David had. 'Except he couldn't market it while it was classified,' she pointed out.

'Yeah,' agreed Bailey. 'He must have been

foaming at the mouth when he lost his animal licence and had to go to the MoD for funding. Well, your friend Shahid is right: Somers had every reason to get the spies interested and to keep them dangling – and they had reason to feel thoroughly pissed off with him. Shit!'

'Detective Inspector Bailey, I really don't think Jeremy Firsby did it,' Janet declared, pressing her advantage. 'I think David was playing some stupid game with Elena and Tao Pharmaceuticals, and it went wrong. He only made a lot of noise about Firsby to distract attention.'

'Hmmh,' said Bailey neutrally. 'Well, Dr Morley, thank you for your help.'

He cut off, leaving Janet feeling oddly triumphant: she understood perfectly the import of that carefully neutral 'Hmmh'. She wondered why she should feel so relieved about Firsby, when she barely knew the man and found him terminally boring.

On Wednesday evening, Professor Clark phoned. He had, he said, finished his preliminary study of the Somers Treatment, and he would be grateful if she and Madhab could come in and let him do some tests to see what he could judge of the results. If they had any medical records or notes, he added, it would be helpful if they could bring them.

Janet was, in fact, relieved to hear from

him. She was eager for somebody to check Madhab and provide reassurance that the treatment really hadn't damaged him. She asked only, 'When?'

'This Sunday?' suggested Clark hopefully. 'I can get access to the brain scanners at the Department of Imaging Neuroscience then. They're fully booked during the week, though I suppose I might be able to do it at night if Sunday's inconvenient...'

'No, Sunday's fine!' she assured him, and wrote the date in her diary. 'Where, exactly, is this Imaging Department?'

'They're right next door,' Clark informed her: '12 Queen Square.'

'Regular neuroscience ghetto, Queen Square,' Janet remarked, adding the address.

'Well,' said Clark, a bit huffily, 'it's convenient that way.'

When Clark had hung up, she telephoned Michael and told him that Clark wanted to see them in London on Sunday. 'You'll stay with me again?' he asked at once, as she'd hoped he would.

'That would be lovely.'

There was a pause, and then he said hurriedly, 'Maybe we could drive in together on Saturday again? After the final session of "Build a Robot"? – I was planning to come up to your place again for that.'

'I know!' she exclaimed, smiling. 'How could I forget? It's this week that your machine goes into combat, and I come along and cheer.'

'Yes,' he said, but he seemed nervous, unsure of himself.

'What?' she asked.

He sighed. 'I ... no. I'll discuss it when I see you.'

'Bad news?' she asked, more urgently. 'I spoke to Inspector Bailey on Monday; he sounded like he was beginning to think Firsby might be innocent.'

'Oh, that!' exclaimed Michael, in such a startled tone that she realized that whatever was bothering him, it had nothing to do with David Somers and his fate. 'Yes, that's right. I've been in touch with Bailey too, helping him trace some money. No, there's no bad news. I ... I'll discuss it when I see you. I look forward to Friday, OK?'

'OK,' she agreed. When she had put the phone down, she stared at it for a little, wondering if he'd been assigned back to the Middle East – or if he had decided that he didn't want to pursue the relationship.

She remembered that moment in the car park in London when she had felt part of a family. *No*, she thought, *please*. She was appalled at the strength of that silent plea, at the emptiness looming ahead of her.

She swallowed and told herself that maybe all he wanted to discuss was what to do next. After all, he'd been coming up all summer for 'Build a Robot', and now the course was almost over. A pattern that she'd barely been aware of would have to change.

There would be a lot of things changing. Summer was almost over. Madhab would soon be back in school full time. Probably she ought to start hunting for a job with more regular hours, or even for a partnership in a practice. She ought to find Madhab a new speech therapist, too, and check exactly when his maths enrichment course started and where it would be held. Life would find a new pattern. What place Michael Shahid might have in it, she didn't know.

Friday, besides being the day Michael would come up, was the final day of Madhab's remedial reading class. Janet received an invitation ('To the parent or guardian of Madhab Limbu') to attend a 'performance at The Hawthorns School', which the children would be putting on at three in the afternoon. She managed to get out of her latest work placement early enough, and drove over to the special school, which was on the southern outskirts of Leicester.

Madhab's school always depressed her. Not that The Hawthorns itself was depressing: true, it was housed in a fairly drab modern building, but it had a garden, appropriately ringed by hawthorn bushes and full of flowers, while the classrooms were cheerfully decorated with posters and with pictures painted by the children. She supposed that part of the reason the place depressed her was the children – they all suffered from one form or another of mental or physical disability, and every time she saw their vivid young faces she grieved at how the world would treat them. Mostly, though, it was that nearly all the children were primary school age – much younger than Madhab. The sight of him among them, quiet and dignified amid their noise and commotion, always made her heart ache. She knew it must be humiliating for him, a near-adult, struggling to keep up in a group of eight-to-thirteen-year-olds; she could guess how much courage and determination it took for him to go on. She wished she could have done better for him.

This time there were fewer children than usual, of course – only a dozen had taken up a place on the summer remedial course, as opposed to the school's term-time complement of forty. The handful of parents sat down on the under-sized chairs in one of the classrooms, chatting idly about their holidays, until the head teacher appeared to welcome them. Presently her assistants came in with the children. Madhab was last, pushing the wheelchair of a little girl with cerebral palsy.

The children performed a play of the

268

"Three Billy Goats Gruff". (The girl in the wheelchair was the troll: her speech was unintelligible, but she roared enthusiastically.) Madhab didn't have a part, but helped move the scenery. It was all rather charming. The parents applauded.

The next item was some poetry, which the children read in small groups, each taking a stanza. A Down's syndrome boy did a dance. An autistic child sang a song. Then, it seemed, the performance was over. The parents applauded again and collected their offspring. 'Dr Morley,' said the head teacher, 'may I have a word with you?'

Janet got up from her seat. Madhab waved to the little girl in the wheelchair and came over, but the head teacher frowned at him. 'I need to talk to your guardian,' she told him. 'Madhab, you help Mrs Martin, please.'

Madhab exchanged a mystified look with Janet, then shrugged and went off to see if the assistant teacher needed any help. Janet, feeling increasingly anxious, followed the head teacher back to her office.

The head teacher, a portly grey-haired woman, sank into her chair and folded her hands on her desk, indicating the spare seat to Janet with a stately nod.

'Dr Morley,' the woman said stiffly, 'as you undoubtedly know, The Hawthorns is oversubscribed. There really aren't enough special schools in the area, and the pressure on every place we have here is intense.'

'Yes, I know,' said Janet, her heart sinking further. 'I was very glad when I managed to get Madhab in.'

'Yes,' said the head teacher – and stopped uncomfortably.

Janet now had a very good idea what this was about. 'I know Madhab's had difficulties,' she said, 'but he never had any education at all before. He works very hard.'

'He does,' agreed the head teacher. 'He's very hard working and always very helpful and considerate of others. It's been a real pleasure to have him in the school.' She sighed. 'Dr Morley, I must be honest with you. I really don't think that this school is the best place for Madhab.'

'There isn't anywhere else,' Janet told her.

'Dr Morley, even when we first took Madhab, we were uneasy about it. He's older than most of the other children here, as I'm sure you're aware, and he isn't physically or mentally handicapped – in fact, his native intelligence is very high. We accepted the LEA's view that his difficulties with language and his lack of experience with formal education meant that this would be the best place for him. Now that he's had eighteen months at The Hawthorns, though, he knows how to cope with a school environment. He's made really excellent progress over the summer – that treatment he had, with the, um, thing in his head? – it's worked, hasn't it? His progress has been dramatic since he had it: it's actually been very exciting to see. We feel that his recent progress, taken together with his age, mean that this is no longer the best place for him. He ought to be with children closer to his own age.'

'Mrs Fyling,' said Janet, smiling in a sick attempt at appeasement, 'I would agree, if there was a special secondary school I could send him to. But there isn't.'

The head teacher was unbending. 'I think he would do better in a mainstream school, with some support from Special Needs.'

'No!' Janet protested, appalled. 'He's ... how can you say that? He *can't understand normal speech*. His reading age ... he's reading reception year *primers*: "Look, here is the dog" and "This is the house." How can you say that he'd do better in a mainstream *secondary* school, trying to cope with ... with *regular* lessons, with Jane Austen and French and chemistry, with everyone speaking in complex sentences at a normal speed and—'

'Dr Morley,' Mrs Fyling interrupted, 'no solution is going to be ideal, is it? There are many children beside Madhab who have special needs.'

'That—'

The head teacher raised her hand for silence. 'There's a little boy we've been asked to take – an autistic six-year-old, with very little language and with behavioural difficulties. His mother is desperate to get him in, and we think he would benefit most if we could take him *now* – he's young; we can still influence him. But, for insurance reasons, we can't take him unless someone else leaves. We have to prioritize.'

'You're throwing Madhab out to take this other child?'

Mrs Fyling winced. 'We think Madhab would be able to cope with a mainstream school, if he had a Special Needs assistant to help him. This other child obviously could not.'

'It's only a week until term starts!' cried Janet.

Mrs Fyling made a quieting gesture. 'Obviously, we'd allow some overlap. Madhab can stay at The Hawthorns while the Special Needs people sort out the help he needs.'

'Sort out the help they're willing to *pay for*, you mean!' Janet said furiously. 'Which won't be much, and you know it! He's fifteen: as far as the LEA is concerned, he can leave school at sixteen, and it'll take them so long to "sort out what he needs" that by the time they've sorted it, they won't be obliged to do anything for him. They never wanted to help him in the first place: they think he should go back to Nepal. I bet this child you want to take in his place is

Anglo-Saxon and white!'

Mrs Fyling winced again, and Janet bit her lip. It wasn't fair to attack the head teacher, a good woman utterly dedicated to helping disabled children. It was not Mrs Fyling's fault that there wasn't enough money to help all who needed it. She had no choice except to 'prioritize'.

'I'm sorry,' Janet said, quickly. 'I know you do the best you can, in very difficult circumstances. But ... but Madhab has been denied so many opportunities all his life! He's suffered so much from the inequality and unfairness of the world, and to take this away when it's the only education he's ever had...'

'I'm sorry,' said Mrs Fyling, sounding as though she meant it. 'I agree. But you can't change the past. From my point of view, Dr Morley, the real opportunity to help Madhab was when he was small, and it was missed. It's terrible, yes, and it's unfair, but I have to be concerned with the opportunities I'm offered *now*. I've already notified the LEA.'

'But the treatment he's been having is *over*,' Janet told her. 'The man who was doing it is *dead*.'

The head teacher flinched. 'I'm sorry,' she said again. 'But ... even so. He was only marginally suited to this school to begin with, and he really doesn't need to be here now. The mainstream Special Needs unit will probably contact you early next term. Obviously, he can start the new term here, but you ought to prepare him for a move before Christmas. I'm sorry.'

Janet went back into the main part of the school, and eventually located Madhab helping to tidy shelves in a storeroom. He looked a question at her, and she shook her head: she did not trust herself to discuss it yet. He frowned, obviously guessing something from her expression, and accompanied her to the car in silence.

'What?' he asked, when they were back home.

She bit her lip. 'My love ... Mrs Fyling says...' She took a deep breath. 'She says you should not go to The Hawthorns any more. She says you should go to an ordinary school.'

He began to grin – then caught her grim look, and frowned. 'Bad?'

She winced. 'Yes. They wouldn't...'

She didn't know how to explain secondary schools to him: the large classes, the speed and bustle where the vulnerable got lost; the loud, thrusting pupils, the sink-or-swim carelessness of the staff; the threshing sharks among whom a linguistically impaired innocent would struggle and drown.

'Not stupid,' Madhab pointed out. 'Gifted at maths.'

'Yes,' she agreed. 'But, darling ... you've been to school for a year and a half. The other children will have been to school for more than eight years. They wouldn't...'

She stopped herself. It was going to happen, she realized numbly. Mrs Fyling had already set the wheels in motion. Given that it was going to happen, she should try to be positive about it, to help Madhab.

But he was being thrown back on to the scrap heap: how could she be positive about that?

Maybe there was something else she could do. Another school, in another town. She would try. God, she would try!

'I think it would be very, *very* hard for you,' she said honestly. 'The teachers will talk fast, and the other children will know more than you, and no one will explain things. Mrs Fyling says they will try to get someone to help you, but probably they won't succeed.'

Madhab was frowning now. 'Work hard,' he suggested. 'Read gooder this summer, after...' He touched the place where the shunt had been.

'I know,' she agreed. 'But I think ... I think it would be *too* hard, even for you.' Then she promised recklessly, 'I think you need a school that is harder than The Hawthorns, but easier than an ordinary school. I will see if I can find one. Mrs Fyling says you can start next term at The Hawthorns, but they want you to leave before Christmas.' She added, careful of his pride, 'She said nice things about you. She said you work hard, and you are kind and helpful, and you are intelligent. She said they liked having you at The Hawthorns, but the treatment has helped you so much, she thinks you should go to a harder school. She said you should be with children your own age.'

He was starting to grin again, which didn't help.

'I will try to find a good school for you,' she promised, and he nodded, happily ignorant of what that might involve.

When Michael arrived, she was on the Internet, looking for a good school. If she'd had an extra ten thousand a year to pay private fees, it would have been a lot easier. Not easy, even then, of course – most independent schools wanted bright eleven-year-olds who'd eventually score well on exams and push them up the league tables, not mathematically gifted teenagers with a reading age of five and less than two years of formal education. Still, there were a few special boarding schools that might ... only not at short notice, and not without money. Anyway, how could she put him in a boarding school? He wouldn't like it, and she'd hate it.

The doorbell rang, and she lifted her head

and stared blankly at the wall while Madhab went to answer it. Presently Michael came into the study with Madhab, chatting happily about robots. They both fell silent at the look on her face.

'Hello,' said Michael uncertainly.

This is where the natural order of the world reasserts itself, Janet thought wearily. *Madhab kicked out of school, and Michael about to disappear off over the horizon. But I'll fight it – God, I will! I'll remortgage the house. If I do nothing else in my life, I'll see to it that Madhab gets the education he deserves.*

In the pit of her stomach was the awareness that the world order might have yet another blow in reserve. Madhab was a Nepalese national who had entered Britain to receive medical treatment, and that treatment was over. Janet had not been able to adopt him. He had no right to remain.

I'll go to Nepal with him, if I have to, she thought grimly.

She quit the search engine. 'Hello,' she said, trying to sound casual, and began to shut down the computer. 'Sorry. I, um, was looking at schools for Madhab.'

'Oh!' Michael said, surprised. 'I didn't realize that was in the air.'

'Well,' she said, and hesitated, unsure how to go on.

'Janet look for harder school,' Madhab explained. 'The Hawthorn school is little kid school. Now I read gooder, I need harder school.'

'That's great!' exclaimed Michael, brightening. 'Well done! Um. It's, uh, my turn to provide supper. Indian, Italian, or Chinese?'

They went to a Chinese restaurant in the city centre. On the drive over, Madhab and Michael talked about schools, but Janet was silent and preoccupied. When they were seated at the table, and Janet stared blindly at her menu, Michael at last asked, 'Is something wrong?'

She shook her head and swallowed. 'It's just ... the schools business was a shock. It just happened this afternoon. The head teacher wants Madhab to leave the school before Christmas.'

'Just like that? It's rather late for you to arrange somewhere else, isn't it?'

Janet nodded. 'She needs the place for another child, and she said Madhab's been doing so much better since he had the treatment that she doesn't think he needs to be there. She's arranging for him to go to a mainstream secondary school, but I don't think he could cope. Hence the...' She gave a vague wave of the hand to indicate her own preoccupation.

'Oh.' Michael was quiet a moment, then said, 'So you're not as happy about it as Madhab.'

She laughed weakly. 'No.'

Michael swallowed. 'This ... um.' He looked at his own menu, then put it down. 'I, uh, was intending to, well, discuss this later, but ... I don't know, this business with the school might make it easier.'

'What?' she asked suspiciously.

Michael took a deep breath. 'I was wondering if you'd consider moving to London.'

She stared at him, and he made an uneasy brushing-aside gesture. 'I, uh, know it's really too early to ask. We've only known one another a few weeks. I know you have your house here, and um, probably friends ... family, your family are in the Midlands, aren't they? And even if Madhab's going to change schools anyway, I know he was going to start that enrichment course. But, well...' He stopped, then said apologetically, 'I keep seeing things during the week, and wishing I could share them with you two. Yesterday there was this machine they were using to demolish a building, the most amazing ... well, it was something I thought you'd like, Madhab. And there was an exhibit of Scottish landscapes at a gallery, and I wished I could take you there.' He sighed. 'The truth is, seeing you only at the weekend isn't enough. I want you around all the time.'

Janet could feel her face going hot. 'You...' she began. 'I...'

'You and I,' agreed Michael. He licked his lips. 'Look, I ... I know I'm no great bargain.

279

Forty-year-old MBA and computer geek with a job he can't talk about and a lot of weird Egyptian relatives. But I love you, and I would do my best to make you happy – both of you. You don't have to answer at once. I know it's a big thing.'

'I...' she tried again – then made herself stop and collect her wits. 'What, exactly, are you proposing?'

'Marriage,' he said, surprised. 'Obviously. It wouldn't be fair to ask you to move to London otherwise. London house prices being what they are, I mean.'

'Oh!' she said stupidly – then, looking at his face, at his dark, anxious eyes behind the spectacles, her heart leapt into her throat and she said, 'Yes.'

There was a moment of silence. 'You mean, "yes"?' he asked incredulously. 'Just like that? You don't need to think about it?'

Desperate Divorcee after all, she thought – but it wasn't that; it was him, just him. 'I don't need to think about it,' she agreed. 'Yes.'

Eleven

She decided afterwards that she should have consulted Madhab before replying – not because it would have changed her answer, but because not to consult him excluded him from a major decision that would completely change his life. Later that night, back at the house, she went to his room, knocked on the door, and went in to apologize.

Madhab was in his boxer shorts ready for bed, looking at *The Way Things Work*. He set the book down and listened to her apology with serious attention. She thought he was relieved and pleased to receive it, though when she finished, all he said was, 'You love Michael?'

'Yes,' she agreed, her face flushing. 'But, Madhab, one *reason* I love him is that he cares about you. I think we can be a family together – you, and him, and me. I really do think it will work.'

'Good man,' said Madhab thoughtfully. 'I like Michael.' He frowned. 'London ... very big city! Good schools there?'

'There are many, many schools there,' she

told him. 'One of them is certain to be good for you.' She did not let herself think about how much easier it would be to find one, with a pot of money from selling her house and another income-earner to share expenses with. It seemed mercenary to think about that – almost a betrayal of the impulse that had forced that 'Yes' to her lips without any hesitation.

There was another thing, though, that Michael could give them, and that might give Madhab a reason to feel happier about the engagement. 'Madhab,' she said, nervously, almost afraid to endanger it with a name. 'When I'm married it will be much easier to adopt you.'

Madhab picked his head up at that, looked at her a long moment, then held both hands up, fingers crossed. She crossed her own fingers back at him, then went over, kissed him on the forehead, and said goodnight.

Michael was sitting downstairs, finishing his coffee. During the afternoon Madhab had moved the folding bed into the lounge, and it was still sitting, folded, in a corner of the room. When Janet came in, Michael looked at it pointedly, then looked at her and raised his eyebrows in a silent question. Janet shook her head, and a wonderful smile spread over his face.

'I did hope,' he told her, getting up and putting his arms around her. 'Though I'd understand it if you didn't want to upset Madhab.'

She kissed him. 'I think Madhab knows it will happen now,' she told him. She lowered her head against his shoulder, breathing the scent: aftershave, cotton and sweat. 'He's anxious about the whole business...'

'Understandably,' Michael put in.

Janet lifted her head again and smiled at him. 'But he's making a real effort to be positive. He was asking about schools in London.'

'Good,' said Michael. 'Good.' His arms tightened around her and he kissed her. She reached up and took his spectacles off.

They went upstairs very quietly, so as not to upset Madhab, and embarked on the awkward, anxious, thrilling, tender and deeply satisfying business of discovering how to make one another very happy.

In the morning, waking with Michael beside her for the very first time, Janet propped herself up on an elbow and studied him. His face without the spectacles looked younger, unguarded and gentle in sleep. There was a frown line in the centre of his forehead, but his lips were curled in a smile. She felt as though the world had been made anew, and the natural order of things was overthrown. *It won't last*, she told herself – *not like this, anyway. One thing or another will go wrong. But this, this proves that evil doesn't govern every-thing. This is purely and wholly good.*

She tried to remember if she had felt like this when she had first woken up beside George. No. She had been exhilarated then, intoxicated with love – and so much young-er, so painfully young. She hadn't really believed in evil then – hadn't believed that patients might die in agony, despite all she could do, or that love could ever fail.

She wondered if this love could fail, too. *No*, she promised herself. *I won't let it. I'll make it work.*

Some small corner of her mind whispered to her, in shame and glee, that maybe it *had* to work. They hadn't used any form of con-traception. No, no of course she wouldn't do a Fran; she wouldn't get pregnant just to oblige him to marry her...

But, oh God, oh God, it would be so wonderful to have a baby! And there were only a few years before it really would be too late. She hoped, she really hoped, he wanted one *soon*.

She kissed Michael, and he woke up. 'Mmm!' he said, smiling, and put an arm around her.

'Mmm,' she replied, putting both arms around him.

He rolled over on to his back and fumbled on the bedside table. 'I need my glasses.'

She put her lips against his ear and

whispered, 'Why do you need your glasses?'

'So I can see you. You're just a blur now, and I want to see you.'

She reached behind her to the dresser, found the glasses she'd set down there the night before, and handed them to him. He put them on and looked at her. His smile widened.

'What's that grin for?'

'Waking up next to a beautiful woman.'

'Oh, flattery!' she observed, laughing. 'It'll get you everywhere.'

'But you *are*!' he protested earnestly. 'You *shine*. All the things you are inside, all that kindness and strength and intelligence – they show in your face. You're just beautiful, Janet, just lovely. When I first met you I kept looking at you and wondering why on earth you were single. I still don't understand how I got to be so lucky. I mean that.'

That was how he saw her? It robbed her of speech. She put her head down on his chest, felt his heart beat against her cheek.

'What's the matter?' he asked her anxiously. 'Are you sorry you said yes?'

'No,' she whispered. 'Never. Are you sorry you asked?'

'Not in a thousand years.'

Janet had anticipated a certain awkwardness with Madhab when they got up. Madhab, however, said nothing about the fact that the folding bed was still folded in the

285

corner of the lounge – largely because he was very eager to get to 'Build a Robot' in good time, and they were running late.

They scraped into the technical college only a few minutes after the hour, and Michael and Madhab proudly showed Janet their robot. It was considerably smaller than she'd expected – not one of the converted lawnmowers that Madhab loved to watch battling on television, but a converted radio-controlled car. It was, however, armour-plated (they'd cut up a baking tin, Michael explained) and painted silver. It had been named 'Swordfish'.

There were twenty-three other robots produced by the 'Build a Robot' class – twenty-four being the ceiling for class numbers. Janet was prepared to cheer and groan for Swordfish as it struggled through the tournament, but, after the first combat, found herself embarrassed to say anything. Swordfish didn't merely defeat its opponents: it crushed them. Under the baking-tin armour at its nose was a thin rod that sprang out and whipped upward. It could be used to flip another robot over, to damage its tyres or controls, or to right Swordfish if it was flipped by somebody else. It completely outclassed the flimsy devices used by all the others.

When the tournament was over, the teacher presented Michael and Madhab with a medal and shook their hands. '*Wicked* machine,' he congratulated them. 'Particularly the spring on that sword-thing. I've never seen anything like it.'

'That's Madhab's,' said Michael.

'Yeah, well, it's awesome. If I were you, I'd check whether anybody's patented anything like it. You never know, there could be some money in it. Look, if you two ever decide to go in for the television version of this and build a full-sized machine, let me know, huh?'

Madhab's eyes gleamed. 'We'll think about it,' said Michael.

They took Swordfish and the medal home. Madhab arranged the robot prominently on the mantelpiece, then sat down to gloat over the medal, a mass-produced gilt shield shape engraved with a gear and the words 'Champion Robot'.

'You'll have to keep that somewhere safe,' Janet advised him.

He looked up quickly. 'I keep on necklace, maybe?'

She was about to laugh when she thought of what it must mean to him: stupid deaf-mute Madhab, champion robot builder. She went upstairs and fished in the jewellery box until she found the silver chain which had, until the Bleickens visited, held a single crystal of amethyst. She gave it to Madhab, and he strung the medal on it and put it around his neck. Then he looked uncertainly at Michael.

'Go ahead,' said Michael. 'It was the sword that won it, and that was your invention.' Madhab grinned and tucked the medal under his T-shirt.

It was, Janet decided afterwards, the most perfect day of her life. After lunch the three of them went to London and spent the afternoon touring the Science Museum, one slightly eccentric-looking family among all the others crowding the displays. They went out to supper at an Italian restaurant and wandered through the streets for a while afterwards, looking at the people, eating ice cream, laughing. At last they went back to Michael's flat, sat in the lounge for a while talking, then made up the folding bed for Madhab. 'Have to buy a bigger flat,' Michael said, regarding the bed with a sigh. 'Or a house.' He looked at Madhab. 'Some place with a workroom, maybe, where you could build things?'

Madhab grinned eagerly. 'Bigger robot?'

'We could try.'

Things will go wrong, Janet reminded herself, as she went off to bed with Michael. *Things will certainly go wrong. Nothing perfect can last.* With a chill, she remembered that the following morning they were to take Madhab to have his brain scanned.

All of David Somers' records, including brain scans, had been lost. However, Madhab had also had a lot of tests both before and after the operation on his ears, and Janet had access to all of those. They did include one brain scan – done not because Madhab was expected to receive any treatment at the time, but because a consultant at the hospital in Leicester had been interested in the effects of language deprivation on the brain. Janet was thus able to present a thick folder to Professor Clark. He pounced on it avidly – then put it aside: 'We've only got the scanners for two hours, so we need to make the most of our time.'

Madhab was an old hand at brain scans. He sat down and let Professor Clark tape the sensors to his scalp, then kept patiently still under the helmet of the scanner. He listed words or repeated sentences as required. The scanner created a strong magnetic field around his head, and the resonance of blood in the living tissue of his brain created an impression of which areas were working hardest. A computer processed the results to produce an enhanced image.

Janet watched the images as they emerged from the computer. After a little while, she opened Madhab's file and picked up the pictures from the scan done a month after his ears were fixed. The difference she'd expected wasn't there: the language areas on the left side of the brain didn't look any bigger in the new scans than they had in the old ones. Their activity had become more concentrated, though. In several of the older scans there was activity in patches all over the brain. In the new scans, the activity was confined much more to the classical language areas which David Somers had treated.

She wondered if that meant that Madhab had previously had to use every mental tool at his disposal when he tried to speak or understand, while now he could rely on a purpose-built language module. She supposed that Clark, who didn't believe in language modules, would say no.

Whatever the explanation, she thought, with relief, it didn't look as though Madhab had suffered any harm from the treatment. Her forebodings had been wrong.

After slightly more than two hours, another neurologist came into the room and informed Clark, with rather strained politeness, that he, the other neurologist, had a research programme scheduled. Clark mumbled an apology and helped Madhab out of the sensors.

They went down to the foyer of the building. 'Everything looks normal,' Clark told them, as they prepared to part, 'though, of course, I'll want to study the scans more carefully. Could we meet again next week to discuss it?'

The intervening week was a very busy one. The pressing need to get Madhab a place at a reasonable school *soon*, before he missed too much of the new term, meant that Janet had little time to sit down and think. Several times she found herself stopping in stupefaction. Had she really agreed to marry a man she'd only known for six weeks? Was she really going to *sell her house* and move to London? Was she honestly going to get a new job, and find an expensive private school that would take Madhab?

The details of what she did began to convince her, terrifyingly, that she was. She visited an estate agent. She began sorting through the contents of the house, deciding what to keep, what to put into storage, what to throw away. She looked at information about schools; she enquired about practices in south-east London that might want another partner. Soon, she realized, it would be too late to back out.

The evenings always reassured her. That was when she phoned Michael to discuss plans, and every time she heard his voice she remembered that backing out was not something she wanted to do.

The friends she phoned with the news were stunned. 'That's sudden!' was the commonest response. 'What does he do?'

'He's a civil servant,' Janet would reply. 'I

met him when he was seeing about the funding for Madhab's treatment.' Her mother was almost the only person who asked, 'What department is he in?'

'MI5,' Janet informed her, 'but keep quiet about it, OK?'

There was a silence. 'You're joking,' said her mother uncertainly.

That, actually, was quite a good moment.

By the time she saw Professor Clark again, she had a shortlist of schools and she and Michael had begun house-hunting. The three of them – Janet, Michael and Madhab – arrived at the Institute of Neurology slightly late, distractedly discussing the merits of a house in Lewisham that they'd arranged to view that afternoon.

Clark was waiting impatiently in the entrance. With him was a psycholinguist he'd roped in to evaluate Madhab, a plump, bright-eyed woman by the name of Barbara, whom Janet liked immediately. While Barbara was introducing herself to Madhab, Clark turned a suspicious stare on Michael.

'Mr Shahid,' he said disapprovingly, 'I know I've agreed to share information with you, but I'm a bit...' He hesitated.

'You're a bit what, Professor?' asked Michael politely.

'Concerned to find you here today,' replied Clark, drawing himself up. 'It's not really the MoD's *business* to listen in on what I say to

Madhab Limbu's guardian. I'll send you a memo of everything that concerns you later.'

Michael exchanged a look with Janet. She stifled the urge to giggle. 'Michael and I got engaged last week,' she explained. 'He's not here professionally. He's here *in loco parentis*, like me.'

'Oh!' exclaimed Clark, utterly taken aback. After a moment he added doubtfully, 'Er ... congratulations.'

Barbara the psycholinguist suggested that they all go to a café where they could have something to drink as they talked, and presently they were all sitting around dinner plate-sized marble tables with cold soft drinks, Barbara chatting to Madhab, and Clark with Janet and Michael.

Clark had a black nylon backpack from which he extracted the images from the brain scans. 'First off,' he said, putting as much of them on the table as would fit, 'I'm very happy to say that Madhab's brain function looks normal.'

He went over the pictures with them, pointing out the changes that Janet had noticed herself – and, to her satisfied surprise, giving them exactly the interpretation she had. She listened with a wide smile; when Clark finished, she asked eagerly, 'Will his language go on improving?'

Clark grimaced and shrugged. 'I don't know,' he admitted. 'Certainly, I expect that it will carry on getting better for the next year or so. Whether it will ever be completely normal, I can't say. But...' He swallowed, then said, 'Have you noticed anything ... unusual since he started the treatment?'

Janet looked at him in puzzlement. Dread began to settle coldly in the pit of her stomach. 'He hasn't had any psychological problems, if that's what you mean.'

'I don't mean *problems*, necessarily,' said Clark carefully. 'It might be something like insomnia, or particularly vivid dreams. Or it could very well be something positive.'

She wasn't sure whether or not to be relieved. 'I'm not sure what you mean.'

Clark picked up his marker pen and bit it. 'Increased energy, bursts of creativity, striking achievements...?'

Janet thought of the recommendation for the maths enrichment programme; of the robot that adorned her mantelpiece at home.

Her face obviously gave her away. 'Ah,' said Clark, eyes gleaming.

'He's a very bright boy,' Michael said reprovingly. 'And he works very hard. Some of that has been beginning to pay off recently. It's not clear to me how anyone could distinguish what he's achieved by himself from something he's achieved because of the Somers Treatment.'

Clark lifted his hands in surrender. 'Point taken. The thing is, the way I read the scans is that the Somers Treatment genuinely does seem to have improved the function of the areas of his brain devoted specifically to language. Before he had it he was trying to work out language by using a lot of generalized problem-solving skills; now he's using the specifically linguistic programming of the language areas—'

'I thought you were a – what you call it – a globalist,' interrupted Janet.

'I am!' agreed Clark. 'But that doesn't mean that I've ever denied that some areas of the brain are hard-wired for certain specific tasks. It just means that I think those areas don't work in isolation, that they talk to one another all the time – and that's what I'm getting at now. I think the fact that Madhab was formerly devoting a lot of his problem-solving skills to language, and that he now doesn't need them for that, ought to mean that he starts using them for other things.' He looked at their faces a moment, then added, defensively, 'I'm not saying that the treatment increased his IQ or anything! You say he was always very bright, and I entirely believe you: if he hadn't been so bright, he'd have suffered much more social impairment than he did. All I'm saying is that now I'd expect him to start making faster progress in general problem-solving *as well as* in the language problems he was treated for.'

Madhab was in a good mood as they left UCL and walked back to the car. 'I like Barbara,' he informed Janet. 'Much more nice than David Somers' psycholinguist.' He skipped a step. 'She say I talk good, learn fast. She want talk me again, help me learn. She say she phone you.'

'That's great,' Janet told him.

He nodded. 'What Professor Clark say?'

'He says that your brain is just fine. And he says...' Janet hesitated.

'Madhab,' said Michael, 'he wanted to know if things other than language are easier for you now. Maths, or solving puzzles – that sort of thing.'

Madhab gave him a startled look. 'Yes,' he agreed at once, as though it were a matter of course. His hand went up and touched the dry scab on his left temple. 'Very good treatment. Make my brain bigger, like other kids' brains. Build very good sword for Swordfish, yes?'

'That wasn't from the treatment!' Janet burst out. 'It didn't help you with anything but *language*. Whatever else you've got is your own!'

Madhab shrugged. 'Stupid boy never understand, no talk good. More clever now.'

Michael laughed and shook his head. Janet gave him an irritated look. 'It isn't funny!' she protested. 'If people started to get the idea that the Somers Treatment improves general intelligence ... it would be a nightmare! There'd be a storm of publicity, and we'd get hate mail from a lot of fanatics who'd accuse us of playing God, and there'd be ambitious parents who'd pay for their kids to have dangerous and unnecessary surgery at black-market clinics and ... and God only knows what! It'd be a disaster!'

'But Clark was very clear that Madhab's general intelligence *hasn't* been improved!' objected Michael, sobering. 'That this effect is just the result of the way language used to absorb so much of it – if it's a real effect at all, and not just Madhab's own natural progress. There's hardly anybody else in the world who's in the same position he was, who'd benefit the same way!'

'Would you trust the media or the public to understand that?' asked Janet. 'This would be "Miracle Treatment to Raise IQ", and details be damned. We're going to have to ask Professor Clark to keep quiet about this.'

'I guess so,' said Michael, shaken. 'I'll speak to him about it.'

They walked on a little way in silence. 'I never realized that language was so difficult,' Michael said thoughtfully. 'Madhab was struggling to produce two-word sentences; when he had the same brainpower free for mathematics, he started working out non-Euclidean geometry *for fun*.'

'I hadn't thought of it that way,' admitted

Janet, staggered by it.

'My boy, you'll go far!' Michael told Madhab, half joking and half-serious. 'That's quite a brain you've got there.'

Madhab grinned shyly. 'I want good school now,' he confided. 'Learn maths, learn science.'

'Sounds good to me,' agreed Michael. 'What then?'

Madhab walked a few steps in silence, then looked up at them with a sudden air of nervous determination. 'Make things. For Nepal.'

'For Nepal?' Janet asked, puzzled.

He shrugged. 'In Nepal very poor people. Not like here. No electricity, no heater, no computer. My cousin – everybody think he very rich man, very important. In England...' He made a dismissive brushing-away gesture. 'I want make things for Nepal. Have idea...' He trailed off, struggling for words.

'An idea for a machine?' asked Michael softly.

Madhab nodded, his eyes bright. 'Little generator. Put on little stream, make electricity. Little one, easy to make, cheap. Give people electricity for heater and light. Now people cut wood, fetch wood, very hard work. Little generator much better.' He grimaced. 'Hard to make, I think. Need learn many thing first.'

'I think that's a *terrific* idea!' said Michael

warmly. 'We'll find a good school for you.'

They found the school during the course of the next week. It was a small private school in Dulwich: it was aimed at helping bright children with dyslexia, Asperger's, or other moderate-to-severe learning disabilities. It was clean, attractive, had a high staff:pupil ratio and was flexible about such things as curriculum and exams. Madhab, massively impressed by the science lab and the computers, was eager to start at once. Another child had been withdrawn at short notice, so there was space for him.

It was expensive.

'We can afford it,' said Michael firmly that evening, when Janet told him about it and agonized over the cost.

'We still have to buy a house!' she objected.

'Selling my flat and your house will certainly cover that.'

'I was planning to use the money from my house to cover the fees.'

Michael caught both her hands. 'We can afford it,' he insisted. 'Janet, love, we're going to have two good incomes, and I have savings as well.'

'I don't want to use your—'

'Why not?'

She had no answer ready, and looked down unhappily.

'We're going to be married, yes? You haven't changed your mind about that?'

'No.'

'So what happened to "for richer or for poorer, in sickness and in health"?'

'I just don't ... don't want to push.' She was aware of the immensity of her good fortune, shining before her like a land of dreams (so various, so beautiful, so new!). It had no certitude: push and it might vanish.

'You're hoping we can legally adopt Madhab, yes?'

She nodded.

'That will make him legally my son. Why shouldn't I spend my money on getting my son the kind of education he needs?'

It was an unanswerable argument. She wanted him to be a father to Madhab: how could she object to him behaving like one? She took her hands from his, then linked them behind his back. 'Sometimes I think you're too good to be true,' she whispered.

He kissed her. 'No. I'm expecting to get a lot back. I don't think he's going to be the sort of son to be ashamed of. I think we're going to be very proud of him.'

Twelve

The new school's autumn term was to start the following week – a week later than The Hawthorns. Madhab was eager to begin the term with everyone else, so the decision was made that he and Janet would move down to London at once, and sell the house in Leicester as and when they could.

The hurried move, combined with the job-hunting and house-hunting, kept Janet very busy. Introductions to relatives loomed large in her mind as well. As Michael told her more about his 'weird Egyptian' family, they sounded merely numerous and colourful, and, to Janet's relief, it seemed they were all strongly disposed to welcome her. ('They'd about given up hope,' Michael explained drily. 'If I'd said I wanted to marry a camel they'd have been relieved – and a *doctor* is a real catch.' He looked at her nervously, then added, 'I'm afraid my parents *will* drop hints about grandchildren. Just ignore it.') Her own family were far more suspicious, but were eager to meet the prospective new in-law.

The phone call from the Leicester police on the Friday morning was an irritating and highly unwelcome distraction. It seemed that her house's state-of-the-art alarm had gone off during the night, and when the police had investigated, they'd found evidence of an attempted break-in. The alarm had switched its sound off after an hour, but the police couldn't switch it off completely without getting into the house, and they wanted Janet to come and deal with it.

Janet had a job interview at a south London practice scheduled for that morning, and that evening she was to have dinner with Michael's family in Hackney. She was very reluctant to drive to Leicester. The police, however, were insistent: she expected them to respond to her alarm system; she could cooperate with their response. She silently cursed the alarm system, agreed with the police, and phoned the London practice to cancel the interview, with apologies. She left Madhab playing on the computer in Michael's flat, and got into her car.

The Datsun was, by this time, parked in a slot outside Michael's flat, looking even older and shabbier than usual among the Rovers and BMWs: she'd driven it back and forth between Leicester and Thamesmead a couple of times, ferrying clothing and computers. That did not mean, however, that her feelings about driving in London had changed. As she struggled through the traffic to reach the M1, she cursed the alarm system all over again. She told herself that probably it had *invited* the attempted break-in: Leicester's young hoodlums must have noticed it and decided that the house contained something worth stealing.

The possibility that the attempted break-in was connected to the Somers Treatment was one she considered, but rejected. Tao Pharmaceuticals presumably *had* all the details and no longer needed to burgle anybody, and it seemed improbable that somebody else had suddenly become interested, now that David was dead.

She arrived in Leicester at about noon and went straight to the house. From the outside it looked untroubled. She unlocked the door and went in.

She saw immediately what the police had meant by 'evidence of an attempted break-in'. The kitchen window, next to the newly mended back door, had been covered over with thick brown package-strapping tape, then smashed: the cracked and splintered glass sagged heavily in the frame, held up only by the tape. It hadn't been peeled out, however, and the back door was still firmly locked.

She went to the controls for the alarm system. All the lights on its little display panel were red, and two were flashing. She remembered belatedly that she *could* have reset it by phone, and spared herself the drive. She cursed it again, then examined it for a minute or so helplessly. Finally, she went to dig the instruction manual out of the filing cabinet in the kitchen. The relevant section was called 'How to reset the system manually'. It was only on reading through it that she remembered that the system was also equipped with cameras.

She read the manual some more, then carefully went to the controls and, following the instructions, accessed the record of the cameras.

Being state-of-the-art, they were, of course, digital. There were two: one at the front of the house and one at the back, both set unobtrusively into the security lighting. When the alarm was triggered the lights came on, and the cameras were programmed to focus on motion and take a series of thirty five snaps over three minutes. When Janet downloaded the images, the first one – labelled 'Camera 2, 1:03 am' – showed her two black-clad figures by the back door, one of them at the window, the other holding a torch. In the second image, taken immediately afterwards, both figures had turned toward the camera with expressions of horror and amazement, undoubtedly reacting to the unexpected light and the sound of the alarm going off. They were both middle-aged Chinese men in suits.

Janet stared at the image for a long minute, trying to contain her shock. Then, bewildered, she began to check the rest of the images.

The two would-be burglars gesticulated at each other for several shots. Then they fled: Camera 2 had three shots of their retreating backs. Camera 1, at the front of the house, took over a few seconds later: there were several shots of the men running to a car, which was parked just down the road from the house. A door in a neighbouring house opened just in the last shot, taken as the car drove off. She couldn't quite make out the number plate on the car, but she suspected that it would be distinguishable if the picture could be enhanced.

Janet flipped back to the second image: the two besuited Chinese businessmen staring at the camera in horror, one clutching a torch and the other a hammer. *Why?* she wondered in bewilderment. What in the world did they think they could learn from her *now?*

It wasn't a question she could answer. On the other hand, she did know what to do with the pictures. She went to the phone and dialled the number of Detective Inspector Bailey.

He wasn't in. She left a message with a flunkey, then went back to the instruction manual for the security system. She saved the pictures, reset the system, and tele-phoned the local police.

Leicester Constabulary, when they eventu-ally arrived, were delighted with the pictures, though slightly puzzled by them. They wanted a printout. Unfortunately, Janet had taken her computer down to London the week before, and had no printer in the house. The two young police officers debat-ed whether one of them could go borrow a printer from police headquarters. They phoned to check, and the answer, appar-ently, was no. Janet was beginning to think she'd have to fetch her own printer back from London the following day when one of the officers checked the instruction manual for the security system and discovered that the pictures could be despatched down the phone-line to a police computer, if there was a police computer ready to receive them. They got back on the phone. Nobody they spoke to at police headquarters seemed to have any idea how to hook-up to the security system to receive the pictures.

By this time it was half past three, and Janet was acutely aware that she would be arriving back in London during the rush hour. Michael's parents were expecting them at seven, and she doubted that she could find the house on her own: she needed to get right across the city to Thamesmead. She told the two policemen to sort it out for themselves and to lock the door when they left. They protested; she ruthlessly gave them some phone numbers and departed.

It was twenty past six when she arrived back in Thamesmead, flustered and exhausted. She rushed upstairs into the flat, and found Michael and Madhab both waiting anxiously for her in the lounge.

'I need to change,' she told Michael.

'No you don't; you look just *fine*,' he replied, glancing at his watch.

'Then I need to use the loo!'

Five minutes later they were back on the road, this time in Michael's Peugeot.

'What was it you went to Leicester for?' Michael asked, as they stopped for a traffic light in Woolwich. 'Madhab said the police wanted to talk to you?'

'Yes. There was an attempted break-in at the house last night.'

'Oh. You could reset the alarm from here, you know. By phone.'

'Yes, I remembered that – when I got there,' she admitted. 'But...'

He glanced across at her, beginning to frown.

'It was Tao Pharmaceuticals again,' she told him.

With the words, she became aware that she was frightened. It was odd: at the house and on the drive home she'd felt only anxious impatience and irritation – at the slowness and incompetence of the police, at the traffic and the roads. Now, safely back in London, surrounded by those who loved her, the image of those two faces turned toward the camera gave her the same panicky, unstable feeling that she'd experienced in the empty yard.

Had the spies known that the house was empty? Probably not. She'd moved to London very suddenly and the Bleickens, who'd been reporting on her, were gone. Probably the two men had believed that she and Madhab were in the house asleep. They had taped over the window, so that the sound of glass breaking would not wake them.

They certainly knew that David was dead and Madhab's treatment was over. So why had they wanted to come in?

Michael stared at her. Behind them, a car hooted its horn loudly: the light had gone green. Michael drove forward with a jerk, then pulled over in front of a row of shops and stopped the car.

'Tao Pharmaceuticals,' he repeated.

'Well,' she said helplessly, 'two middle-aged Chinese men, anyway. In *suits*.' That ludicrous detail was one she couldn't quite get over: two middle-aged burglars in *suits*. 'That alarm system has cameras. It took their pictures.' After a moment, she added, 'I left the Leicester police trying to download the pictures. And I tried to phone Detective

Inspector Bailey, but he wasn't in. I left him a message.'

Michael stared at her a moment longer. Then he shook his head angrily and got his phone out.

'I can't think what they might have wanted,' Janet told him.

He glanced at her, and she saw that he had an idea, and that it wasn't a pleasant one.

'What?' she asked sharply.

He sighed, lowering the phone. 'The police have dropped charges against Firsby. They released him yesterday. I know that Bailey has been trying hard to make the case against Wong and Tan. He's questioned them several times.' He hesitated, then met her eyes and added, 'I think he may have told them that he has a witness who saw them at Somers Synaptic at the time of the murders. Now that Firsby's been released...'

It was the same cold shock she'd felt herself when she'd seen the images. She had buried it then, refusing to acknowledge any threat; now it chilled her. 'You think they wanted to eliminate the witness?'

'I don't know.' He picked up the phone again and dialled a number.

Janet sat silent while he spoke to someone on the other end about 'asking A-branch to increase the surveillance' and 'getting a report on the movements of the suspects last night'.

The two spies would have known at once who Inspector Bailey's witness was. The Bleickens must have told them about Madhab's Friday appointments, and they'd seen the car driving off. As Michael had once pointed out, they probably had a stack of reports from the Bleickens, which would give them not merely the location of her house, but something about its layout as well. They wouldn't have known about the alarm system, though: that had been installed after the Bleickens had gone back to Berlin. They would've expected to get in easily.

She wondered if they were aware that their faces had been caught on camera. Probably not: it was the light they'd turned towards, and the alarm that had made them run. In the dark and the dazzle and the confusion, that little lens tracking them would have gone unnoticed.

Michael made a couple more phone calls, then started the car again, signalled, and pulled out on to the road.

'You've obviously been keeping up to date on the case,' she observed neutrally.

'Yes,' he agreed. 'I told you I helped Bailey track the money.'

'What money?'

'The money that was paid into Elena Simonson's bank account, that none of her friends could explain. It came from

Tao Pharmaceuticals, through a dummy account. One of several, in fact – Wong was clearly guilty of breaching UK banking regulations, if nothing else.' He glanced across at her, then said defensively, 'It wasn't a secret. I would've told you if you'd asked. It's just that it wasn't something I particularly *wanted* to talk about, and we had a lot of other things to discuss that were more important.'

More important than espionage and murder? About to burst out with an angry denial, she stopped herself. It was true, she had *not* asked about the case. She had sunk herself instead into the details of the move, into Madhab's treatment and his school, into house-hunting and job-hunting. She had wanted the murders to be something in the past – a horrible event that she'd once witnessed, but which would not affect the bright future opening before her.

She found, too, that she knew why Michael hadn't wanted to talk about it any more than she'd wanted to hear. He wanted to have some part of his life that was good and whole and entirely separate from terrorism. *I don't get to hear about good people as often as I'd like,* he'd told her, after the first meal they shared together, and: *Sometimes I've had days where all I see is evil. Cruel and violent men doing cruel and violent things.* They had both been deluding themselves.

'You can't shield me from things,' she said quietly, after a long silence.

He looked over at her again, then focused uncertainly on the road.

'I can cope with it,' she promised him. 'I *know* I'm a champion worrier, but honestly, I can cope. And if we're going to be each other's refuge, we need to know when something is hurting.'

He was silent a long minute. 'It wasn't hurting,' he said at last. 'Once I knew that they were going to release Firsby, I wasn't really worried about it at all.'

'No,' agreed Janet. 'I guess I felt the same way. I just meant, in general.'

He glanced at her again. 'I take your point,' he said, after another silence. 'I think you're probably right. I warn you, though: I'll probably go on trying to shield you anyway. I'll try not to take it amiss if you nag me about it.'

She felt herself start to smile. 'Something to work on, then.'

They arrived for the dinner a quarter of an hour late, but there were no reproaches, only cries of joy and relief from the gathered crowd of Anglo-Egyptians. Michael's parents were younger than Janet had expected, still below retirement age: they had married young, and Michael was their first child, and the only son. He had three sisters, however, all of whom were present, with husbands and children ranging in size from tiny toddler to hulking teenager. Janet felt somewhat overwhelmed, but soon began to enjoy herself. Madhab, too, was quickly made to feel at home: two of the nephews liked robots.

It was after eleven before they left again. 'I hope my mother wasn't too overbearing,' Michael said, as he drove back through the quiet streets.

Janet smiled. Mariam Shahid had indeed dropped hints about grandchildren. 'She wasn't overbearing,' she told Michael. 'She's sweet.'

'She is,' agreed Michael, 'but sometimes she *is* overbearing. This whole grandchild business ... we have Madhab, and you don't need to feel that...'

It was a sensitive subject, and one that was beginning to cause Janet a queasy sense of guilt. They still hadn't been using any form of contraception, but she suspected that Michael simply assumed that, as a doctor, she was well able to deal with the matter. She kept intending to – but, so far, hadn't been able to bring herself to do so. Several times she'd gone to the prescriptions program on her computer and contemplated the array of options available to her, but on each occasion had shut the program down again without choosing any of them. She'd told herself that she would never do a Fran,

313

and she'd meant it – but the possibility of a child, a real live baby of her own, had been so potent and so desirable that she hadn't been able to bring herself to take steps to prevent it. *Tomorrow*, she kept telling herself, and, *I'll discuss it with Michael* – but somehow she hadn't discussed it with Michael and hadn't done anything at all.

She hadn't realized that she was that hungry for a baby. In general practice she saw them all the time – fat, happy babies, cranky, crying babies, floppy, ill babies – along with their proud, exhausted or anxious mothers. She'd dealt with them gently and professionally, and had been almost resigned to never having one of her own. So where had it come from, this sharp ache for a child in her arms? It was alarmingly irrational. She had Madhab, as Michael said, and beyond a doubt she loved him as dearly as any child of her own blood.

He'd been twelve when she'd met him, though – another woman's baby. She wanted one of her own.

She braced herself, took a deep breath, and asked bluntly, 'Do you want a baby?'

Michael hesitated, and she realized with a thrill that, yes, he did.

'I want one,' she told him now. Suddenly she was free to confess that small and silent evasion, with its potentially enormous consequences.

'Oh!' he exclaimed, and began to grin. 'I was afraid to ask.'

'I want a baby so much that I haven't ... that is, if you think I'm on the pill, you're mistaken. Sorry. I know I should've done something. I keep meaning to, it's just ... Sorry.'

'Oh!' he said again, in a different voice; but, after a moment the grin came back. 'I kept putting off asking you about it.'

'So you wouldn't mind.'

'I'd be over the moon!'

Too perfect, she thought, sighing joyfully and settling back into her seat. *If I get pregnant quickly, I'll have to throw the necklace in the Thames or something.*

It was nearly midnight by the time they arrived back in Thamesmead, tired and happy. Michael pulled the car into its usual slot outside the building and switched off the engine. He was just opening the door when the two men emerged from the shadows at the side of the building. One of them held a gun, its barrel shining silver in the light of the lamps set into the front of the building.

'Stop where you are!' he commanded, in a vehement accented whisper, and they all froze.

Janet had seen the two, caught by her security camera the previous night. Until that moment, it had never occurred to her as significant that she had left a forwarding

315

address at the post office.

Michael stood motionless in the open car door. His hands went up slowly, empty. The light gleamed on his spectacles.

Wong and Tan moved forward. Above their black suits, their faces showed white with strain. She guessed that Wong was the older man, the one who held the gun. 'If there is noise, I shoot,' he said, his voice still pitched very low, but sharp with suppressed panic.

'We won't make any noise,' Michael replied, also speaking in a whisper. He sounded unnaturally calm. 'But you're making a mistake.'

Wong shook his head. 'Turn around. Put your hands behind your head.'

Michael obeyed, and the second man, presumably Tan Yiji, frisked him, then stepped back with the car keys and the phone. Wong took a step closer, levelling the gun at Michael's head. 'Move!' he ordered, jerking his head towards the back of the car.

Michael moved away from the open car door. Wong looked across at Janet in the passenger seat, who had watched paralysed, afraid that at any moment one bullet would demolish the whole of her new world: love, marriage, adoption, baby and all. He frowned, his eyes flicking nervously from her to Michael. 'Your hands up!'

She raised trembling hands. At once Tan

got into the driver's seat of the car beside her. He picked up her handbag and was about to toss it into the back, when he realized that Madhab was there, and stopped. He glared at the boy. 'You,' he ordered, 'open the door!'

Madhab looked at him a moment, then looked at Janet. She nodded.

Madhab opened the rear door of the car, then scooted over to make room as Wong forced Michael back into the car and sat down beside him, keeping the gun pointed at his head all the time.

'Do not move,' ordered Wong. 'If anyone moves, I will shoot.'

Nobody moved. Tan looked at the handbag he was holding with some confusion, then tossed it into the back, next to Wong. Then he sorted through the keys he'd taken from Michael, started the car and drove slowly round the green and back out on to the street. They turned left along the quiet road, then pulled over and stopped. To their right, below an embankment, the Thames flowed darkly under the street lights.

'You're making a mistake,' Michael said again, still calm and quiet. 'Wong Xinpei, Tan Yiji, you're making a mistake.'

The gun jerked, and the senior man stared at Michael in disbelief. 'You know our names?'

'I've had you under surveillance for weeks,'

Michael told him. 'Didn't you look at my ID?'

Wong said something in Chinese to Tan, who replied, angrily and defensively.

'This won't work,' Michael said, very gently. 'You'll be caught, and your problems will be worse than ever. Please. So far you've done us no harm: there's nothing we could charge you with. Let us go.'

'We cannot!' Wong declared abruptly. 'Better you than one who knew nothing.' Keeping the gun against Michael's ear, he reached under his coat and drew out a bottle. 'Please to drink this.'

It was, Janet saw, cheap brandy. She understood the plan at once: the car in the Thames, with Michael in the driver's seat, drunk. An accident.

'It isn't going to work!' she said loudly. 'It's already too late. The security system at my house in Leicester has cameras. It took pictures of both of you last night. The police have already seen them.'

There was a silence. Wong and Tan stared at her, eyes wide in their shocked faces. She abruptly remembered her own advice to Madhab: *People can be dangerous when they're scared.* These two were terrified. She should not have said anything to frighten them more.

'Just let us go!' she said urgently. 'Look, whatever Inspector Bailey told you, he

318

doesn't have any evidence against you that would stand up in court. We saw two men at Somers Synaptic, yes, but not close-up: there's no way we could give him a secure identification. He was just trying to scare you into confessing: he can't touch you unless you do something more – something like this! Killing us won't help you; it'll destroy you!'

'All lies!' replied Wong shrilly. 'Of course you tell lies now! Drink that!' He thrust the bottle at Michael.

Michael took it and held it in both hands, but made no move to unscrew the cap. 'If I'm going to die either way, why should I?' he asked quietly. 'If I make you shoot me, they will identify the bullet. I told you, you've been under surveillance for weeks: my people *will* link you to the gun. This won't pass, Wong. Give it up. It isn't your only option. I don't know why you killed David Somers, but I suspect that there was provocation. A good lawyer—'

'It was *justice*!' exclaimed Tan shrilly. '*They* were the murderers! They sold us lies that *killed* ten people!'

'I'm sorry,' Michael said into the tense silence. 'I'm sorry they sold you lies. I know Somers was a callous liar. He lied to us, too. We can testify to that – if we're alive. But killing us won't help you.'

'You'll testify in *China*?' spat Wong. 'Oh no.

It must not come to court. It need not. There is no evidence, apart from one witness.'

'*She* saw us,' Tan added. 'At the lab.'

'No,' Madhab interrupted suddenly. '*I* saw you. Not Janet. Not Michael. *Me.*'

The two Chinese stared at him a moment in surprise. Madhab held their eyes a moment – then abruptly threw the door open and dived out.

Wong yelled and swung the gun towards him. There was a flash of movement and the crash of the gun going off, both together: the screaming seemed to begin in the same blinding instant. Janet tried to swallow the terrible sound even as it emerged from her throat; Tan was shrieking something in Chinese – and Wong was screaming too, clutching his face with both hands, blood gushing from under them. Michael thrust the barrel of the gun directly into Tan's face. 'Don't move,' he ordered.

Tan sat frozen. Wong sobbed and cursed. Madhab picked himself up off the street and stared into the car, his face blank with shock. Across the street, lights were going on in apartments.

'Are you hurt?' Janet shouted frantically, dividing the question equally between Madhab and Michael.

Madhab shook his head. 'Janet,' said Michael composedly, 'get your phone and call the police.'

The police arrived about ten minutes later. By that time Tan was sitting on the ground beside the car, his hands secured behind his back by his own tie, and Wong was lying flat on the pavement under a street light while Janet gave him first aid. Michael had rammed the brandy bottle into his face with all the savagery of a man defending his family, and she didn't think that even the most skilled ophthalmologist would be able to salvage the right eye. Michael stood over her protectively, still holding the gun.

The first action of the Metropolitan Police on arriving was to yell at Michael to drop the gun. When he did that, they tried to arrest both him and Madhab who, as a teenage male, was obviously among the guilty. It was several minutes before Janet could convince them that the two Chinese had been the assailants, not the victims. However, once the police allowed Michael to extract his ID card, things became very much easier.

There followed several horrible hours of interrogation and statement-drafting. At seven o'clock in the morning the three of them were released and driven back to Thamesmead by the police.

'I'll make us some cocoa,' Michael announced, when they staggered back into the flat. He went into the kitchen.

Madhab sank down on the sofa and wrapped his arms around himself. Janet came and sat down next to him. She brushed his hair back from his face. The place where the shunt had been was already almost invisible. 'Darling,' she said softly, 'you shouldn't have jumped out of the car like that. He nearly killed you.'

Madhab shrugged. Michael came back into the room, carrying three microwaved mugs. 'He was trying to draw their fire,' he explained to Janet. 'Weren't you?'

Madhab nodded. 'I think, they know I am the witness, they want me most.' He met Michael's eyes. 'He move that gun, you will stop him. I know that.'

'You took a terrible risk,' said Michael. 'I might not have been fast enough.'

Madhab shrugged. 'They want kill us *anyway*.'

'We might have convinced them to let us go,' Janet said.

'Maybe,' said Michael. 'But they were pretty desperate.' He handed round the cocoa and settled on the sofa next to Janet. She put an arm around him, and at once he set his mug down and held her, burying his face in her neck. She put her other arm around Madhab, and clutched both of them at once. They all smelled of sweat and the stale-cigarettes-and-coffee odour of the police station. She could feel her pulse beating in her arms, pressing against the warmth of their flesh: alive, whole, and free.

'Oh, my darlings!' she whispered to them. 'I was so afraid I would lose you. I was so *stupid* not to worry about it; I *knew* I'd left the forwarding address!'

Madhab pulled loose and punched her arm, and Michael laughed weakly. 'Don't kick yourself!' he commanded. 'And stop worrying. It's over now.'

Detective Inspector Bailey came round that afternoon. His thumb on the doorbell dragged them muzzily from the sleep of exhaustion.

'Sorry,' he said, when Michael, dishevelled in pyjamas, opened the door to him. 'I, uh, wanted to check that you were OK.'

Michael grunted, but allowed him to come in. Madhab, on the folding bed in the lounge, sat up and looked at him blearily. Janet trailed in from the bedroom in her dressing gown.

'I, uh, think I should apologize,' the inspector said, glancing uncertainly around the apartment.

'Yes,' agreed Michael coldly.

'I shouldn't have told Wong and Tan that I had a witness – not when they could guess who I meant like that.'

'No,' said Michael.

'I didn't think they would go after you,' said the inspector.

'Obviously not,' said Michael.

323

'I'm sorry.'

There was a pause, and then Detective Inspector Bailey shrugged. 'Do you at least want me to tell you what happened?'

'Yes,' said Janet, coming into the lounge. 'Tan told us that David and Elena had sold them lies that killed ten people. What did he mean by that?'

The inspector sat down in one of the lounge chairs. 'Well. Apparently that was an exaggeration. David Somers had fed Tao Pharmaceuticals false information about his treatment, and the company's main base in Shanghai started a clinical trial with it last April, using ten volunteers – young volunteers, school and university kids. Only the information they were using was false, and Tao apparently didn't have anybody who realized that. The drugs they used damaged the brains of those ten kids. They're not dead, though. They're just severely a ... a ... what's the word for someone who can't talk?'

'Aphasic,' supplied Janet, appalled.

Bailey nodded. 'Apparently one of the volunteers was Wong Xinpei's nephew and another was Tan Yiji's cousin. They'd got into the trial by recommendation – sort of a company reward to Wong and Tan for stealing the treatment. They thought the kids were going to end up speaking perfect, accentless English. Instead they can't speak at all.'

'Oh God,' whispered Janet. The image of

those ten volunteers leapt in agonizing sharpness before her mind. Ten bright young people who thought they'd been granted a short cut to learning and advancement, stripped suddenly of language: ten lives blasted.

Probably the volunteers hadn't even known that the treatment was stolen.

'Obviously, Wong and Tan were pretty worked up about that,' Bailey continued, with brisk understatement. 'They'd recruited Elena Simonson to spy for them last summer, and they'd been paying her for information on the treatment, which they expected would earn big money. She'd stolen the monkey for them, and she'd been supplying them with information about the drugs – information that she claimed she was able to get from Somers' house while she went to bed with him.' Bailey hesitated, then went on, 'Wong and Tan are convinced that she was lying to them all along. Me, I'm sure she believed that the information she was giving them was good. It doesn't make sense otherwise.'

'What doesn't make sense?' asked Michael.

'The murders. They seem to have been triggered by the fact that you' – Bailey nodded at Michael – 'told David Somers that you suspected Elena Simonson, and he refused to listen. Elena wasn't stupid. She knew her boss; she knew he didn't give a damn about her.'

'She told her friends he was going to marry her!' objected Janet.

Bailey shrugged. 'Probably just wanted to give them an explanation for why she stayed with him. She couldn't very well tell them, "Oh, I'm earning twice what he pays me by selling his secrets to the Chinese," could she? Anyway, I think when she saw Somers protesting about how loyal she was, and accusing Firsby instead, she realized that he *knew* what she'd been doing – that he'd been using her all along. He wanted a threat from a foreign company to use as an excuse for pushing his research through into production without too much scrutiny. He used Elena Simonson to hook Tao and string them along – but he made sure that the information they got from her was false.' He paused, frowning. 'Would he have *known* what would happen to the people who used the fake treatment?'

'I don't know,' said Janet, after a moment's thought. 'He ... he may have thought it served them right.' She swallowed in horrified disgust. 'On the other hand, he may have believed that nobody *would* use it – that Tao would have somebody in Shanghai who'd be able to see that the information was wrong. It was incredibly stupid of them to run a clinical trial of a new experimental treatment if they really didn't have anybody on hand who knew enough about brains to evaluate it.'

'Huh,' said Bailey, unconvinced. 'On the other hand, he knew they were greedy, and that they'd want to rush through the trials fast, so they could claim priority. And I bet he could've fed them some false information that was *harmless*, if he'd wanted to. He was a bastard. He got what was coming to him.'

There was an uncomfortable silence. After a moment, Bailey cleared his throat and resumed, 'Anyway, Elena Simonson contacted Wong and Tan on Thursday evening – the night before the murders – and told them that she would get them the *real* drugs.' He paused. '*I* think that she probably felt bad about what had happened to Tao's volunteers, and was trying to make amends, though Wong and Tan insist that she was trying to set them up.

'By that stage they knew that the information they'd had before was bad. Tao's trials of the treatment had gone wrong by the end of May. At first Wong and Tan didn't know, though, whether that wasn't just because Somers himself had got it wrong. That was why they hired people to spy on you.' He nodded to Janet. 'By that Thursday, though, they knew that the treatment Madhab was getting worked, and they were desperate to get hold of it. They hoped it could be used to undo the damage of the fake treatment, and cure the kids back in Shanghai. So they jumped at Elena Simonson's offer.'

'Which they now think was a set-up?' asked Michael.

Bailey nodded. 'They picked Elena up from Somers' house in Abingdon at half past eight. She told them that she'd put sleeping tablets in David Somers' coffee and stolen the key to the lab fridge from his pocket. They drove her to Somers Synaptic. When they arrived, however, Firsby was there, so they dropped her off and went to park in a lay-by down the road, to avoid notice. She went in, and Firsby saw her and had a row with her before driving off. Tan and Wong arrived on foot as soon as he was gone. The lab security system was still switched off, so they squeezed in through the gate. Elena unlocked the fridge for them, and they'd just finished unloading it when David Somers arrived.' Bailey grimaced.

'Wong and Tan reckon that it was planned – that Somers wanted them caught in the act and deported, so that they couldn't cause any more trouble. They think he'd arranged the set-up with Elena Simonson. I don't think so. I think Somers had guessed that Elena Simonson was up to *something*, so instead of drinking the drugged coffee, he poured it down the sink or something, and followed her at a safe distance. I don't think, though, that he'd realized that Tan and Wong would be there, or that they were armed and very, very angry. I mean, if he'd realized that, he wouldn't have gone, would he? At any rate, they say he burst in while they were packing up the drugs, yelled at them, and got out his phone – so they shot him. Then they turned on Elena Simonson. She ran out of the biology lab, locked the door behind her, and went into the office, probably to try to phone for help; but they just opened the back door, came round the building, and shot her at her desk.'

Bailey was silent for a moment, then added, 'The gun belonged to Tan Yiji. He'd bought it on the black market, as a collector's item, I think, not as a weapon. He was a big fan of westerns. He says he only brought it along that day because he was afraid it might be a trap.'

'I feel sorry for him,' said Janet.

'Nnn,' Bailey replied, neutrally, then burst out, to Michael, 'Christ, what you did to that man Wong's *eye!*'

'He had a gun,' Michael replied flatly. 'He intended to kill us. I had to disable him – but, yes, it was horrible.'

'Mmh,' said Bailey. 'Anyway, once Tan and Wong saw they had two bodies on their hands they tried to destroy the evidence. They smashed the computer that had all the records, then went to the chemistry lab and started cleaning themselves up. They were still doing that when you arrived. Then they knew they'd been spotted. They drove off in the Mercedes to get away as fast as possible. Wong picked up their own car from the lay-by, and then Tan dumped the Mercedes at the station, just to confuse things. They hot-footed it back to London and denied everything.'

'Until you frightened them by telling them you had a witness,' said Michael.

'Yeah, well, you kept telling me to let Firsby go, because *they* were guilty!' protested Bailey. 'I thought maybe if I leaned on them they'd say something. But I hadn't realized how scared they are of being deported back to China. They think their bosses will blame them for everything, and they'll rot in some hell-hole prison for the rest of their lives.'

'What happened to the drugs?' asked Michael.

'They took some samples from them and dumped the rest down the chemistry lab sink. They still have the samples, though, hidden in – would you believe it? – a Chinese takeaway box in Wong's fridge. They'd realized they were being watched, and figured they couldn't smuggle them out of the country until things calmed down.'

'You should give those drugs to Professor Clark,' said Janet firmly. 'And ask if he might be able to help those poor kids in China.'

Bailey looked at her a moment. Then he looked at Michael. 'That's a nice woman,' he commented.

'I noticed,' said Michael smugly.

'For an MI5 man, you're almost human,' Bailey told him approvingly. 'Look, I really am sorry. You've been unusually cooperative, and I fucked up and put you and your girl-friend and her kid in danger. I'm sorry.'

'Well,' said Michael, after a silence – then sighed. 'I've got no right to be angry. I'm as much to blame as anyone. I didn't expect them to come after us like that, either. All along I've told myself that this was industrial and I didn't need to worry. I had them under surveillance, but I didn't increase it until yesterday evening, after Janet told me about the attempted break-in at her house in Leicester – by which time it was too late. It never occurred to me that they'd come after Janet *here*, either. I assumed they would simply cut and run. I didn't consider them a risk any more than you did, and we were both wrong. Still – it turned out OK.'

Bailey grinned.

When the Detective Inspector had left, Michael took off his spectacles, rubbed his eyes, then put them back on again and blinked at Janet from behind them. 'You OK?' he asked.

She nodded listlessly.

Michael came over and rested his hands on

her shoulders, looking into her face. 'Those ten Chinese kids,' he concluded.

She winced and nodded. 'I got help for Madhab,' she told him, 'and now there are ten more like he was.'

'You're looking at it the wrong way,' Michael told her gently. 'You got help for Madhab – and because of that a treatment has been developed to help those ten kids, and the tens of thousands of others who, because of strokes or drugs or accidents, are like them.'

'That's not because of me and Madhab,' she protested. 'It was *David*'s treatment.' She grimaced. 'And what happened to them happened because of David's treatment. How can one man's action be good and evil *at the same time?*'

'Always good and bad, always together,' stated Madhab matter-of-factly.

The natural order of the world, Janet thought – and then realized that it was a far less gloomy natural order than the one she usually assumed. Her ordinary expectation was that everything always went bad, not that the two were always mixed.

She remembered her youthful ambitions to change the world for the better and, for the first time in years, wondered if she'd really been such a fool after all.

'Maybe we *can* make things better,' she said thoughtfully, 'if we work at it.'

'You need luck, too,' said Michael, smiling. 'But I think the three of us have had enough bad luck between us to be owed some more good for a change.'

Madhab shook his head. 'We *have* good luck. We are all here, all OK. Now if we work hard, we can make everything good.'

'Madhab!' exclaimed Janet in delight, 'You used "if"!'

Madhab looked at her in surprise for a moment, and then a huge grin spread over his face. 'If,' he repeated softly. 'If I work hard, I will talk good. I have good luck already.'